PHANTOMS

PHANTOMS

MICHAEL LEON
CHRISSIE ANTHONY

Published in Australia by Australian Inspiration 2018

www.australianinspiration.com.au

Cover, design and typesetting by Luke Harris
www.workingtype.com.au

ISBN: 978-0-9944731-6-5

CONTENTS

CHAPTER ONE

THE COMING

The water gently lapped on the man-made shore, dampening the mirror black of Erik's infantry boots, the only flaw in his freshly pressed military outfit. Dressed in jet black formal uniform with only his cape of royal blue providing a splash of colour, he gazed out on to his private lake. He tenderly held a bouquet of fresh cardinal roses and studied his reflection. It took Erik back to a past life, so far removed from his present, that he wondered if it really had happened. He smiled cynically. It could have been his wedding day.

Rose's enchanting smile haunted him. He turned to look behind, certain he saw her standing in the shadows of the gothic pillars that surrounded his subterranean water world. Rose faded from his mind, before he studied the bouquet he fastidiously prepared. Then he remembered there would be no wedding this day. Not any day.

He dropped the bouquet on to the tightly bound woman he cradled in his left arm. She was peaceful now, free from the terror that had been inflicted on her.

"This is for Rose. You will not be forgotten, my love."

Erik caressed the face of his victim before taking her rope-entwined torso in his powerful arms to stand up on the water's edge. He peered out to the middle of the lake and watched the current of the man-made cistern suck the murky water to its centre. The current was at its most powerful as he tested its flow. The bouquet drifted quickly to the focal point before disappearing from Erik's sight. Water was his world now. Strange that the creator of life could just as easily extinguish it.

Erik shouted "As per your orders, Sir!" Desperately repeating the words as if his life depended on it. The calm he usually felt from water turned, like the current that was about to suck his victim down to the depths of the Seine. He studied every angle of the flowing lake as if each droplet contained the memories that had destroyed his life. Water engulfed his mind, endless flows threatening to extinguish his tenuous grip on the world.

"Will I feel these seething shadows for an eternity? The world shall feel the darkness that stirs in my mind. Then they will know," he vowed, before releasing his corpse to the powerful flow of the current, her youthful beauty now extinguished so that the water could claim her. This was the second life to be taken and would not be the last. A distorted, deformed history surrounded him as the body fell into the abyss. Corpses piled up in every corner of the prison that was his mind. Rotting corpses no more than feed for savage beasts. He wanted the currents to take them all and rid him of his torment, but the motionless bodies remained, tearing at his life like the hunger lust of wild dogs.

Erik would extract his brutal vengeance. He'd make everyone aware of the ugly horrors that haunted his life, an ugliness that masqueraded beneath his handsome features. The world admired people like him, unaware that he was uglier than that monster, *Le Fantôme de l'Opéra*, who had haunted this domain a century earlier. Beneath the cool charm was a true phantom, willing to extract far more vengeance. He sniggered, confident that his mask was more effective than the first creature to rule these shores. He was normal to the world, until he allowed his unwitting victims to witness the wild gaze that revealed his intent.

"Do you love me now, father? Do you know where I am?" Erik shouted to the eight stone pillars that held his subterranean refuge below the Palais Garnier, the famous Paris opera house, in place. His voice echoed back as if his father had responded. He walked victoriously from the lake and spread his arms wide, repeatedly crying out to the echoes. "Am I not the perfect soldier, mon Général?" The echo in his defiant pleas made him laugh uncontrollably. Then the noise subsided. *Perhaps not*, he thought in a quiet moment of reflection. "But I will be remembered long after your precious decorated career quickly disappears from the memory of this fucking world. I will be remembered for an eternity," he proclaimed, proudly.

The echoes again died, leaving him alone in his kingdom. He thought he saw someone peer from behind one of the pillars as the reflections and shadows played tricks on his mind, momentarily unnerving him, before he cast his satisfied gaze a last time to the centre of the lake. It flowed freely into the lake's release valve, the work done, his prey flushed into the murky depths of the Seine.

Erik triumphantly ascended the steep stairs, gliding through darkened hidden corridors as surely as if it were day. As he entered his private retreat, music drifted from his computerized security monitor. It gave him 24-hour access to centre stage where the Witches' chorus was rehearsing for the music from the forthcoming opera, *Macbeth*. He loved this opera. He loved Macbeth and his wife, Lady Macbeth. They understood ambition and revenge. But unlike them, he would not be destroyed.

Erik's lair was filled with candles that lit his damp, subterranean home. Copious half written musical scores littered the floor beside his beloved grand piano. The ballerina's clothes still lay beside his wood-fired furnace. He hastily picked them up and held them close to him, before casting them into the furnace.

"Mother won't be pleased," he mumbled, as he went about removing any evidence of the victim. The fire brightened, illuminating his home. Dampness was all around, except for the immediate area in which he stood. Erik had spent many long nights casting unfinished drafts of his music into its warming fiery pit. His retreat, like his life, was in two parts. There was the home of his music which was chaotically creative and then there was the orderliness and precision of his military retreat, filled with wardrobes each adorned with perfectly pressed uniforms from a time past.

Erik stripped and placed his wet uniform on a table near the furnace, then towelled dry his tall, taut and muscular body. He sat naked for a time, staring at the flames and listening to the music as the new opera ensemble rehearsed.

Eric randomly selected an early music score he had

written in his late teens. In that life, he held high ideals. He was in love with life, more particularly with music and his beloved, Rose. He was a budding virtuoso and Rose his first and only love, a gifted opera singer and his princess. They spent hours in the family music room imagining the fairy tale future that awaited them, sometimes under the watchful eye of Erik's mother, Caroline, who maintained some semblance of work ethic to help them achieve their dreams. For more often than not, they spent long hours in each other's arms enjoying the sweet charms of each other's caress.

Erik played for a time, consumed by his sweetest memories, oblivious to the darkness that would follow. He almost smiled, but the sound of a female voice practising above, broke the spell. It was a voice he recognised, the angelic sounds of Christine Dubois. However, her sweet melodies incited rather than soothed Erik. When he closed his eyes, she became Rose reincarnated, and he was in love again, with another dark-haired angel. One with stunning green eyes, whose voice was heaven sent. Someone who could touch his very soul.

Erik angrily thrust the cruel thought from his mind. He'd seen Christine often enough and spoken sparingly, choosing to observe and listen to her conversations. Like the previous phantom, nothing went unnoticed as he and his team cast their deadly web over the Garnier and its occupants. In time, he was sure this Lady Macbeth in waiting would expose herself as the third interloper of this incestuous trio who dared to cast her meddling gaze on his hidden world.

Erik also kept his distance, fearing love's cruel barbs may return, for she had an uncanny likeness to his beloved, Rose. His experiences had taught him that what followed love was excruciating pain and loss. Consequently, she knew nothing of him, or his knowledge and love for music. And, he wasn't about to share his 'secret place' with her.

Christine Dubois, born to privilege and showing it every chance she had. Also born with beauty and a quiet confidence that deservedly earned her popularity. Amongst a highly-competitive and jealous opera community, most of the cast considered that because the lead diva, Renata Fleming had pulled out due to illness, Christine, as understudy, was the natural choice for the role of Lady Macbeth. But if Erik had his way, she would wait a lifetime for her chance, just like his precious Rose. At least one of her key connections, Philippe, her lover, supporter and financial backer had been taken care of. He had seen to that. Erik stood up from his piano and looked upwards to where Garnier's centre stage would be.

"It will give me exquisite pleasure to extinguish the life

from the next female lead of the new opera, Macbeth. I will delight in watching Lady Macbeth's beauty forever removed in front of her adoring fans. She will feel the perdition of losing everything that she holds dear. I have taken her dearest Philippe from her and next I will remove her hopes and dreams," he said, fists clenched, barely containing his rage. It was not until the echoes quietened that he regained his composure.

"Now, now, Mother. Let's not be too disappointed," he said quietly into the empty darkness, hoping the spirits of his parents were in ghostly attendance, ready to witness and approve the revenge he would exact on opening night at the Palais Garnier.

He recommenced playing, but the music was sharper as his anger returned and overflowed. An anger born from the bleakest of worlds, darker than the deepest caverns in the Garnier. Such wretched terror could not be satiated by any melody, no matter how exquisite. This was once Erik's world and he wanted everyone to know the pain he felt from his loss. In this place, they would learn that the Phantom had indeed returned.

CHAPTER TWO

ENCOUNTERS

C hristine and Danielle sat in the front row of the Garnier opera hall immersed in conversation during a break from rehearsals, oblivious to the scurrying of the stage manager and stagehands on centre stage, but when the rest of the girls in the Witches' chorus who sat nearby, started chattering loudly and excitedly amongst themselves, Christine turned to her closest friend, Danielle, and said,

"Come on, let's get a breath of fresh air. Even if only for a few minutes."

They walked outside and turned to look back at the Palais Garnier. It was one of Paris' most celebrated monuments; the sumptuous opera house symbolised the opulence of a bygone era. They stood there, contemplating the lavish façade — a mélange of sculpted figures, friezes, mosaics and columns dedicated to music and the arts, and, it must be said, to the vanity of an era that demanded the flattery of an audience that was there for one sole purpose to see, and be seen. Both girls were thrilled to be playing in this wonderful theatre, in the roles of witches, even if Christine coveted the main role of Lady Macbeth. Still, it was work.

When they returned to the auditorium, Monsieur Laloux, the Artistic Director, was still shouting directions to the hapless team as they tried to follow his instructions.

"Put the window to the left, Victor. Mais non! The fountain goes to the right of the window, Gerard. I have told you that three times now!" Monsieur Laloux turned to Christine and Danielle, shrugging his shoulders in frustration, much to the amusement of both girls. His eccentric and artistic character, was reflected in his shaven head and immaculately groomed Salvador Dali moustache. And also in his dress, which was as changeable as his moods. Today, tight striped silver, black and grey trousers and a grey turtle-necked shirt, under a black velvet jacket with satin lapels.

"My precious beauties. Save me from these imbeciles!" He shrieked in his high-pitched theatrical voice. Both ladies laughed in mild amusement before returning to their conversation.

"We won't be practising for hours at this rate and I'm already famished," said Danielle, gaining a nod of agreement from Christine.

"He'll never change, Danielle. It's always been perfection or nothing for him."

"Does it matter? Formal rehearsals don't start for another two days."

"Well that's when the new Opera Manager commences. Then he will have to handle Monsieur Laloux's moods. He means well, but his emotions get the better of him. He just needs a strong director to guide him and everything will be fine." Christine replied, letting out a tell-tale sigh that Danielle recognised.

"Still no word?"

"Philippe?"

"Who else would I be referring to?" Danielle replied sarcastically. But Christine's sad expression was sufficient reply.

"He was probably called away on another one of those urgent overseas contracts. You know Philippe. His life has always been filled with endless work commitments. Remember when he flew to Montreal for two months and you didn't hear from him until a week before his return."

"It's been a year, Danielle!" She protested, and a

knowing silence ensued. This topic had been raised on more than one occasion.

"Maybe it's time to consider moving on?

"Please, Danielle. Let's not go there again!"

"I say this as your friend. How many more months do you want to waste on him?"

"He's warm and gentle and kind...."

"Too kind, Christine. Everyone knew his generosity was beyond even his privileged means. There was rumour of a financial crisis."

"Just rumours. Not that it mattered to me. I didn't love him for his money."

"I know he adored you. He showered you with gifts, but he was generous with everybody. Philippe always had to be the life of the party and everybody's best friend. All those parties we attended. Who do you think paid for them?"

"He was supporting our futures."

"Yes. We all appreciated his generosity as patron of the opera house. But what if it was all on borrowed money? His brother, Raoul uncovered serious overseas debts Philippe owed and even spent time in Rome trying to uncover the money trail. Remember his findings?"

"Never proven."

"In all likelihood, Philippe disappeared in Rome. He was last seen leaving his hotel to attend a meeting with one of his financial backers, a known criminal in that country."

Christine became increasingly agitated with her friend, and raised her hands in defiance. "No more. I don't want to hear another word about Philippe."

"But....."

"No! Promise me, Danielle." The silence resumed, as it normally did when they spoke of Christine's lost love, before Monsieur Laloux broke the impasse.

"We are finally ready. Witches' chorus to the stage, please," he said, his contagious smile breaking the sombre mood, but failing to shift them from their seats. "Come, my adorable angels, we have work to do," he demanded, clapping his hands, showing his stricter side. When the twelve witches assembled on stage, Monsieur Laloux turned to the pianist, Paul Pidoux, signalling him with a flourish.

"Monsieur Pidoux, s'il vous plaît." In short time, the chorus were practising the concluding song from Act One of Macbeth, *Schiudi, inferno, la bocca* (*Shut up, hell, your mouth*) from the opera to be launched for the new winter season. The women sang in perfect unison, to the accompanying pianist, showing a musical harmony only possible after many years of singing together. Monsieur Laloux guided them expressively, delight in his eyes.

"Christine, the final chorus, solo, please." All those

working around the stage stopped their chores to listen to her angelic voice. There was little doubt she had the power and control of a prima donna, destined — with luck, hard work and a good manager — to sing many of the greatest arias.

"Bel canto, Christine! Brava, my darling!" Christine responded diva-like, quickly changing Monsieur Laloux's excited mood. He turned to the chorus. "Of course much work remains. Danielle, you must work on the contralto elements of the piece so that you better support Christine's soprano. Both of you have great harmony, but your vibrato can quickly lessen the impact. How do we fix these issues, my darlings?"

"Practice."

"Yes. One more time, girls please," he said, signalling to the pianist to commence. The admiring cast and crew which had momentarily gathered to hear Christine soon returned to their daily duties, as the key closing scene was sung repeatedly, filling the huge auditorium with the voice of sirens, mixed with the incessant demands of their Artistic Director.

CHAPTER THREE

HEAD OF SECURITY

Erik cast the music score to the ground with the same passion he had just played it. He walked across the paper-strewn floor, naked. Now satiated, he suddenly felt the damp cold of his lair. The familiar voices of Christine and Danielle on the monitor filled the labyrinth as he selected one of an array of freshly pressed suits, fastidiously hung in his large Edwardian storage unit. A dozen stylish suits lined the cupboard like a military parade, ready for his assessment and selection.

Erik dressed with a meticulous stylishness that signalled his lofty aims. His ambition was obvious to all but none could imagine the extent to which he sought to control the Garnier. Erik gazed into his full-length mirror, admiring his new mask, Head of Security. The stranger stared back at him. Tall, toned, and tanned. The strong lines of the face and nose were partially offset by a neatly trimmed full beard and the wavy, light brown hair, falling softly over the forehead. But the steely resolve in the blue eyes, was riveting.

His outfit selection was graceful, modern and colour-coordinated, from his polished Italian shoes, to the perfect Windsor-knotted silk tie. When in company, Erik's arrogant air of confidence was seldom questioned. That made sense to him as he was good at his job. The best. There was little he didn't know about any potential threats that may befall a famous Parisian landmark. From hand-to-hand combat, to counter-terrorism, Erik was well versed in all the deadly games known to professional soldiers. He buttoned up the top button of his Gucci suit happy with his selection. He was about to start his day, when his mobile sounded, breaking the silence of his lair.

"Yes, Bernard."

"I'm in Storage, Level 3. Can you meet here?"

Erik contemplated one of his security guard's request, as he went about making last adjustments to his coat. "Is it important?"

"Delivery shortage issues."

"Okay. Wait there," Erik replied, promptly turning his mobile off and placing it into his inside coat pocket. His day had begun as he made light work of the three flights of stairs that had to be ascended to Level 3, no more than a light training run for an elite soldier. He could run all day through the twelve hidden layers of the Garnier with a hundred kilogram back pack if he chose. But that would wait until tomorrow, when he trained with his team of security guards.

Erik crisscrossed a maze of dark corridors until he reached a hidden doorway that could only be opened via a hidden keyhole behind one of the many low-level wall lights that lined the passages. Bernard was waiting for him as requested. He stood beside a shipment of boxes that Erik's team had carried to the underground storage area the night before. Dozens of boxes piled three high filled the back wall of the shadowy expanse, one of many heavily secured areas known to just a few of his select team.

"The lamp hasn't been moved fully back to its secured position," Erik said sternly.

"Sorry. It won't happen again," Bernard replied nervously, knowing Erik never tolerated mistakes to be repeated.

"That's two mistakes in one week?"

"Like I said....."

"What's the other problem?" Erik asked, talking over Bernard, not allowing him to finish his answer.

"We haven't received all of the armaments."

Erik cast his gaze toward the large and expensive pile of boxes. His stern mood was growing worse by the minute. "What's missing?"

"We got the full stock of explosive devices and all Beretta M9 pistols and M12 holsters, but were short changed on the 17-round SB magazines. Seems like there are shortages in Rome."

"How many?"

"We got half."

"That should do, as long as you don't fuck up again, Bernard!" Erik threatened, causing Bernard to raise both hands defensively to Erik's stern gaze.

"And the rifle?"

"Got it. One Remington 700 M24 and all 6MM cartridges."

Erik raised the slightest hint of a smile, before issuing his next orders. "Plant all armed-pistols and spare sniper rifle in the appropriate security caches. I'll talk to Rome about the remaining orders. You just make sure we're set up before opening night."

Bernard didn't ask any more questions. He simply nodded and went about following his orders immediately, as he had done for Erik over a long period of time. As he left Bernard alone to carry out his orders, Erik's faint smile grew broader. His terrible plan that would forever change the face of the Garnier was coming to fruition, a feat to emulate that of the original phantom. He quickly ascended the many dimly lit stairs to the main stage with an extra spring in his step.

CHAPTER FOUR

PRACTICE MAKES PERFECT

After the rest of the chorus had moved off, Monsieur Laloux studied his two favourite singers for a time as if he had hypnotised them, tweaking his moustache, until finally he gave his verdict. "You cannot improve on how you both sang that chorus," he said, smiling and kissing them in the French way on both cheeks, to show his delight, before a final serious look. "Just remember to sing that way opening night. Okay?"

Danielle replied with relief in her voice. "I will most certainly do that Monsieur Laloux, but I do not think Christine will."

"And why would you think such terrible thoughts of your beautiful friend?"

"She will most certainly be singing the role of Lady Macbeth on opening night, Monsieur. I believe that and you surely know that, too."

Monsieur Laloux looked toward Christine who was peering down, hiding her embarrassment. "I know nothing of the sort, young lady. The decision as to who plays the lead will be made by our new manager, who starts with our company in the next two days. I love you, my little flower, but sometimes you should keep your opinions to yourself!"

Monsieur Laloux was about to say more, but something caught his gaze out to the darkness of the seating area, before he smiled. Erik appeared from the shadows, as if an apparition. The truth was, Erik could walk around all corners of the Garnier unnoticed by anyone should he choose.

"Don't you agree, Monsieur Destler?" Monsieur Laloux called out, taking Erik by surprise.

"A good security officer never agrees to a question when he does not hear the context of it, Monsieur Laloux."

"I said that Danielle should keep her opinions to herself, when it comes to selecting the diva of our forthcoming opera. Don't you agree?"

Erik considered his answer, as he was prone to do. Laloux was a man of endless optimism because he loved beautiful things, especially voices. He generally looked toward the positive possibilities, particularly when it was to do with his beloved opera. Erik preferred to work with people of that ilk. They had a naive view, never looking too deeply into a person's soul. He much preferred to befriend and use those types of people as they were rarely suspicious of anyone who may mean them harm. He looked to Danielle, who appeared embarrassed by his attention, no doubt due to the sexual feelings he knew she harboured for him. He enjoyed playing with her emotions, using his physicality and air of mystery to stir her desires.

"Well, I have no doubt someone as talented as Danielle would have the ability to see skills in others."

"Ahh! Our security manager remains as diplomatic as ever! We are so lucky to be protected by our Head of Security, don't you agree, my lovelies?"

Erik studied the two girls' reactions. Danielle, unsurprisingly laughed before agreeing wholeheartedly with Monsieur Laloux and casting a quick glance in Erik's direction. Christine remained circumspect, showing her ambivalence toward him.

"One hopes so, Monsieur Laloux. We open to the public in less than a month." Christine replied, looking directly at Erik with a playful but accusing stare.

"I am certainly ready for any contingency. Just as I suspect any professional diva would be equally prepared."

"Practice would not be necessary for a true star," Erik

replied, artfully, knowing full well, the contrary was true — that practice is essential, even for a diva.

A chilly silence ensued, before Monsieur Laloux intervened nervously. "Well there it is. You have your answer from a professional. You will both have to practice!"

Danielle laughed nervously, whereas Christine stood in stony silence with a glare that was worthy of a wounded diva.

"But for now my hardworking darlings, a thirty minute break. We will use final practice for the aria from Act One, Scene Two — *Vieni! T'affretta! (Come Hurry!)*," he said, turning his gaze to the back of the stage and waving the girls to go away and rest. "Did you hear me stage hands? Props for Act One, Scene Two, s'il vous plaît!"

Erik walked up the stairs on to the stage, brushing Danielle as he walked past her, and deliberately ignoring Christine, as he headed to the back of the stage to begin his daily inspections. Danielle took her friend's arm, guiding her down the stairs to the seating area to rest.

"Why do you push him, Christine? He has a job to do."

"He's filled with too many opinions that don't concern him. What would a security guard know about opera? Christine retaliated, her gaze still on Erik.

"He's not a guard. He's Head of Security and he is the last man you want off-side in this day and age.

"You're just like everyone else. The man pretends to know a lot about opera and yet he is no more than a glorified thug."

"A cute thug, don't you think? When he looks at me with those piercing eyes I feel like he can see straight through me."

"He's toying with you, Danielle. As for mysterious, I'd call him a loner who gets his kicks out of bullying people, so he can impose his huge ego on others."

"He could impose his huge ego on me any day!" Danielle quivered at the thought, gaining the first glimpse of a smile from Christine.

"Honestly, Danielle, that is all you ever think of. One day your libido is going to get you into a lot of trouble. Why can't you focus as much on your singing? You have the capability to be a star, if you practiced more."

"More practice! Sacré bleu! Monsieur Laloux is already killing me with his incessant criticisms and you want me to do more? I'd rather be out in our beautiful city every night. It is the lovers' city."

Christine shook her head in frustration. She and her friend had spent many long nights after practice arguing over commitment to singing. For Christine, singing was her whole life. She had always been surrounded by the beauty of music. Her mother, Francine Dubois had been the most successful opera singer in France, who regularly performed at the Garnier to her adoring French fans. As a young girl, Christine would spend countless hours watching her mother practicing, before she'd disappear to her make-up room and practice her own performances in front of the mirror. That was why Erik's words riled her so. She had practiced more than anyone, to perfect her craft. Yet a security officer had the gall to tell her to practice more!

CHAPTER FIVE

PAST LESSONS

Erik moved as freely as a trapeze artist as he inspected all levels of the backstage, from the fly system to the lighting and sound. The Assistant Stage Manager, responsible for backstage operations, was briefing his specialist operators in props, when Erik approached.

"Any problems to look at, Henri?"

"No. It's all coming together quickly."

"When does the full team arrive?"

"Soon. I have selected the final applicants. Around a dozen and all good at their specialties."

"Let me see the resumes, won't you?"

"I put copies of them in your mail."

"Thanks, Henri. I'm going to take a closer look at the fly system. Where are the overalls?"

"There's a bundle just near the pulleys system," replied Henri, pointing to the main operating area for ropes, wires and pulleys. There was also a long black leather bag, zipped and locked with a note tied to the shoulder strap, with his name on it. He picked it up and carried it over to the bundle of clothing.

Erik half smiled as he turned toward the intricate system. It was here that the flyman transformed scenes from high above, turning the blank canvas of the stage into an array of scenic wonderlands. But there was something else that he liked most about this specialist position. A flyman had to be a master of the ropes and wires that held scenes in place. It was a precise art, where every knot had to be understood and assembled in an instant to ensure the safety of the performers and the enjoyment of the audience. Ironically, Erik had all the flyman's skills, but his craft had a deadlier intent, ensuring he controlled his prey and bring about death if required.

Erik too, like the best flyman had no fear of heights. He looked up to the small platforms that hung precariously high above the stage and felt only excitement for the climb. He quickly undressed and put on the black overalls, soft shoes and tight gloves, ready for his ascent up a combination of aluminum framed steps, ladders and knotted rope to the narrow viewing platform. With a heavy shoulder bag strapped to him, he hardly raised a breath, before obtaining sweeping views of the most famous opera house in the world. Erik always felt a special power when he stood on the elevated platform. Only one other person could walk his bridge with the same level of confidence and joy, and only Erik knew this bridge held secret connections to his undercover world, afforded no one else.

Lights suddenly changed in intensity, making him look down to the stage. He had a clear view of the performers rehearsing their new scene. Erik slipped a dark stocking mask over his face to maintain anonymity. Suitably camouflaged, he freely roamed his world undisturbed by the puppets he would control, delighting in the fact that he was soon to become the world's most deadly marionette.

As the singing wafted gently to the highest levels of the grand opera house, Erik climbed a single knotted rope higher toward a small platform just below the iconic ceiling, containing the large number of emergency ropes that safety standards required. Erik picked out one special rope from the bundle and wrapped it securely around his underarm before descending back down to the bridge. Then with a confident silence, he stalked across the narrow platform toward a concealed ceiling entry that would allow him to crawl to his own personal viewing confine, the infamous Box 5 — the Phantom of the Opera's box. His *oubliette*. The perfect word to describe his hiding place, he mused, smiling at the thought – a secret dungeon with access only through a trapdoor in its ceiling.

Erik then tied a perfect double fisherman's knot, securing his makeshift rope ladder between the bridge and the ceiling entry, before climbing to the ceiling. Once there, he moved a false cover that looked like a support beam, revealing the narrowest of openings to the premier cache of the myriad of secret rooms that lined every level of the Garnier. He quickly positioned his body into the narrow duct that connected to the Box 5 *oubliette*, silently and deftly closing the cover with his feet, before making the challenging three hundred metre crawl and descent through the darkness of the shaft. To simply climb to the shaft would be challenging enough for most, but to crawl through a long, confined space would be physically and emotionally daunting for even the fittest person.

But Erik was no ordinary man. He had faced more than any human should, enduring long periods of solitary confinement, waiting for his tormentors to reign their terror over him. The suffering he had faced prepared Erik for anything. No one would have the endurance or the motivation to reach his most precious secret space. A hundred metres along the pitch black shaft and his arms and shoulders ached from the exertion. The final two hundred metres would turn most back, as the shaft further narrowed, creating an Everest-like confrontation. His body heat and quickening breath reverberated off the small chamber, creating a feeling of entombment. By half way, most would face a fear similar to being buried alive and back away, but in this deathly world, Erik always heard the cries of the phantom wolves that sought to claim him. Saliva drooled from their hungry mouths and dragon hot breath filled the narrowing enclosure, subjecting him to a dread he knew too well, giving him the strength to crawl through the impossible, to claim his destiny.

Erik fell through on to the many soft pillows that lined the narrow entry to his secret dungeon. Still hearing the howls from the deadly pack, he quickly closed the sliding entry door behind him, before slumping in the dark on the softness of the pillow-bed, to recover his strength.

The pure high notes of Christine's vibrato woke Erik from his micro-slumber. He reached for a small torch that was packed in a box containing an assortment of useful items and he switched it on, lighting up the small confines of the cache that bordered his own private viewing box. The soundproofed wall allowed no sound to emanate from his lair, except for the smallest of spaces that provided viewing to the main stage and another to Box 5. Both were concealed by false ornaments that he could slide open if required. He stood up and walked the two paces to open the front viewing space and peered down at Christine who stood centre stage, practising *Nel dì della vittoria (In the day of victory)*, willed on by the expressive Monsieur Laloux and the piano accompaniment.

Erik then unlocked the shoulder bag and unzipped it, revealing its deadly contents — the loaded Remington 700 M24 sniper rifle and two extra rounds of 6MM cartridges. He wasted no time aiming the rifle toward centre stage, carefully lining its sight on Christine. Bright spotlight rays illuminated her, making it the perfect opportunity for a kill. He kneeled in sniper position to make a shot, all the while wishing it were opening night, but Monsieur Laloux's insistent interruptions reminded him that he too was in rehearsal. Yet the taste of the kill filled his senses like the voice of his tormentor and his team of wolves.

"You will do exactly as I say, or die like the miserable band of soldiers who lay there with my children," ordered the Captor.

Erik could smell the mound of corpses that had dared disobey their Captor as did the smell of ravenous wolves standing like statues, awaiting their reward. One by one, the Captor circled each soldier, their pride long extinguished by the terrors they had endured.

"You would even kill your own for me, should I require it."

The Captor's words repeated in his ears as he again sighted the sniper rifle. The spotlight remained on his prey as if the Captor had willed that Christine sing the most beautiful notes. Her beauty, so like his beloved Rose, made him flinch as he trained the rifle sight directly at Christine's heart.

"You would extinguish the life of your nearest and dearest, should I request it," taunted the Captor.

Kill your own, kill your own, kill your own, repeated in Erik's ear until he could not distinguish his *oubliette* from the torture chambers he endured in another life. Sweat trickled from his forehead on to the barrel of his sniper rifle. He felt the dampness on his trigger finger as he began to squeeze the loaded killing machine. The image of Christine in yellow dress, then Rose in blood red gown, filled the telescopic site. *Kill your own* filled his mind as Erik slowly capitulated to the torment of his past. He was in the kill spot, ready to murder for the Captor, waiting for the singer below to reach the highest crescendo before he would light the Garnier with a single deadly flash.

The moment arrived, but suddenly all light from below was extinguished, leaving Erik in the darkest of spaces. He released his finger from the rifle trigger. All he could hear was the sounds of people scurrying somewhere out in the darkness. Was he back in the Captor's prison? He could not be sure, as the muffled sounds tortured his mind. Endless nights he had sat in his small prison hearing the sounds of voices coming close. Sometimes they stopped at his prison, but mostly they went to others claiming their prey, before the sounds of terrified pleas cried out into the unending night.

Then all went quiet around him. His dark memories faded, before the momentary peace gave way to real whispers that echoed in the confines of his *oubliette*. Had someone gained access to his private lair, he wondered, before shaking his head in disbelief. No one had his capabilities to scale such formidable terrain. And yet the whispers continued. At first, he could not make out the words as they seeped into his secret dungeon like a gathering fog, but then the whispers grew louder, demanding his attention.

"My opera house, my rules. My opera house, my rules." A challenge repeated over and over. Erik wanted to squeeze the trigger and end his torment, but doubt clouded his mind. He dropped the rifle to his side. He would wait until the opening night to enact his bloody vengeance.

CHAPTER SIX

INSPECTOR MOREAU VISITS

VIPs, politicians, journalists, critics, the cast and their guests started to file into Garnier's Great Hall filling the gothic expanse with an atmosphere of expectation. Formal rehearsals for Macbeth were to begin next Monday and the new Opera Manager was to be announced this evening.

Conversation flowed as freely as the champagne, and with it, many forthright opinions about who deserved the part of Lady Macbeth. In the absence of Renata Fleming, Christine Dubois was the popular choice, but rumo urs swirled around the Great Hall about a surprise contender. Who would be available at such short notice?

A second dreadful event also filled the minds of the guests, Camille, a popular ballerina, had suddenly disappeared, leading to much conjecture over the reasons. A recent mysterious love who had showered her daily with gifts of bouquets, was the favoured reason. Had Camille eloped? The more fanciful conjecture centred on the return of the Opera Ghost. Most scoffed at the idea, but secretly feared it might be true.

Raoul D'Arenberg, Philippe's younger brother, was engaged in deep discussion at the top of the grand staircase with Inspector Claude Moreau. Standing together, the two were a contrast, looking more like an athlete and his craggy old coach. At nearly two metres tall, Raoul towered over him Amazon-like, lean and lithe. Formal black attire was contrasted by his fashionably long black hair resting on his collar, and a two-day growth. Raoul's alert, dark brown eyes maintained a fixed gaze as if he were a prize fighter. Whereas Claude restlessly moved about as his attention turned from Raoul to the scene below, seemingly scanning all the attendees as if every one were potential suspects in a crime scene. His round face and large eyes were accentuated by dark glasses, and his short, stocky frame similarly accentuated by a favourite sand-coloured, knee length coat he always wore. Claude was a man who liked to stand out as he went about his investigations. Quiet observation was not his style. Everyone quickly knew why he was in attendance, further stirring the rumour mill below.

"Raoul, Camille has been missing for two days now. Early investigations have revealed very little. It is likely that she has simply left France with her mysterious lover."

"And who might that be?" Raoul asked.

"We are yet to find out. It seems none of her friends has met him. That's why I'd like you to carry out informal investigations. You know most people here. Spend some time with them. There has to be someone who knows a little about him," Claude continued in his usual rapid way, firing words like a machine gun.

"You said she could be abroad?"

"That was our only lead. Camille did mention to a friend her excitement about possible travel," said Claude, but Raoul looked unconvinced.

"It's not much, I know, but that has been our only lead to her possible whereabouts."

Raoul shook his head wearily as he spoke. "This all sounds familiar."

"Yes it does. That's why I thought you would want to be involved."

"I don't know Claude. I wasted my time for the best part of a year, last time. Why don't you use one of your young up and coming officers?"

"You know these operatic people better than anyone. They trust you and may be more inclined to open up to you."

"That simple?" Raoul said, cynically.

"Alright, I don't want to waste any more valuable resources on this. That's the truth."

"But it's okay that I waste my time on your behalf? I have enough on my plate trying to pick up the pieces of the management of our family estate."

"Just a few days, Raoul. If there is nothing, we will pay you handsomely. But imagine if there is something in this disappearance? Who knows, there could be a connection to Philippe. Would you not want to give this some time?"

Both men turned and leant over the marble balcony and gazed down toward the enthusiastic crowd that had gathered. All were impressively dressed in their finest clothes, befitting the dazzling Grand Hall. The twenty chandeliers shone like jewels, accentuating the baroque paintings that lined the one-hundred-eighty-seven metre long walls. It was implausible, but nevertheless possible, that a killer walked among them. Unlike Claude, Raoul had little doubt his brother Philippe was murdered. Why else would he have not returned? The thought that the murderer was in this room, remote as that may be, was enough to at least consider Claude's offer.

"I'll take a look for you, a few days, no more," he said, casting his gaze across the room below, until it stopped at a face he knew. Christine Dubois stood in the centre of the mingling crowd, dressed in a stunning yellow organdie full length gown. With long sleeves, pinched at the waist and flared at the bottom, it showed off her svelte body to perfection. Her glorious brunette mane, parted in the middle, fell softly over her back and shoulders, with tendrils seeming to circle her generous breasts. Not surprisingly, she was drawing a crowd of admirers to her, for she was as bright as the grand chandeliers above her. Raoul would not admit it to Claude, but the truth was he always liked Christine, at times thinking there could be more, but for the fact she had always deeply loved his brother. The ring-tones of Claude's mobile phone interrupted Raoul's thoughts.

"Yes. I'm at the Garnier, so thirty minutes. Yes. Okay then." Claude switched off his phone and turned to Raoul. "A few days is perfect. Thank you, mon ami," he said, shaking Raoul's hand.

"You have to leave?"

"Yes. Another case at Montmartre. Paris never sleeps," he said, raising his hands, signalling his frustration with the demands of his position. Claude buttoned his coat in preparation for the chilly winter breeze outside and the next case he was about to face. "I have assigned Detective Inspector Sophie Giroux as your support. She can provide you any research or contacts, should you need it. You know our number," he said, shaking Raoul's hand again, before disappearing into the crowd below.

Raoul leaned against the rail for a time, lost in his memories of Paris's wonderful opera house. Like his brother, Raoul loved the opera, but it had been some time since his last visit to the Palais Garnier. Sadly, it now harboured some dark memories for him, spoiling his natural love for this most dramatic of art forms. Still, he'd made his commitment to Claude, deciding to waste no more time in reflection and begin his search for clues.

CHAPTER SEVEN

THE NEW KING AND QUEEN

Raoul's first port of call was Christine. She shone like an early sunrise in her organdie gown, looking every bit the diva that most of the cast expected her to be. Her natural friendliness drew people to her. People liked her because she radiated charm and a clear love for her vocation, and was always prepared to share her experiences, to teach younger singers. Her lively green eyes danced and she almost sang as she spoke, such was her enthusiasm. Christine was the first to see Raoul as he approached her circle of friends.

"Well here's a face I haven't seen in a while."

Raoul approached smiling, before kissing her on both cheeks. "Too long," he replied, sharing a knowing glance. Both knew Philippe remained a shadow in their lives. "But when I heard Macbeth was playing at the Garnier, I had to return." A warmth in his voice, flooding his usual aristocratic reserve.

Christine smiled graciously, before taking care of formalities. "Raoul D'Arenberg, I think you know most people here: Danielle; Julien; Marias; Jean Claude our illustrious doorman."

Raoul nodded, showing his familiarity with all except one attractive young lady who stood next to Danielle. "I don't believe we have met?"

"Raoul, this is Angelique, one of our senior ballerinas who is part of the Witches' chorus."

Raoul stooped and kissed Angelique's hands. She was small but elegant in her strapless red satin dress. Her lithe body had the exotic shape of a ballerina, accentuating her beauty.

"Pleased to meet you, Monsieur."

"Don't be too pleased, Angelique," Christine interjected. "Raoul is not only here to enjoy the opera. He is no doubt here to investigate Camille's disappearance. Would I be right, Monsieur D'Arenberg?"

"That is unfortunately correct. Inspector Moreau asked me to see if I could uncover this mystery. With luck it is no more than a mysterious romantic entanglement. Given you are one of the ballerinas, I would be extremely grateful if you could spare a few minutes to speak to me privately, Angelique?"

"See, I warned you!" Christine said, as Angelique

nodded her acceptance and walked with Raoul to a quiet corner of the grand hall.

"Thank you, Angelique. I will try to be as brief as possible. Are you good friends with Camille?"

"All the dancers are close. She was not my best friend, but we talked often, mostly to do with our performances."

"Can you tell me anything you might know about Camille's movements just before she disappeared or anything she may have said that seemed strange or out of place?"

"How can you answer such a question in this place," she replied, sharply.

"What do you mean?"

Angelique looked around the Great Hall before hesitated before replying, as if there was danger close at hand. "The Garnier has not changed. It is an opera house filled with secrets and strange occurrences."

"Would you care to elaborate?"

"It's as if the walls have ears, Monsieur D'Arenberg. Who knows? Perhaps the Opera Ghost still lives. Do you believe in him?"

Raoul tilted his head as if to indicate he had an open mind. "I only believe in what I see. Two people associated with the Garnier have disappeared. One my brother, and now Camille. Are you saying the Opera Ghost is responsible?"

"No, I am not saying anything. I only know that rumours run through this building quickly, then they take on a life of their own. People who express their opinions openly do not fare so well in this cavernous building."

"Tell me what you know, Angelique. This conversation will go no further. I promise."

Angelique looked around the Great Hall until her gaze finally rested on the group gathered around Christine, before speaking hesitantly, "I can tell you nothing with certainty and I wouldn't risk revealing anything, even if I knew what you sought. But there is possibly someone who could, but you must approach that person with extreme caution," she replied, holding her gaze in Christine's direction.

Raoul was about to ask Angelique more, but their conversation was interrupted.

"Mesdames et Messieurs, could you gather around the grand staircase, please? The new Opera Manager is about to be introduced," Enzo, the Stage Manager, announced.

The chatter of the mingling crowd quietened as a spotlight pointed to the top of the stairs, illuminating the new manager, a face most in the crowd recognised.

"Mesdames et Messieurs, please welcome our new Opera Manager, Monsieur Victor Marchand!"

A collective sigh of disappointment reverberated around the hall. Monsieur Marchand had been attempting to take over the Garnier Opera for many years. He already owned the Opéra Bastille, where he had earned his reputation for being overbearing and ruthless. He was an ambitious man, small in stature, but as he strode down to join Enzo at the midpoint of the marble stairway, his confidence permeated around the grand hall. He was unaware of the reaction the shocked guests had shown as he took the microphone from Enzo's hand.

"Ladies and gentlemen, I am honoured to become the new manager of this, the most illustrious opera house in all of the world. You and I are destined for even greater achievements, I promise you," said Victor, effusively. "Starting with the most important announcement that you have all no doubt been waiting for."

Monsieur Marchand stood silently, signalling for a second spotlight to be directed to the top of the stairway, shining a light for the imminent entry of their new diva. Raoul glanced across to Christine who stood tall. He looked for a reaction, but Christine's expression remained inscrutable. Her friend Danielle held her arm, giving a hint of the disappointment most were about to feel. It appeared another had been chosen for the key role of Lady Macbeth.

"Ladies and gentlemen, may I introduce you to the most famous soprano in all of France, in fact the world, *La Divina*, Carlotta Caccini!" Monsieur Marchand proudly announced. Shock gave way to applause as Carlotta entered the spotlight, and responded to the reception as if it were her fifth standing ovation. She wore a magnificent Chanel black crepe de chine ball-room gown, flared from the knees with thousands of black feathers, which showcased her statuesque beauty. Her dark brown hair was tied back, and elegantly looped around her long neck, accentuating her high cheekbones, a mouth painted deep red, and eyes heavily ringed with kohl. Expressive green eyes, which were taking in all before her, with an aplomb befitting a woman who had commanded stages all over the world.

Beside her, Erik Destler, Head of Security, assisted her in the steep walk down the marble staircase. Indeed, it could have been Lady Macbeth herself as she regally descended the staircase to join the new manager, her partner, Monsieur Marchand. Erik escorted her safely to Marchand, who lightly kissed her hand in admiration, turned to present her to the audience and then invited more applause. All followed his signal, except Erik who dutifully fell back from the spotlight into the background, his role to defend his new king and queen. *La Divina* was back. After a hiatus, reasons for which speculation abounded, Carlotta Caccini had chosen the Garnier and the role of Lady Macbeth to continue her glittering career.

CHAPTER EIGHT

AT THE RECEPTION

Raoul observed the unfolding scene with mild amusement. From a distance, there were striking similarities between Christine and the new diva, although Carlotta's imperious carriage, self-possession and age disguised the fact, somewhat. Mother and daughter, he mused, before dismissing the thought, and his mind returned to the group that stood with Christine. Many passed consoling glances to her, except for Jean Claude. His gaze remained firmly fixed on Erik as he moved further into the shadows.

Raoul recalled Angelique's words that someone may know of Camille's whereabouts, but they must be approached with caution. She was looking at Christine's group at the time. Was one of the group he now studied the person who could supply him the answers he needed? He could not be certain, but one thing was sure, Angelique was fearful of someone or something in the Opera House. Whether it was a person or group of people or simply the rumours of a ghostly phantom still haunting the performers who chose to walk its stage, he could not be sure. But Raoul was beginning to believe that the mysterious disappearance of his brother and now the sudden disappearance of the ballerina could possibly be linked.

Victor Marchand and Carlotta with Erik, their new, ever-vigilant guard in tow, descended the final section of the grand stairs, to mingle with the star-struck crowd. Whatever misgivings they harboured for the new power couple, the regency of their new diva's presence made them forget.

"Darling Chloe and Ivan! It has been too long! Victor, I sang with this beautiful lady in the Merchant of Venice. When was it darling?"

"In 2008, Carlotta. To an appreciative crowd."

"Appreciative. Chloe has always been the modest one. Sellout crowds for three months and rave reviews!" Carlotta cried, more to the surrounding throng than Chloe or Victor. Her expressive hand gestures showing her Italian origins as much as her accented voice. Carlotta had been a star of Italian opera for decades and she showed it, with a performance befitting her reputation.

Victor glided Carlotta through the Grand Hall with the polished assurance of a seasoned politician, ensuring his star mingled with all in attendance. An hour flew past before Carlotta showed any signs of weariness.

"My darling, Victor, I could mingle with these beautiful people all night, but my shoes will not allow it!"

Victor looked mildly annoyed by Carlotta's complaint and at a loss what to do, before he turned to Erik. "Beautiful women? What do you do?"

"We are but small players sent to do the bidding of a goddess. I can have security bring you more comfortable shoes, if that helps?"

"My darling security manager! I feel safe in your hands!" Carlotta declared, offering her extended hand in gratitude. Erik smiled as he gently kissed her manicured fingers, all the while holding his gaze toward her, long enough to signal their growing mutual attraction. Victor, used to Carlotta's excesses, quickly put an end to the flirtation.

"Thank you, Erik. I have every confidence in my manager of security to do the right thing." He intervened, before taking his partner's hand to continue mingling with the crowd.

They soon met with Monsieur Laloux. Looking resplendent in a royal blue velvet suit, with matching satin lapels, shirt and tie, he took it upon himself to introduce them to the cast of Macbeth.

"Carlotta and Victor, it is my pleasure to introduce you to Christine. She will be your understudy for the season."

There was a moment's pause as the two divas – one firmly in the lexicon of stars, the other a youthful aspirant — met for the first time, as if both were sizing each other up. Victor intervened, aware of the awkward moment.

"I feel as if I know you well, young lady. I have been to some of your performances and you have indeed come so far in a very short time," he said, effusively. Victor accepted Christine's extended hand and kissed it gently, retaliating for the earlier flirting incident between Carlotta and Erik.

"You are too gracious Monsieur Marchand. It is a pleasure to finally meet you. I have followed your career closely. We are indeed fortunate to have an important businessman such as yourself support the arts in France."

"Merci beaucoup. May I introduce my beautiful partner to you, Carlotta?"

"Madame Caccini needs no introduction. She has been the most famous soprano in all of France for as long as I can remember. It is an honour to finally meet you." Christine nodded her head ever so slightly, as a gesture of respect for Carlotta's eminence, but received none in return from Carlotta, who extended the briefest of smiles, before taking Victor's hand and turning to Monsieur Laloux.

"You are welcome my dear. Now Monsieur Laloux, where is my handsome fellow lead? Is he here this evening? Are you keeping secrets from me?"

Monsieur Laloux turned to Victor for help, unsure of his reply.

"Yes, it was a secret, my darling. Entirely of my doing. We will return to the grand staircase where I will introduce you to your male lead in Macbeth," he called out to the excited crowd.

Both assembled at the midpoint of the stairway. A spotlight again fell on to the top balcony above them, which would reveal the male lead. Although he had been contracted some time ago, it was the first time he had sung at the Garnier.

Victor turned to Carlotta, "Why don't you introduce him, darling?"

Carlotta, arms outstretched, looked upwards, adding as much drama to the occasion to ensure attention remained with her as long as possible.

"Let me introduce, the lead for Macbeth, the delightful, the handsome, and the talented........René Bourdin!"

René walked into the spotlight on cue. He was young for a male lead, but he was extremely popular with French women. He stood tall and smiled down to the crowd below, flashing blue eyes and long black hair, accentuating the intensity of his gaze and immediately winning female hearts in the main hall. On Victor's signal he walked down the stairway to admiring applause, extending his hands in stylish appreciation, befitting the male lead, before joining Carlotta. They stood together hand in hand, raised high in appreciation for the applause.

Raoul nodded his approval for the choice, although the pairing did not look right. Carlotta was resplendent in her gown and powerful in her presence, whereas René was gifted, not only with a distinctive baritone voice, but with youth and natural good looks. He was not alone in his opinion. Many murmured their thoughts as they applauded.

"They look more like mother and son, than husband and wife," came one whispered comment close to Raoul. In truth, he had to agree.

He looked toward Christine who stopped applauding long before anyone else. She merely gazed at the two leads, stony faced, holding back any emotion she felt. A gracious loser, Raoul thought. Her friend, Danielle was not so coy. She openly shook her head in disbelief and

held Christine's arm ever tighter as the applause continued. Then he looked at Jean Claude, who he thought for
a moment was staring back at him. But someone walked
past him quickly and glanced his shoulder. It was Erik
carrying shoes, the pair he had promised for Carlotta.

Raoul knew Erik, but he had never spoken to him
at length. He had been appointed as Head of Security
sometime after the first investigations of his brother
Philippe's disappearance. He appeared to have a rapport
with Jean Claude and others on his security team. Erik
was tall and lithe, and very capable in the art of defence.
Not a man to be crossed.

Then Angelique's words struck him. "The walls have
ears, so be careful what you say." It would certainly be in
the Head of Security's interest to know everything that
was happening at Garnier. If anyone had a fix on problems, it would surely be Erik. Raoul had unveiled many
lines of enquiry already, notating his key leads on a small
notebook he always carried in his coat pocket. *'Christine,
Danielle, Angelique, Jean Claude, Monsieur Laloux and
Erik'* were notated — his first leads in what was turning
out a fruitful night.

CHAPTER NINE

AN EVENING OF SURPRISES

While Victor and René stood at the bottom of the staircase enjoying a champagne and conversation, Erik assisted Carlotta with her change of shoes at the top of the staircase, just out of view. He kneeled on one knee by Carlotta's feet removing the more comfortable shoes from a pink box, before asking her to extend first her left foot then her right. Carlotta sat with her legs crossed accentuating the curvaceous lines of her body beneath the black crepe de chine gown. Erik held Carlotta's ankle and removed her Parisian designed stiletto shoes, revealing perfectly manicured toe nails and soft, pampered feet. She squirmed slightly to his touch and arched her toes back as he stroked her foot with his other hand.

"That is such a relief," said Carlotta, resting her head back against the chair and closing her eyes.

"Beautiful feet and stilettos. Such a delicious mix of beauty and pain," said Erik, as he massaged one foot, than another.

Carlotta kept her eyes shut as she luxuriated in the relief. "It seems we have a multi-talented Head of Security. How wickedly delightful."

Erik responded by slowly, seductively massaging ever higher, from her toes to her lower thigh. "Talented beyond anything you could imagine."

"Well, aren't we a bold one? Are you brave enough to take me on this balcony, now? I do love to take risks," said Carlotta, suddenly opening her eyes to gaze down at Erik.

"One evening, Carlotta, I might just accommodate your wishes," he replied, slowly gliding his hands higher to her inner thighs. Carlotta breathed heavily, enticingly parting her thighs as far as her dress would allow, inviting further exploration. Erik teasingly slid his hands higher, building her desires, until a voice from the shadows interrupted their moment.

"Excuse me, Erik. Monsieur Marchand is asking for Madame Caccini."

Erik reluctantly stood up, and, business-like, adjusted his jacket before signalling to his henchman that they were coming. Alone again, he held Carlotta's hand and pulled her up from the chair, drawing her close to him.

They gazed into each other's eyes, not needing to say another word. Two uniquely disparate forces of will were in each other's captive gaze breathing in the addictive taste of expectation. Both wanted each other, but for different reasons that would require time to reveal. But for now, reasons didn't matter, only primal desires. Erik was the first to break their spell.

"Is Lady Macbeth ready to return to her adoring fans?"

"She has never been more ready," Carlotta replied, inviting Erik to take her arm and accompany her back to the guests and her devoted partner.

Raoul watched them return from the shadows. Carlotta brought with her a reputation for having many lovers and she appeared not to be wasting any time in her new opera — starting with the Head of Security. He wondered if it was as obvious to others. Certainly not Victor, who remained in deep conversation with the new male lead. The evening had been filled with so many surprises, he couldn't but help shake his head.

"Something amusing you, Monsieur D'Arenberg?" Came a voice from behind. It was Jean Claude, carrying two glasses of wine. "One for you, Monsieur. Do you like champagne?"

"Am I French?"

Jean Claude smiled and passed him the chilled glass. "Are you enjoying the evening?" A harshness evident in his speech.

"Of course. Who could not enjoy such sumptuous surrounds?" Raoul looked him over. Despite being in formal attire, Jean Claude had the bearing and muscular build of a soldier, as well as the shaven face and closely cropped hair.

"Yes, we are lucky to be able to work in the most beautiful opera house in the world, are we not?"

"Yes. I wish I was here for more favourable reasons."

"Ahh, yes. Camille's disappearance."

"Most here seem to think she has run off with a mysterious lover. So if that is true, my time here will be very short."

"I hope that is true. Although, it must be difficult for you to return to the Garnier, given your brother went missing here. Has there been any more news of his whereabouts?"

"I'm afraid not. But I have not given up hope."

Jean Claude nodded in apparent sympathy, before drinking his wine and placing the empty glass on a nearby table. "Then I should not hold you up any further on your quest, Monsieur D'Arenberg. I wish you luck," he said, before shaking his hand and leaving Raoul.

Raoul too, finished his champagne, ready to leave the Garnier, but he wanted to see Christine one more time. The group that stood with her had dispersed and only her friend, Danielle remained at her side.

"I'm about to head home, but wanted to pay my commiserations to you for not being picked for the Lady Macbeth role."

"Thank you Raoul. That is so sweet of you. I admit disappointment, but I will have many more opportunities ahead of me than Carlotta. So in a way, I'm happy for her."

"Yes. There is an age difference and you are on the right side of that equation."

Christine smiled. "Carlotta will be wonderful. Now is her time, where the future will be mine," she said, as she gazed around the Grand Hall.

Its opulent restoration was breathtaking. Eighteen metres above them was a grand ceiling lovingly painted by Paul-Jacques-Aime Baudry, reflecting the history of music. Hanging from the art-filled ceiling were twenty crystal chandeliers. History abounded in this place. The chandeliers made Raoul think of the premier seven-tonne bronze and crystal chandelier designed by Garnier that made up the main feature of the auditorium. It had a deadly tale to tell. In 1896, one of the chandelier's counterweights broke free, bursting through the ceiling into the Grand Hall, killing a member of the audience. To this day, they attributed the incident to the Opera Ghost.

"With luck, the Opera Ghost will smile on you, as he did your mother," said Raoul, reflectively.

"He always smiled on those who genuinely love music, so I feel I have his spirit with me."

Raoul nodded his agreement, continuing to gaze at the one-hundred-eighty-seven-metre long walls. Marble columns, interspersed with paintings completed this most perfect of settings. Raoul held his gaze at one particular painting, its gold frame bordering golden angels and ogres in equal measure. One of the ogre's faces caught his attention, for in one brief moment, Raoul thought he saw real eyes gazing at him, before just as quickly disappearing. He blinked a number of times, then looked up to the painting again.

"Is anything wrong, Raoul?" Christine asked.

"To be honest, I'm not sure," he replied.

Raoul simply smiled and said good night to both ladies, deciding it best he have an early night. His mind was spinning from the events of this special evening and the champagne. He wanted to remain, but more importantly he needed rest and an early start to investigate the people and surrounds of this beautiful but dangerous opera house.

And this time he would find the answers he had been seeking for a very long time.

CHAPTER TEN

REHEARSALS BEGIN

Deep in thought Raoul exited the subway. First, he had been forced to take leave of absence from his work as a scientific researcher to manage the family estate and to sort out the financial mess left behind when Philippe disappeared. And now, he had been asked to investigate the disappearance of the ballerina. His career and his life in abeyance, once more. He shrugged away the disturbing thought.

"Where will I start my investigation? With whom? So many hiding places. So many secrets. Will I ever discover what happened to my brother? Philippe is all that is left of my family." Emerging into the light disrupted his train of thought. Ahead, glistening in the sunlight, was the magnificent Palais Garnier. Raoul's eyes glanced upwards towards the sculptures that topped the façade.

At the apex, towering above Paris, sat the bronzed Apollo — God of Music, with the gilded figural groups of *Harmony* and *Poetry* at either end. An ironic smile flashed across his handsome, dark, stubbled face.

"Would that is all I was seeking in this magnificent building?" Raoul thought as he resumed walking, his long, rhythmic strides belying the conflicting emotions and troubling thoughts within.

As he entered the opera house, a flurry of activity and noise greeted him. People were hurrying along the interweaving corridors, stairwells, alcoves and landings, this time in less formal attire. Standing in the centre of the magnificent Grand Staircase, was Enzo, that most enterprising and entertaining Italian. His wild hair was dyed the colour of a canary. Wearing a bow tie to match, with his left arm outstretched, baton in the right, he looked more like a ringmaster conducting a circus than the Stage Manager directing people into the right place for rehearsals. All the while a bell was ringing.

"Rehearsals are about to begin, Raoul," called Christine, her elegant voice floating in the air from the top of the Grand Staircase. He watched entranced as she seemed to glide down the ceremonial white marble staircase, her hand touching the red and green balustrades lightly as she moved towards him. She was dressed in yellow again, this time in a stylish buttercup yellow frock cinched with a black belt. Her long dark hair was tied back, emphasising the prominent cheekbones. Her alabaster skin was aglow. Raoul was taken aback yet again by her beauty.

Her green eyes locked onto his, "Come into the auditorium and watch for a while. *Macbeth* may give you some clues as to what happened to Philippe."

"How can I resist an offer like that, Mademoiselle?" he said, offering Christine his hand, then walking with her on his arm into the sumptuously decorated Italian horseshoe-shaped auditorium. Red velvet, stucco, marble and gold leaf adorned the five tiered auditorium with its sixty-metre high ceiling and two thousand seats, but the assembled cast and crew looked curiously at them as they walked past and sat close together on the far side. All too soon the hushed whispering and gossip began.

"Did you see that?"

"What a handsome couple they make."

Danielle's voice reached them. "Brava. She's been pining for Philippe too long." Hearing them, tears started to well and Christine trembled.

Raoul squeezed her hand reassuringly. "I'll find out what happened. No more harm will befall you, I promise," he said, lightly kissing her hand.

"I'll hold you to that," she said, squeezing his hand as if her life depended on it. "And now I must leave you, the Witches' chorus is first up for rehearsal."

Kissing his cheek, Christine stood. "I am in the chorus as well as understudy. Beware, I may cast a spell over you."

"You already have," thought Raoul, wondering if Christine would ever love him the way she loved his brother Philippe. Why is it he always thinks of his brother in the past tense? He mused.

Raoul leant forward to kiss her, but sensed someone was watching him. Looking upwards to Box 5 he saw Erik's eyes trained on him like a sniper. Erik quickly turned away, but in that split second, Raoul had seen a glimpse of the menacing side of the man. "What else lies behind that handsome mask?" he wondered.

"Damn that little detective, snooping around! And damn that witch with him as well!" raged Erik internally, angry with himself for having been seen.

He thrust open the door to his waiting henchmen. "Run a second check on the perimeter alarms," he barked at them. "Make sure no one, absolutely no-one, especially the high and mighty Raoul D'Arenberg gets beyond the barriers we have set. No snoopers. Fuck-ups will not be tolerated. Do you understand?" he asked menacingly.

"Yes, Boss." Jean Claude and Bernard spoke and nodded in unison then quickly moved away. The boss was in one of his moods. Best to keep one's head down.

Erik closed the door and sat down again, looking down into the auditorium from the Phantom's Box. His box, now. On stage were Macbeth and Banquo, the king's generals, listening to the witches' prophecy as they sang in dark, but beautiful unison.

"All hail Macbeth, Thane of Glamis. All hail Macbeth, Thane of Cawdor. All hail Macbeth, King of Scotland." Above the chorus, one voice rang clear and true — Christine's voice — piercing him like the knife of his torturer. Rage threatened to overwhelm him once more. Erik breathed deeply, trying to centre himself. With a discipline born of long practice in dark, confined spaces, he closed his eyes and mind to her voice until his breathing slowed and a deadly cold calm returned. Silence enveloped him like a thick blanket. He sat regally on his front row throne, surveying his royal court, breathing in the power he felt. Erik would fulfil his destiny through sheer determination. His years of suffering would be repaid in full, even if it took the blood of many others, starting with the upstart couple below — a pretend detective and a wannabe diva. He clenched his right hand, as if preparing to strike out against his kingdom. Then a whisper...

"All hail Erik, King of the Garnier. All hail Erik, Phantom of the Opera. All hail Erik, Usurper!"

Erik jumped to his feet, already on high alert. "Who is there?" he challenged, looking all around, but the box was empty, except for him.

Then, repeated in the quietest of whispers, a male voice he had heard once before, "All hail Erik, King of the Garnier. All hail Erik, Phantom of the Opera. All hail Erik, Usurper!" Erik withdrew a razor sharp switch blade from his jacket and walked to where the whispers had emanated. Knife drawn and ready to strike, he pulled the curtain open, but again Box 5 was empty. Erik froze, foreshadowing the lyrics as first Macbeth's deep baritone voice penetrated his consciousness.

"Bloody thoughts, from whence have you come?

Fate offers me a crown, which I will not stretch out my hand to snatch."

Banquo's bass voice answered, *"Often the evil spirit of hell tells us truths and betrays us, and cursed, we are then abandoned above the abyss dug out for us."*

Erik retaliated, tearing the curtain with swift gashes, as if a ghost stood between him and the velvet shreds. He repeatedly attacked as if he were surrounded by a hundred phantoms, but to no avail. A shiver ran down Erik's spine. "Is history going to repeat itself?" he asked the empty air. "No fucking way. I rule here," he retaliated defiantly, storming toward the Box 5 exit. "If anyone gets in my way, I will kill them," he spat out to the empty room, before throwing his knife hard into the back seat of his throne. As he turned to leave, he thought he saw blood trickle from the velvet chair, but he shook his head in disbelief at the thought, not daring to look back.

Raoul watched as Christine, the Witches' chorus, Macbeth and Banquo, exited the stage. Even singing with the chorus, Christine's voice rose above the others. Despite her disappointment at not being chosen for the lead role, Raoul knew she was a consummate professional and would perform any role to her utmost.

"Time to have a look around," he thought and pulled out his notebook before he headed to the exit.

"Next on stage, please Lady Macbeth and her Lady in Waiting," called Monsieur Laloux. Danielle appeared and looked around expectantly.

"Where is Lady Macbeth?" he asked impatiently.

"I don't know, Monsieur," responded Danielle. "Perhaps she is too good to rehearse," well knowing his reaction.

"What nonsense!" Laloux spluttered. "Only practice

makes perfect." He gestured to a small woman dressed all in black standing at the side of the stage.

"Yes, Monsieur?"

"Madame Giraud, find Madame Caccini at once and bring her here."

"Of course, Monsieur." With a small nod of her head, Madame Giraud moved off in her usual unobtrusive manner.

"Christine, come back on stage," called Monsieur Laloux, waving theatrically for the benefit of the waiting cast and crew. "You can be Lady Macbeth for the time being."

Sottovoce and smiling to himself, he muttered, "Let's see what *La Divina* thinks about that."

"Yes, indeed," echoed Danielle mischievously in more audible tones, "Let's see what *La Divina* thinks about that."

CHAPTER ELEVEN

THE MYSTERIOUS MADAME GIRAUD

Rumour around Paris had it that the ubiquitous Madame Giraud had been concierge at the Palais Garnier for thirty years or more, although no one remembered exactly how long ago she came here. Or if indeed, if she even lived here. Not even her Christian name was known. The mysterious Madame Giraud was short in stature but not in status. She moved with minimum fuss to the stage door, long black skirt trailing behind. In stark contrast was the short dark hair which hugged her head like a helmet. The hair was shot with grey, and if one was able to get close enough to look behind those black steel rimmed spectacles, one would see the same steel grey in her very alert eyes.

Many familiar with Paris' operatic world suspected

that Madame Giraud was more than an unassuming concierge, and that she knew every nook and cranny of the cavernous opera house, as well as all its secrets — past, present and future. Rumour had it she was able to see into a person's soul, but few dared to ask how or why. She held her counsel wisely, so zealously did she guard the Palais Garnier. Few were permitted into its inner sanctum, although rumour also had it she and the Opera Ghost were friends.

As Madame Giraud turned into the corridor nearing Madame Caccini's dressing room, she paused. Raoul was coming at a fast pace from the other end. Head down studying his notebook, oblivious to anything else, he barely avoided cannoning into her, snapping him back to his surroundings.

"Pardon, Madame."

"You are looking for me, Monsieur D'Arenberg?"

"No, Madame." He had seen the woman before. She was everywhere but he had no idea who she really was or what she really did, although her old-fashioned Parisian French spoke of another era.

"I am Madame Giraud, Monsieur and you are look-ing for a guide to the Palais Garnier. N'est pas?" Raoul looked at her a little confused. "You are investigating the mysterious happenings here. N'est pas?"

"Yes," he said, even more confused.

"Well then, follow me. First I have to deliver Lady Macbeth from her dressing room onto the stage for Monsieur Laloux, before he has apoplexy. Then I will be your guide."

She turned and started hurrying down the corridor. Raoul put his notebook in the breast pocket of his jacket and followed, wondering where this would lead.

Raoul stood behind Madame Giraud as she knocked on the leading lady's dressing room door. Moments passed before the door was opened.

"Pardon, Madame Caccini, I am Madame Giraud, the concierge. Monsieur Laloux requests your presence on stage for rehearsals."

"But I am not dressed yet. Tell him I will be there presently," Carlotta said with a moue, pointing to the sheer silk robe that did little to hide the contours of her svelte body. Raoul politely averted his gaze in amazement. Up close, this statuesque beauty bore no resemblance to the dumpy, overweight diva he had seen on stage performing *Norma* at La Scala over a decade ago.

"Monsieur Laloux asks that I bring you, Madame."

"How tiresome that little man is. And who is this? Your enforcer?" she said nodding towards Raoul.

"No, Madame. Monsieur D'Arenberg is waiting for me."

"Didn't I see you with Christine Dubois the other evening?"

"Yes, Madame."

"You are her patron, her lover, la Grande Passione, perhaps?"

Taken aback by her directness, Raoul answered a little wistfully, "No, Madame, my brother was."

"Very well, come in and wait." Madame Giraud entered the dressing room. As Raoul followed, Carlotta moved closer so that he brushed against her. Raoul hesitated.

"Scared of a real woman, Monsieur?" asked Carlotta artfully. She paused seductively, maintaining the contact. "What is your name, young man?"

"Raoul. Raoul D'Arenberg," he said, summoning all his willpower to speak in the presence of such a powerfully dominant sexual being.

"Well Raoul, Raoul D'Arenberg, amuse yourself here while I dress." Carlotta gestured around the dressing room, then traced her finger enticingly across his lips, before disappearing behind a huge screen.

A very uncomfortable Raoul looked at Madame Giraud but her face was unreadable. Seeking a distraction they gazed at the photos adorning the huge mirror and walls which showed photos of Carlotta Caccini's glittering career and her various roles in all the major opera houses around the world.

The universally acclaimed *La Divina*, was gifted with a rare voice, that of a dramatic coloratura soprano. At her height it was powerful, rich and emotive with a darker timbre. A voice that could hold notes longer and could sing over, or cut through, a full orchestra. As well, she could act. Dramatic weight loss had weakened her diaphragm and years of overwork and over-indulgence had damaged her remarkable voice. These days her jet set elegance, temperamental celebrity and fiery love life had made her legendary international reputation as a diva on and off stage. Her stormy personal life had eclipsed her professional one — clashing with opera companies, fellow singers and numerous lovers, walking off the stage or only singing when she felt like it.

"I need help with this zip, caro mio," Carlotta said, emerging from behind the screen and headed towards Raoul. Madame Giraud quickly stepped in between them to assist, eliciting a scowl from the diva.

"I wish to be conducted to the auditorium first. Monsieur Laloux can wait," she said, pursing her crimson lips in a pout, then flouncing towards the door in an exquisite, figure-hugging navy blue Chanel frock. She turned and extended her hand regally to Raoul.

"Your arm please, Monsieur D'Arenberg." Raoul quickly obliged as Madame Giraud led the way.

As Carlotta, Madame Giraud and Raoul entered the auditorium, it was filled with the lush sounds of René Bourdin's baritone voice contrasting exquisitely with the crystal quality and clarity of Christine's, lyrical soprano. They were rehearsing *Fatal mia donna (Fatal Woman)* from Act One. Already apparent was the harmony and chemistry between these two singers.

"Not nearly dramatic enough! I will show you how it should be sung," cried Carlotta, gesturing wildly, before storming towards the stage. René and Christine stopped mid-song, dumbfounded. René patted her hand reassuringly. Christine coloured and moved off stage.

"Ah, Madame Caccini has finally arrived. Please, let's start *Fatal Woman* again," said Monsieur Laloux pretending nothing untoward had happened. A gasp and wave of chatter ran through the watching cast and crew at the deliberate humiliation of the two singers. Only Erik, back in Box 5, was amused by the insult and the irony.

"I find the machinations and machismo of this power hungry woman very appealing, very appealing indeed. A woman who is prepared to sacrifice everything on the altar of her ambition and lust," he mused silently.

"Indeed, I think Carlotta Caccini and I have much in common," he said aloud, smiling to himself.

Meanwhile, Raoul, appalled at the treatment of Christine, moved to console her, but Madame Giraud, seeing Erik in the auditorium, nodded to Raoul and then at the stage door. Reluctantly he obeyed.

CHAPTER TWELVE

IN THE CELLARS OF
THE OPERA HOUSE

"Once upon a time, all this machinery was moved by hand." Madame Giraud and Raoul stood in the huge space underneath the opera stage, looking around. Accessed by a wooden bridge, a row of giant cog wheels with ropes and pulleys for set changes, stood idle. Faint sounds of distant steps sounding on the floor of the theatre above wafted down to them, but Raoul barely noticed, so intent was he on listening to Madame Giraud.

"The Garnier is a vast subterranean network of cellars and corridors – catacombs with staircases, trapdoors, sewers and lakes, full of hiding places and escape tunnels. Many unknown passages leading into the opera cellars from outside still exist. I have not ventured very far into this underground world, nor do I wish to." Cold, dank air, swirled around them as if emphasising her distaste.

"I know enough to show you how to access them for your investigations, but you must be very, very careful," she said earnestly, as her hand exerted firm pressure on his forearm.

"Thank you, Madame, but why are you helping me?"

"Evil is afoot here, Monsieur D'Arenberg. I was told to expect you and told to help you."

"Who told you that?" asked Raoul, surprised.

"That is not important, right now, Monsieur. What is important is that you find out what is happening and stop it before any more harm comes to the Palais Garnier."

"I will," Raoul vowed reassuringly, without knowing what was in store for him.

"Over a century ago, this underground world teemed with workers. Some even lived down here, mostly old men," she said as she moved forward. "Worn-out scene-shifters, rat catchers, watermen, maintenance men unclogging sewers, and old door shutters. Draft-expellers they were called. Drafts are very bad for the voice, wherever they come from. Even thieves hid here – believing falsely they were safer in the darkness here than in the world above." She turned to look at him, her face serious. "Many were never seen again."

Stopping at a little staircase, they peered into the darkness below. Madame Giraud reached into her voluminous skirt pocket and removed two flashlights. Giving one to Raoul, she continued her tale, "There are five vast underground cellars underneath the stage. Each level is accessed by a staircase like this one, or by a series of trapdoors. At the bottom, level six, is a lake which, when water is released, can flow out into the Seine."

"How do you know all this?" asked Raoul.

"A friend of mine lived here a long time ago," she said enigmatically. "He told me about it. Come, I will take you down to the first cellar to show you what to expect. You can come back later on your own to explore further."

"I'll go first," said Raoul, his flashlight barely registering in the gloom at the foot of the steep staircase. He stepped down two treads, then turned and offered his hand. Madame Giraud took it gratefully, using the flashlight in her other hand to light their way. As they slowly descended, the air became noticeably colder. Nearing the bottom step their flashlights played around the walls. It was a catacomb, a series of enormous stone archways and pillars. Corridors led off in all directions. Deep niches had been carved out of the walls. Directly ahead was a sign saying *Entry Strictly Forbidden*. They stepped around either side.

"During the days of the Paris Commune, these corridors were used by the revolutionaries to store food and ammunition," whispered Madame Giraud. "Some say the bodies of those massacred in the riots were left here."

Raoul took a few more steps forward, but Madame Giraud suddenly grabbed him.

"Turn off your flashlight, and don't move," she whispered. He did as he was told. The cellar was plunged into darkness. A blast of cold air hit them. Something moved in the darkness ahead. Raoul's skin crawled.

"What is it?" he whispered. Fear gnawed at him, but whatever was there was moving away, the sound of something cloth-like brushing against the walls receded as it moved further down the cellar.

They waited a few more moments, before Madame Giraud said, "It was a warning. Look." They turned on their flashlights. One step ahead of where Raoul stood, a trip wire glinted. Knee high, strung from one pillar to the next, with what looked like a security camera at the foot of the nearest pillar. Raoul took a deep breath. A narrow escape. Disaster had been averted. This time.

"Who comes down here now, Madame?"

"Only Monsieur Destler, the Head of Security, and his cronies are allowed here, now."

"Well, there must be something down here they want to hide. And I'm going to find out what it is," said Raoul determinedly. "But first I must find out more about this overly zealous security manager, Monsieur Destler."

CHAPTER THIRTEEN

THE CHANDELIER WOBBLES

Madame Giraud entered the auditorium at the rear while Raoul entered from the stage door. Raoul looked up at Box 5. Erik was sitting there watching. He smiled knowingly at him. Raoul glared back. Very little escaped Erik's notice at the Palais Garnier. His security cameras had alerted him to the breach on Level One. Thinking of Madame Giraud's foolishness and naiveté, brought another smile. An interfering old busy body. As if choosing not to enter the auditorium with Raoul would make any difference to his knowing whose side she was on, or where they had been.

"Interfering bastards, you will keep," vowed Erik, wrenching his eyes from Raoul to Carlotta. She was still on stage, an hour later and, judging by her body language, she was fuming. Eyes flashing, body rigid, furious at being held over for so long. He looked around. Nearly all the cast and crew were watching expectantly, waiting with bated breath for an explosion, one that looked like it would surely come.

"Act One, *Nel dì della vittoria (In the day of victory)*, one last time, Madame Caccini. Even the best can be better," said Monsieur Laloux obsequiously, tweaking his Dali moustache. He was making the most of the opportunity. Judging by Madame's pouting and flouncing, the hiatus wouldn't last much longer.

Erik looked down at Christine. She sat apart in the audience, tense and upright, wanting to be alone. She would be angry, still smarting from the public humiliation of Carlotta's dismissal. Typically, Carlotta had not endeared herself to Christine or the rest of the cast and crew, but they had stayed on, watching and listening closely, secretly hoping the diva's voice might falter again on that high note. Just a slight wobble, but he had heard it. So had Christine and Monsieur Laloux. And so had Carlotta. That was why she was so angry.

Erik watched as Raoul slipped into the seat beside Christine, surprising her. She flashed him a lukewarm smile, but her eyes betrayed her. Wordlessly, he put his arm around her shoulders and hugged her warmly.

Christine rested her head on Raoul's shoulder. Erik scowled as he watched the tender display.

"I will have the greatest of pleasure ensuring they come to the same sticky end as his interfering brother, Philippe. No one gets in my way," he vowed.

Monsieur Laloux signalled to the pianist and then to Carlotta who stepped forward gracefully to centre stage. Even in rehearsal and without costume, she had an impressive and commanding presence. He nodded to her. As if by magic, Carlotta disappeared and Lady Macbeth took centre stage, imbued with a statuesque solemnity. As the dramatic dark timbre of her voice took hold of him, Erik closed his eyes and became lost in the lyrics of the aria.

"You are ambitious Macbeth. You long for glory, but shall you be wicked enough?"

"Yes, my Lady, I shall. I am not weak like your partner, Marchand," Erik responded from his eyrie, opening his eyes and leaning forward. Carlotta's eyes locked on to his.

"The path to power is full of misdeeds and woe to whom sets an uncertain foot on it and retreats." Pacing the stage and clasping her hands to her heart, her voice filled the auditorium — full, rich and powerful, singing only for Erik.

"Come on hurry up. I want to set a fire in thy cold heart. I shall provide you the necessary strength to carry out the bold deed," she challenged him.

"*You were promised the throne. Why are you delaying? Accept the gift. Ascend to it.*" As Carlotta's passionate voice rose and fell, Erik was enraptured by her electrifying performance. It was a dare, a challenge.

Mouth wide open, arms outstretched, reaching ever higher for the final glorious sound, "*Reign!*" Carlotta's voice wobbled tremulously on the high note, in concert with the seven-ton bronze chandelier, which swayed ominously above an awestruck Erik.

CHAPTER FOURTEEN

THE DIFFICULT DIVA

Please, Carlotta, opening night is only three weeks away." Victor Marchand, was pacing in his partner's dressing room, a worried frown, etched deep into an already lined forehead. He was followed closely by a fluffy red toy poodle barking at his heels.

"Stop pacing Victor, you're making Fifi anxious." He stopped suddenly and Fifi bumped into him, squealing, and then barking at him loudly and crossly.

"Heavens above, Victor. Be careful! Come here Fifi, come to Mama," she said patting her knee. Fifi jumped up and nestled into her lap. "Mama loves you," Carlotta stroked her soft fur lovingly, ignoring an exasperated Victor.

"You spent all last week resting your voice, now you must return to rehearsals. The opera needs you. Paris needs you. I need you, ma chérie," pleaded Victor.

Carlotta looked at her ageing partner dispassionately. Now sixty-five, twenty-five years her senior, she remembered when she first met him. He was a wealthy, opera-loving impresario, a short, dapper man in his late forties, head of the family entertainment business, and very much a ladies man. The Romeo of Rennes, as he was known, had been assigned as her official escort for her premiere performance at the Rennes Opera House. After touring Greece, America and Italy, the new and exciting opera singer, who had won praise wherever she sang, had come to conquer France.

Love had played no part in her life until Victor started courting her. He said he admired her for herself, not just her voice. He was gentle, affectionate and supportive, a constant source of strength when her fears and anxieties threatened to overwhelm her, as they often did, especially before a performance. She had learnt to love him, certainly not to rely on him. Had perhaps even fallen slightly in love with him. With her career and love life blossoming in those days, Carlotta had never been as happy. Were she not a slave to her art, she may have considered giving up singing for him and getting married. Instead, she allowed Victor to assume control over her career by becoming her personal manager, agent and sponsor. Even if there were some things she kept secret from him.

Victor's voice now broke into her reverie, sharp and chiding. "The damage to your reputation will be irreparable if you pull out of this opera, too. And we will be sued, again. It could ruin us financially, mais non?"

Carlotta looked at her husband with disdain. "That's all you care about, Victor. I'm just a cash cow to you," she said, her voice rising. Fifi barked, echoing the sentiment. Meeting Victor had given her the security and affection missing in her childhood. For him, Carlotta's rising career meant the cards were stacked in their favour. The financial dealings became a bonanza. Driving a hard bargain was heaven itself. The more international and glamorous Carlotta's career became, the more her talent was acclaimed, the harder he bargained, and the more diminished his own reputation became. The truth was that wherever possible Victor asked for payment in cash, and soon was siphoning off some of Carlotta's money for his own use.

"Remember your first performance as Lady Macbeth at La Scala, ma chérie?"

"I certainly do. It was a triumph," replied Carlotta, haughtily. "How could anyone forget?" Drawn into the conversation against her will.

Carlotta sighed, her fingers unconsciously twirling round and around Fifi's long, fluffy ears, as the memories flooded back. The sleepwalking scene had electrified the audience. They applauded for a full fifteen minutes before they would allow her to continue. In the lead up to that performance she had shed eighty-pounds. Before that performance, she and Victor had spent months apart, she to secretly diet and exercise, he to engross himself in contracts and business affairs. Her magical transformation had stunned him, her audiences and captivated the world. The ugly duckling had become an exotically beautiful swan, and, combined with her divine singing, was quickly acclaimed as *La Divina*.

She could not forget that after that performance, she had been introduced to the man who became the love of her life, Antonio Biasini, a wealthy, debonair Italian business tycoon, whom she called Tony. The one man who had the power to make her forget the world of opera.

"You were perfect for the role," said Victor, trying to charm her back to the present.

"I was," replied Carlotta. "Once upon a time," she thought, shrugging off the compliment, as she wandered wistfully back into the past. The master composer, Guiseppi Verdi, had wanted Lady Macbeth to be ugly and evil. Carlotta agreed with him, and made her voice deliberately harsh and dark — yet somehow glorious — to create the atmosphere the music demanded; for she regarded herself not just a sublime singer, but a dramatic artist who could breathe life into the characters she played.

Never a naturally beautiful voice like Christine's, her voice had always been in some respects a flawed instrument, but through sheer determination and unrelenting hours of practice, she had triumphed over her limitations. Just as she had triumphed over a childhood and family background where music and art had no place. It was sheer luck that she had been heard singing in the local church by one of the best teachers in the country.

By virtue of her voice, musicianship, magnetic stage presence and her flaming temperament, she attracted attention from the world's media and theatre critics. Even more so after Tony came into her life as she moved amongst his world of billionaires and the highest echelons of international society. Carlotta Caccini, was glamour incarnate, but controversy followed her everywhere. It still did. She was sick of it all.

"But not you, my darling little girl," she thought as she stroked her beloved Fifi. "It is only you whom I can count on, to remain truly loyal."

Victor again broke into her thinking. "*La Divina*, made opera mean something again. You, still do." His voice had taken on a desperate, whining note. Carlotta looked at

Victor dispassionately again. Theirs had been a sexless partnership for over a decade. She realised money was the god Victor worshipped. He had turned a blind eye to her passionate and tempestuous five-year affair with Tony, the tycoon. Whereas she would have given up everything for him, Tony had left her for a widow, not even a wealthy one, but an aristocrat with a title. Despite the devastation of hurt and public humiliation, she refused to criticise him. She still loved him and desperately wanted him back. Yet she knew it was impossible. Never again would she be hurt like that.

"Victor, every year I want to be better than the year before. Otherwise I retire. I don't need the money. I work for art." It was true. In spite of her extravagant lifestyle and profligate spending, she didn't sing to become wealthier. What Carlotta still craved was the limelight, the need to be loved, adored. To hear that avalanche of applause, the roar of cheers growing steadily louder followed by a standing ovation, curtain calls, brilliant reviews and bouquets. How she loved that.

Carlotta had always felt isolated from her colleagues and the musical and operatic world around her. Despite the presence of Victor by her side, and the younger lovers that amused her, she increasingly felt very alone and fearful. Haunted by a gnawing doubt that her ageing voice, was no longer an instrument she could rely on. That fame and fortune were behind her.

"Well, if you feel your voice is no longer up to the role, perhaps I should ask Christine to play Lady Macbeth," said Victor, deliberately provoking her.

"How dare you say that, Victor?" An outraged Carlotta leapt to her feet, sending Fifi flying. "Don't you dare offer that young upstart my role," she screamed at him. Fifi cowered in the corner, whimpering. Carlotta leant down and picked her up. Cradling her in her arms, she turned on Victor again, challenging him, "See what you made me do. This is all your fault. Wanting to put that ambitious bitch in my place. How could you?"

Victor judged it better to remain silent.

Carlotta calmed, "A couple more days' resting my voice and then I will return to rehearsals."

"Wonderful, ma chérie," said Victor smiling smugly. He knew his partner so well.

CHAPTER FIFTEEN

HIDDEN AND FORBIDDEN PLACES

Christine was hurriedly coming out of her dressing room as Victor was leaving Carlotta's. She paused.

"Hello Monsieur Marchand. How is Madame Caccini today?" she asked solicitously.

"Thank you for your concern, Christine. Her voice is gradually recovering. She'll begin rehearsals again in a couple of days."

"I'm pleased to hear that. Please pass on my regards."

"Where are you heading in such a hurry Mademoiselle?"

"I'm late for a meeting with Monsieur D'Arenberg. He has asked me to give him a tour of the opera house above ground, above the trap doors for a change. He's been coming to the opera since he was a school boy but has never seen beyond the grand public spaces. Into the hidden corners and the forbidden places of the Palais Garnier."

"Perhaps, Mademoiselle," said Victor, holding onto her arm proprietorially, "you might do the same for me."

Christine's skin crawled, but she replied politely. "Of course, Monsieur Marchand, but I must go now," moving her arm away.

"Please call me, Victor."

"Very well, Victor." Christine flashed him a winning smile, as she walked away, hating herself for being so obsequious.

Raoul was waiting impatiently in the entry foyer at the rear of the building as Christine rushed out of a nearby door.

"You're late," he called, a frown on his face.

"I'm sorry," she said, flushed and breathless.

"Is everything alright?"

"How I detest our new Opera Manager and his partner," she said, scowling.

"What's happened?"

"Forget it," she said, dismissing the question with a wave of her hand. "And now you want me to help you with your investigations." Her green eyes were flashing with irritation. "It's a wild goose chase, if you ask me." Her voice was rising.

"Christine, please. I'm sure Philippe disappeared around the opera house somewhere. This is where he was last seen." Raoul touched her arm gently. "He loved you, Christine. Philippe would never have gone off and left you willingly. And he would never have gone off without telling me either." Tears welled in Christine's eyes. Raoul's heart melted. He loved her, too. He had to find out so he and Christine could move on and not forever be left in this limbo.

Raoul went on, "I'm convinced something has happened to him. Some evil has befallen him, and I'm determined to find out what."

Christine patted his arm reassuringly. "So am I, now, but it's been so long. How can I help?"

"Show me all the hidden and forbidden places above ground in the opera house, anywhere at all, where someone could hide."

"Alright," said Christine with a wan smile. "There are so many. I only have an hour and a half before I start rehearsals again," she said checking her watch. "Let's start from the top and work our way down. But first..." she said brightening up, "there's a special hidden place I want to show you."

Christine opened the door to the seventh floor roof at the back of the building. She signalled to Raoul to follow

her up a spindly iron ladder and out a narrow glass door
onto a parapet about two feet wide. There a verdigris roof
sloped away to empty air on one side and the cracked
panes of a skylight sloping up the other. In between were
five weathered wooden boxes from which bees crawled to
launch themselves lazily into the crisp winter sunshine.

"Beehives," said Raoul, amazed.

"Yes," said Christine, 'the apiarist is a Mr. Paucton.
Originally he was a prop man for the Garnier, then the
opera house fireman. He used to raise trout in the building's huge underground lake, too."

"I thought bees died out or hibernated in winter," he
said ducking and waving away a bee that came too close.

"No, they reduce numbers and are a little less active."

"Not around me, they're not," said Raoul, dancing
wildly on the parapet, slapping and swearing at the buzzing creatures.

Christine laughed and warned him. "It's best to stay
back of that hive in case they get angry."

Raoul walked further out onto the thirty-foot-square
roof overlooking the mansards, steeples and domes of
Paris. They could see for miles. "Paris is such a beautiful city."

"Yes, isn't it?" said Christine.

His eyes travelled towards the corner of the roof at the

front of the opera house, where one of the two bronze statues of *Fame Holding Pegasus* reared up. "Magnificent," he thought and leaned out over the parapet to look down onto the street below. Ant-like people were scurrying to and fro.

"Aha, I wonder what they're up to." Raoul recognised Erik and two of his cronies coming out onto Rue Scribe from the Palais Garnier, walking quickly. Raoul remembered something he'd heard about a gate opening into Rue Scribe from the lake. Rumour? Or had he read about it somewhere? No matter, time to investigate. He headed towards the glass door.

"See you later," said Raoul.

"Where are you going?" a surprised Christine asked, "don't you want me to show you anymore?"

"Yes," he replied, "but not today. While the cat's away the mouse can play," he said, blowing her a kiss and headed down the ladder. Christine smiled and shook her head.

CHAPTER SIXTEEN

THE GARNIER'S SECRETS

Raoul's long, lithe legs raced down the seven flights of stairs two at a time, heading for Rue Scribe. Outside in the street, he went round, looking for outlets, his hands seeking out cracks, of stones that could be moved, a gate or a door, made of bars, iron bars. "Was it this one? Or this one? Or these? Could that be an air hole?" He peered through gaps and gates, through bars. How dark it was! He listened... All was silence! He made his way all around the building. More gates, bigger bars, but leading to where?

He raced inside to an inconspicuous office on the ground floor at the rear of the building. He leant over to catch his breath before knocking. The door opened.

"You need my help, Monsieur D'Arenberg?" asked Madame Giraud.

"Can you see through doors, too, Madame?"

Madame Giraud smiled enigmatically, and waited for Raoul to speak.

"Could you tell me where to find a gate or a door made of bars, iron bars, opening into Rue Scribe, and leading to the underground lake?"

"I know about the lake under the opera, Monsieur, and I have heard about a door leading to it from Rue Scribe, but I have never seen it!"

Raoul shrugged and sighed, disappointed. "Well then, I will search Box 5. Could you stand guard for me, please?"

Madame Giraud nodded, quickly closed over the door to her office and turned around. Raoul had already started to move off.

"No, this way, Monsieur. It is quicker." She led him through a nearby fire door into a stairwell. They exited on the first floor, onto a small landing at the rear of the stage.

"The place is like a maze," said Raoul, astounded. "How will I ever find my way around the Palais Garnier in a few days?" he wondered, ruefully.

"Along here," said Madame Giraud, leading the way along a narrow corridor. They emerged onto the rich, circular-patterned, mosaic tiled gallery. Ahead were the doors to the boxes, carved mahogany doors. The entrances were lipped with lush red carpet. Madame pointed to the second door on the right. "There, Monsieur. Box 5."

"Thank you, Madame Giraud." Raoul cautiously looked around. Nary a soul was in sight.

"Please hurry," she whispered urgently, "we haven't got long."

Raoul entered the lavishly decorated box and closed the door. Rich, red, floral-patterned- fabric lined the walls. The box was framed by two ornately carved golden pillars either side. A single red velvet upholstered mahogany chair and a small shelf fixed to the wall was the only furniture. He walked to the ornate balcony overlooking the empty amphitheatre. On stage, two men were manoeuvring a large banquet table into place, whilst another two were rigging lighting. Both teams were being directed by a man with a shock of yellow hair. Raoul recognised Enzo, the Stage Manager, and his prop team. Behind-the-scenes people like him and Madame Giraud, he thought, wryly.

He tapped on the walls of Box 5. Solid enough. Not enough room for a man to hide. The pillars were much larger, they could accommodate a person, but there was no access to them. Which only left the ceiling. Perhaps a crawl space in the ceiling. He started to climb on the chair when the door opened. He started. Madame

Giraud's face was pale, shocked. She entered the box and closed the door.

"Is someone coming?" Raoul asked with concern.

Madame Giraud put her finger to her lips, shushing him. She leant her head slightly to the left listening intently to something he could not see or hear. Goosebumps peppered his body, chilling him.

"Who are you?" she asked quietly, then listened intently again.

"Who are you talking to?" Raoul whispered, but she ignored him.

"Where are you?" She nodded, straining to listen closer, then looked at Raoul and sighed deeply. "He's moved away. I can't hear him anymore."

"Who's moved away? For God's sake, Madame," he cried in frustration, "who the hell were you talking to?"

"It's not safe to talk here. The walls have ears. Hurry, they'll be back soon." Madame Giraud turned and headed back the way they came. Raoul followed, questions pounding in his head all the way to her office.

"Madame. Tell me, please."

"Please sit," she said calmly, looking at Raoul who was ready to explode with frustration. He sat down heavily while Madame Giraud explained. "I heard voices coming from inside the box while I was waiting."

"How could you? No one was in there, but me," he said firmly.

"These were voices, many voices from the spirits, from another realm."

"From another realm, indeed! What kind of a fool do you take me for, Madame?" Raoul scoffed.

"There are spirits trapped below, some from long ago, some more recent, men and women."

"Spirits?" Raoul asked in disbelief.

"Yes, spirits. Their souls cannot depart until things are righted."

"Spare me this nonsense, Madame."

Madame Giraud looked directly at him. She had met with this kind of unthinking and obstinate opposition all her life. The most deluded people were those who choose to ignore what they already know. She was reminded of the old adage, *there are none so blind as those who do not see.* Instead she said, kindly,

"In time you will come to understand, Monsieur. For now, please trust me."

CHAPTER SEVENTEEN

REHEARSAL INTERRUPTED

I want the image of Banquo's ghost to show up at this end of the banquet table." Monsieur Laloux was instructing Georges, his lighting manager. He went on to explain, "Macbeth killed his rival but he comes back to haunt him at the banquet. I want the ghost to appear then disappear. Can you do this?"

"Of course, Monsieur. We are using Ray Optics. It was used for the classical Pepper's Ghost illusion," said Georges. "We put it in this small room here, out of direct sight of the audience, with a wall of glass angled between the stage and the room. The audience can see the stage but not the glass."

"Yes, yes," said Monsieur Laloux, impatiently, "but can the image of Banquo's ghost appear exactly here?" he says pointing to the end of the table.

"Wherever you wish, Monsieur. I'll show you." Georges

placed the dummy in the corner of the small room and indicated to his offsider, "Richard, turn the lights on, please." Banquo's ghost appeared, but away from the table. "The light propagates from the 'ghost' to the glass. Some of the light is reflected and reaches the audience."

"Please, Georges, I'm not interested in the how," he said, his high-pitched voice becoming more voluble, "I just want him standing pressed up to the table."

Georges pointed to Richard who adjusted the dummy, and the illusion of Banquo's ghost was perfectly positioned.

"Now turn the light off and on and make Banquo appear and disappear." Georges did this three times. "Wonderful," said Monsieur Laloux, effusively, happily clapping his hands. "Thank you, Georges and Richard."

Turning to the actors waiting in the auditorium, "Now let's try it with the four main actors in the banquet scenes in Act Two, starting with *Salve, o re! (Hello, O king!)* Clapping his hands once more he called, "On stage please, Macbeth, Lady Macbeth, Macduff and the Lady-in-Waiting." René, Marias and Danielle walked up the steps to the stage.

"And, where pray, is Madame Caccini?" Monsieur Laloux cried, hands outstretched theatrically, as if in prayer.

"Perhaps her voice has not yet recovered," suggested Danielle.

"Merde! That woman tries my patience. I will have no more of this nonsense," he said ignoring her. "Madame Giraud, Madame Giraud," he called.

"Yes, Monsieur," said Madame Giraud, who had quickly appeared from the wings. "Fetch Madame Caccini and bring her here. At once!" He barked the order at his faithful concierge. Madame Giraud nodded and moved away swiftly.

"Christine Dubois, come up on stage. You are Lady Macbeth, again."

"Yes, Monsieur," said Christine, keeping her head down as she stood up, so he would not see the smile on her face. René, Marias and Danielle avoided each other's eyes, trying not to smile, too. Carlotta had won no hearts amongst the actors here at the Paris Opera.

"We'll walk through the scene first, then sing it, alright?" Christine, Danielle, René and Marias nodded. "Macbeth, in the middle of the table, facing the audience." René moved to position. "Lady Macbeth seated opposite, back to the audience. Macduff seated beside Macbeth, and the lady-in-waiting beside Lady Macbeth," said Monsieur Laloux, indicating the chair in each position. The three actors moved to their respective chairs. "Sit, please."

"Macbeth, draw attention to Banquo's absence. Then go to sit in his place." René moves to Banquo's chair whilst Monsieur Laloux signalled to Georges. Banquo's ghost appeared.

"But only Macbeth can see it," said René, his booming voice a welcome change from Laloux's high-pitched and querulous instructions, "and his wild questions make no sense to the others." Laloux signalled to Georges again and the ghost vanished.

"Then Lady Macbeth browbeats her husband into behaving calmly," said Christine, walking through her part. "She proposes another toast, but the ghost appears again to Macbeth." Laloux signalled again and the ghost reappeared.

René continued, "And Macbeth's raving disrupts the banquet."

"Very good. Back in position for the start of the scene, please." Monsieur Laloux turned to the pianist patiently waiting. "Maestro, *Sangue a me quell'ombra chiede (Blood to me asks that shadow)* if you please," he waved.

René turned to the ghost who had reappeared. Then his deep dulcet tones filled the air.

"Go spirit of hell!
Earth, open a ditch
And swallow him…"

Suddenly pandemonium broke loose back stage.

Sounds of people running. Screams and wailing in the distance, "Catch her, catch Fifi, please. Don't let her escape." A red toy poodle, its tiny feet skittering on the wooden floor, burst onto the stage, its long ears with pretty pink bows streaming behind her. Fifi began doing excited laps around the banquet table, in and out and under the actors' chairs, barking all the while, leaving the actors and crew surprised but amused, but with Monsieur Laloux shaking and mute with rage.

Jean Claude suddenly burst onto the stage, too, following the little dog around, shouting over and over, "Here, Fifi, come here, Fifi." Fifi paused now and then, teasingly, before taking off in fright whenever Jean Claude came close. The shrieks and wails continued to come ever closer.

By this time a crowd had gathered to see what the commotion was all about, laughing at the pantomime unravelling in front of them. Erik moved quickly through the auditorium, onto the stage and skillfully intervened, by scooping Fifi up on one of her laps around the stage. He held her high in the air, then brought her close to his chest to calm her beating heart. Applause rang out as a breathless Madame Giraud, followed closely by an even more breathless Carlotta, appeared on stage.

"Quelle horreur! What is the meaning of this outrage?" spluttered Monsieur Laloux, finally regaining his voice.

"It's all your fault, you odious little man," Carlotta screamed at him, going to Erik, who was stroking Fifi, who, as usual, was lapping up the attention.

"You saved her, Monsieur. You saved Fifi, my precious baby."

"At your service, Madame," said Erik, bowing slightly.

"Could you bring her to my dressing room, please?"

"Of course."

"I need to check she has not been harmed," she said, glaring at Jean Claude.

"But you are expected here at rehearsals, Madame Caccini," said Monsieur Laloux, lowering his voice, his face a flaming red, as his anger threatened to boil over.

"Not now. Fifi is more important," she said, dismissing the Artistic Director with an imperious wave of her hand. "Come, Monsieur Destler." And with that she flounced off as Erik, still holding Fifi, followed closely behind.

"How can I ever repay you for rescuing Fifi, Monsieur Destler?" Fifi was now happily ensconced on a velvet cushion, resting after all her excitement.

"Call me Erik, please."

"Very well. How can I ever repay you properly for rescuing Fifi, Erik?" asked Carlotta provocatively.

"By having dinner with me tomorrow evening." Erik

picked up Carlotta's hand and held it. "A private dinner here at the opera house, Madame, s'il vous plaît." He grazed her hand with his lips, his eyes looking deep into hers. Carlotta was mesmerised by this charming man.

"My pleasure. *Il piacere è tutto mio*," she said, emphasising her Italian accent, as she withdrew her hand from his, but not before running a finger enticingly over his lips.

Erik nodded courteously to Carlotta, before speaking, "9.00 pm at the stage door entrance, Signora. Until then, addio."

CHAPTER EIGHTEEN

AN ASSIGNATION

It was a freezing cold February evening in Paris. Opening night was a fortnight away. Buffered against the chill night air, Erik was wearing his long, black full dress uniform cape and white gloves. He paced to and fro outside the stage door, waiting impatiently for Carlotta to appear. Snow was not far away. Although his handsome features were pinched with cold, there was no hint of the ugliness and torment that lay within. Erik looked at his watch for the umpteenth time. Nearly an hour late!

"Damn the woman," he muttered, angrily. "Damnable diva! She'll soon learn not to play games with me!" A black limousine rounded the corner and slowly drew up beside the stage door entrance, stopping directly in front of him. Erik stepped forward, opened the rear door and offered Carlotta his hand. She stepped elegantly out of, and away from, the car. Still holding Erik's hand, she allowed him to admire her.

Dressed in a full length fur coat — a stunning black onyx mink, Carlotta's dark brown hair was tightly drawn back in a glamorous coil around her beautiful, swan-like neck. A low-cut, long-sleeved emerald green silk crepe dress, slit to the thighs, revealed towering black patent-leather ankle boots which accentuated her elegant slimness and her height. Her flashing green eyes ringed with black kohl, locked onto Erik's, drawing him into her orbit. The only hint of colour was her lips, painted a deep scarlet. She smiled. A noticeable tremor coursed through him. Erik chastised himself silently. Carlotta smiled again, well knowing the effect of her magnetism on men, even so-called 'men of the world', like Erik Destler.

Erik kissed her hand, leaving his lips there while he held her gaze, drank her in. He was becoming intoxicated. Enough! "Let us move inside, Madame." Letting go of her hand, he steered her towards the stage door, "It is too cold to stay out here," he said, opening the door with one hand, whilst his other hand was placed gently, but proprietorially in the small of her back, trying to move her inside.

She stopped, turned and kissed him on the mouth, a lingering kiss, then withdrew to look at him, "Carlotta, please." Erik's lips were stained a deep red. "Oh, dear."

Carlotta took a small white lace handkerchief from inside her voluminous mink coat, then wiped the lipstick away, teasingly, as he gazed, entranced by her eyes that were like liquid green pools.

Trying to regain the upper hand, Erik placed her arm over his, and said, "This way please, Carlotta."

Looking like a glamorous couple going to the opera, he led her past the rear of the stage, into the main foyer and up the grand staircase. Except that being a Sunday night, and pre-season, the opera house was barely lit. They were the only ones in the Palais Garnier. He had given his security guards the evening off. Erik and Carlotta emerged on the first floor landing, leading to the boxes. Erik headed to Box 5. "Welcome to my own private Box, Carlotta. Box 5." With a theatrical flourish of his cape over his shoulder, revealing the royal blue satin lining, he opened the door. Carlotta entered. Erik followed, closing the door quietly behind him.

A single candle mounted in an exquisitely carved gold candelabra sat on the small shelf, giving the small room a warm glow. Beside it, basking in the glow, sat a beautiful hand-cut crystal vase filled with long-stemmed, blood-red roses. Whilst Carlotta looked around, Erik removed his gloves and cape, laying them carefully on the single arm chair. Carlotta had moved to the front of the box and was looking down into the darkened auditorium. The rich red velvet cross-over curtains with their burnished gold embroidery and tassels, were draped in front of the stage.

Erik moved up and stood behind her, his hand placed firmly in the middle of her back once more. "The stage performance will start a little later, my dear." Carlotta leaned back into him feeling his hardness pressing against her. Erik kissed her on the nape of the neck, his breath hot against her skin. Carlotta breathed deeply and turned to face him. Silently, Erik slid the fur coat off her shoulders, then delicately extracted one arm at a time, before letting it fall to the floor. They stood there, looking at each other, minds inextricably locked together, pulses racing. The will to dominate each other paramount.

Erik opened his arms. Carlotta walked into them. They stood there intertwined, arms around each other, holding each other gently, exquisitely, swaying as Erik's fingers slowly danced down her arms, around her neck, over her back.

"Night time sharpens, heightens each sensation." The air was suddenly filled with music as Erik's powerful voice resonated off the walls.

"Darkness stirs and wakes imagination," he sang. Carlotta's fingers echoed the slow, sensuous pace up and down

his arms and back in return, surprised by the lovely quality of his singing. Erik loosened her hair, his fingers sliding their way sensuously through one silky strand at a time, sending quivers rippling through Carlotta. Erik's attention then turned to her face and neck, his lips moving in concert with his fingers, delicately kissing her skin, light as a feather. And between time singing. Carlotta was swept away by the sensation of it all.

"Who is this man singing to me?" she wondered, secretly delighted that he was. As their bodies swayed rhythmically in a sea of sensation, Carlotta found herself letting go and becoming lost in the moment. This wonderful moment.

Erik turned Carlotta's back to him and started unzipping her dress. Mouth pressed close to her neck, his voice softer now,

"And you'll live as you never lived before." Carlotta trembled as Erik slowly slipped the dress from her body, letting it too fall on the floor. She turned and faced him, stark naked, quivering with anticipation, then she closed her eyes, lost in space, in a timeless reverie.

Erik slowly undressed and spread Carlotta's mink coat in the centre of the room. Carlotta felt like she was floating on a cloud as she swayed in time with her phantom and the music of the night. Eyes still closed, Erik caught her and eased her gently onto her back on the coat. Carlotta opened her eyes, sighed, and knew it was time to open up her mind and let her fantasies unwind.

Erik lay down beside her. His fingers delicately traced her nipples, giving them a flick now and then. Carlotta's nether regions twitched with each delicious jolt. The delicate tracery continued, up and down Carlotta's belly, her breasts, her arms. Then Erik turned his attention to her legs, the insides of her thighs, all the while coming closer and closer to her sex, the pace slow, rhythmic, and loving.

"This is not sex," thought Carlotta, "it is a dance of love." She surrendered to the power of Erik's voice and his sublimely, enticing, sensual touch. As their lips and bodies merged, a lightning bolt surged through them filling Box 5 with the sound of sensual pleasures.

Afterwards, they lay together, sated, Erik's strong arms still enfolding her. The flickering light of the candles gave a ghostly appearance to their cocoon. As his lips grazed her neck, a tremor ran through Carlotta's body.

"A banquet awaits, my lady. Here, let me help you up," he said, offering his hand. They slipped on their clothes and Erik zipped up Carlotta's dress. "Over here," he said, indicating the balcony at the front of the box. He stood behind her, as the curtains slowly opened, revealing a darkened stage. Wine goblets and platters of food were laid out on the banquet table adorned with a red velvet cloth. The whole scene was lit by a single flickering candle in a giant gold candelabra, giving a ghostly appearance to the stage.

"Come, let us eat," he said offering Carlotta his hand. He led her through the rear staircase and onto the stage. "Sit here." He pulled out Lady Macbeth's chair, seated Carlotta, then sat opposite her in Macbeth's chair.

Carlotta looked hungrily at the food – a feast of meats, cheeses, breads and fruits. "I am famished," and started eating with gusto.

"Wine, my Lady? Or champagne?" Erik stood with a bottle in each hand – waving first a 1928 Krug then a 1929 Chateau Lafite Rothschild.

Carlotta nodded, her mouth full. She swallowed the food so she could speak. "Wonderful. Champagne first, please," then continued eating.

Erik expertly opened the champagne, then with a flourish, poured a little into each of the exquisitely hand-carved gold goblets, allowing the champagne to rise up then back, before topping them up. He handed Carlotta a goblet, picked up his own, then raised it to make a toast, but Carlotta spoke first.

"To us, to the King and Queen of the Garnier," she toasted.

"And to the Phantom of the Opera," replied Erik, "I shall sit in his place." Suddenly the air was rent with the discordant sounds of an organ before the ghostly apparition of a masked phantom appeared. His loud, disembodied voice echoing off the walls, "To thine own self be true."

Erik leapt to his feet, alarmed, gesticulating wildly and startling Carlotta. "There... there... can't you see it?" The phantom vanished.

"You are mad!" said Carlotta, softly.

"I saw him with my own eyes."

"Sit down, Erik. Let's enjoy ourselves."

Erik went to sit in Banquo's chair again, but the ghostly apparition of a masked phantom reappeared there again. A shocked Erik stood still.

"*Leave me,*" shouted Erik, loudly, now in the mind and body of Macbeth, "*leave me, awesome ghost!*" The phantom disappeared.

"*Shame, my lord!*" Carlotta sang back at him, wondering what was happening, but ready to play this musical game.

Erik paced to and fro, now singing Macbeth's part, pointing to where the phantom had been, acting as if he were truly mad. "*That shadow demands blood from me, and it will have it, I swear it will have it!*"

"What is wrong with you?" a now troubled Carlotta

asked, clearly disturbed by seeing Erik unravel before her. Was this a performance, a scene from the opera, for her benefit?

"The Phantom of the Opera was here," a tormented Erik cried. Carlotta stood up and breathed deeply. If it was a performance, he would have it. Reincarnated as Lady Macbeth, she faced him.

"Cowardly spirit! Your fright has created idle phantoms," she sang, her powerful tones ridiculing him. Now wishing to end the disturbing performance, Carlotta picked up her goblet, and toasted Erik.

"René Bourdin has a rival. You never cease to amaze me, Erik." Unsure of what had happened, he stood there, in the flickering candlelight, stunned into silence, grappling with the phantoms in his mind.

CHAPTER NINETEEN

TESTING TIMES

Erik sat in the shadows of the third row, watching the unfolding drama of rehearsals. It was obvious that Carlotta was a temperamental diva, difficult to tame. For some, like the hapless Monsieur Laloux, she was impossible to control, but that was what attracted Erik. He allowed her the satisfaction of seducing him, but it would be his turn, soon enough.

Carlotta's eyes glazed with anger at the teacher-like treatment Laloux was handing out to her. They had locked horns for the best part of two hours, both refusing to retreat from their entrenched positions. Monsieur Laloux persisted.

"The crescendo of your aria in this act lacks the power required for that special moment, Carlotta."

Carlotta held a lengthy gaze in silence, seemingly not breathing as her cheeks reddened from the strain.

"Monsieur Laloux, do you wish that the most famous prima donna in all of France – the world — not be able to sing to her adoring fans on opening night?"

"My dear prima donna, I wish only that your many fans see you shine like an evening star on that special night. I ....."

Carlotta turned her back from Monsieur Laloux, cutting his outcry short. Defiantly, she walked to the front of the stage to look out to the empty theatre.

"You are a threat to the good name of this famous opera house. If Victor were here, I would have your position as Artistic Director terminated on the spot. The opening night sold out within an hour of making tickets available. That only happened because I am now the lead. No one knows or cares about you, Monsieur Laloux. Do not forget that."

Stagehands stopped their busy preparations, sensing the volatile moment was about to get out of hand. Monsieur Laloux's gaze darted across the various stagehands, highlighting his acute embarrassment at Carlotta's accusations and threats. He rubbed his bald pate, something he always did when drawn to anger, before he purposefully walked to the front of the stage to confront Carlotta, the stern look on his face advertising his intent.

He stood within a metre of her, relentlessly tweaking his moustache, waiting for her to turn his way and acknowledge him. But Carlotta held her gaze on the empty seating, as if she remained alone. She scanned the theatre until her gaze rested on the sole occupant — Erik — bringing an immediate smile to her face.

"Can no one save me from this monster? Perhaps the Head of Security can be my knight in shining armour?"

Erik reacted, immediately standing up, eager to redeem himself from the disastrous end to the night before. Walking toward her, he buttoned his jacket in preparation for playing his part in this confrontation. Carlotta looked down at him, admiringly, revealing feelings towards Erik, that had been fanned from their previous night's encounter. He smiled knowingly, signalling the secret bond they had formed. Erik was also a man who knew when to play his cards. Leaving aside his ambition to gain control of the Garnier, he wanted to secure their lustful bond, winning Carlotta's confidence. He looked firstly at her, then to the downcast Monsieur Laloux, before ascending the stage stairs to join the two intractable combatants.

"What seems to be the problem?"

"Well it's perfectly obvious. This brute of a man will not rest until he sees me collapse with exhaustion. He

fails to understand that he will be the cause of straining the finest voice in France – in the world! If that
should happen, Victor would most certainly sue him
for damages!"

Erik turned to Monsieur Laloux, looking for a
response. "It has always been and always will be my
duty as Artistic Director, to bring out the best in all my
performers. It is my considered opinion, based on thirty
years' experience, that Madame Caccini must rehearse
more, in order to be ready for the opening night."

"See, Monsieur Destler. This monster does not listen
to reason," said Carlotta, extending her hand to Erik's
strong arm. "Please protect me from him, or the opening
night audience will demand his blood when they find out
he was the cause of my absence."

Erik stood tall, holding a steady gaze toward Monsieur
Laloux, who could only hold up his hands in the air in
exasperation. Erik intervened authoritatively.

"Let's call an end to rehearsals, today."

"I knew my Head of Security would rescue me!"

"This is an outrage, Monsieur Destler. You know as
well as me that I am solely responsible for what happens
on stage. You overstep you mark!"

Erik responded by stepping closer to Monsieur Laloux,
no more than half a metre, amplifying the difference

between the two men. Erik was almost half a metre taller, his strong athletic frame dwarfing Monsieur Laloux's stocky, older frame. Erik glared at him now, with the eyes of a prize fighter about to do battle.

"Would you care to tell me what mark I overstepped?" He said in a low deliberate voice, provocatively stepping even closer. Erik unbuttoned his coat as if preparing for conflict, before Monsieur Laloux retreated, muttering to the stagehands, in an attempt to save face.

"Very well. Have it your way. I will be available for Madame Caccini, should she need my assistance. But perhaps she would prefer to use Monsieur Destler as her private coach." He walked away from both of them not looking back.

"What are you all staring at? You all have work to do!" He said, clapping his hands to the scurrying stagehands.

Erik watched Monsieur Laloux disappear behind the stage curtain before he turned to Carlotta, extending his arm for her willing hand.

"Time you rested your precious voice, Madame Caccini."

"Take me to my stage room, darling man," she cried, ensuring everyone heard her. "I want to make love to you right now," she whispered to Erik. "Just like last night."

Erik opened the door to Carlotta's room, as she continued to express her displeasure with Monsieur Laloux, waving one hand in frustration, while caressing Erik's arm with the other.

"Make me forget that old fool as only you can, my darling Head of Security."

She giggled at the promise of unbridled lovemaking, until the sounds of Victor speaking on his mobile phone interrupted their lustful intentions.

"Yes, I know decisions need to be made. I will be better placed once the opening night has passed. Things will settle down then," he said, before looking up to Carlotta and blowing her a kiss. "Look, something has come up. I have to go now, but I'll be at the meeting shortly. We'll talk more, then. Okay?"

Victor had no sooner hung up before Carlotta was seeking his sympathy.

"Darling, our kind security officer saved me from that brute of a man, Laloux."

Victor consoled Carlotta for a time, before turning to Erik. "You have saved my angel again, Erik. How can I ever thank you?" Carlotta intervened before Erik had a chance to respond.

"You must appoint him as my personal bodyguard. The people here have never worked with a diva of my standing before. They think that my perfect instrument should be pushed as if I were no more than an understudy. Please assign him to me, my love. Then you will see my greatest performance ever, come opening night."

Victor shot a helpless glance toward Erik. "What do you say? Could you do that for my beautiful angel?"

"I couldn't do it full time, but if you assign me more staff to take over the more routine aspects of my job, I might be able to keep a more watchful eye on Madame Caccini. It would strain the demands for my time, though."

"I will make it worth your while, my boy," Victor replied, rubbing his fingers together as if counting cash.

Erik nodded in the affirmative and opened his arms toward them both, signalling he would become part of their personal team, much to Carlotta's glee.

"Oh darling, thank you!" Carlotta cried, holding Victor close, "you will not regret this decision," kissing him repeatedly on his fulsome cheeks.

"Our success depends on your happiness, my darling. You rest now and prepare for the next day's rehearsals," he said, effusively, before standing and checking his phone. "I shall leave you in Monsieur Destler's capable hands. I'm sure he'll do the right thing by you. Won't you Monsieur Destler?" Victor asked, his implications clear.

Erik nodded his head, shaking Victor's hand firmly,

well pleased with his day's work and preparing himself for the night's work as he smiled at Carlotta.

Victor's hasty exit signalled the onset of Carlotta's lustful expectations. "I need you, now!" Erik smiled, stroking Carlotta's aroused nipples with an assuredness of ownership. "Your devoted husband may return. As Head of Security, I recommend you wait. It will be worth it."

Carlotta unfastened her hair clip and swept her long hair over bare shoulders like a spoilt girl, before turning her back to him, presenting the long zip of her gown to be undone.

"At least help me out of this torturous dress, so I can change into something more comfortable."

Erik obeyed, slowly unzipping her dress, allowing Carlotta to seductively drop her gown to the floor. She stepped out, revealing her naked body beneath. Erik alluringly stroked her soft back, signalling his own intentions. She squirmed with delight before reaching for a printed red dress from her nearby chair. Carlotta slowly robed in front of Erik, maintaining her hungry gaze toward him through her dressing mirror.

Erik studied her svelte curves. The mirror lights made her smooth skin shine, belying her age. The touch of Carlotta's soft skin, no doubt due to the untold number of pampering massages she had luxuriated in, made Erik desire her even more. Her body was free of hair, bar her long brunette hair. He stroked her womanly curves with his eyes. Her firm breasts shone, accentuated by the desirability of her now erect nipples. Carlotta giggled as she slowly slipped the body-hugging dress over her breasts, but no lower, leaving her exposed to Erik's hungry gaze, taunting him to act.

He came closer, holding his intense gaze, pressing his desire against her willing body, eliciting pleasurable groans. He teased her nipples with one hand while holding her half fallen dress against her belly.

"*La Divina* holds many secrets," he whispered as he slowly slid one hand down to her smooth sex. Carlotta groaned excitedly as he slipped his fingers between her folds, sampling her erotic dew.

"You already know my most personal secrets, my love. I so want you again, like last night."

Carlotta's whispering emboldened Erik to stroke her fires, assuredly controlling her every intense feeling as if they'd been life-long lovers. "I will give you much more than last night, if you let me."

Carlotta was uncontrollably writhing to Erik's foreplay, nearing orgasm. "Have all of me," she said, breathlessly, before yielding to her orgasm. She turned and faced Erik, kissing him deeply, showing her true desires. "You have freed me from that torturer, so the night is yours."

Erik sniggered an ironic smile. "From one torturer to another. Be careful what you wish for," he said, holding her closer to him, both hands firmly grasping her womanly buttocks. Their intense kiss lingered as their tongues explored each other's deep yearnings. All the while, Erik firmed his grasp on Carlotta, making her flinch from the pain.

"Quite the strong man, aren't you," she said, her gaze wild and hungry for more.

"You don't know half of it," he replied, his gaze equally wild.

"Maybe I will unmask your deepest secrets tonight and see who hides beneath those handsome looks."

Erik manoeuvred Carlotta against the wall, showing the intensity of his desire. He grasped her long hair, pulling it back and exposing her bare shoulders and neck. Erik buried his lips into the soft nape of her neck, closing his eyes and smelling her sensuality. How many nights had he imagined Rose like this in his torturous confinement? Endless cries of pain and submission filled his nights then, as one by one, his fellow patriots succumbed to the unflinching cruelty of the Captor, all the time trying to cover his ears from his torment. But withholding sleep too was the instrument of his torture. Captives were never allowed enough sleep to refresh, rather just enough to remind them of what they had lost. He could only hide his head in the dark corner of his cell and imagine Rose lying with him in the dark, caressing away his fear.

She would repeat his name, "Erik, Erik.....," at first in a nurturing fashion, relaxing his mind, but then her tone would turn to a more desperate call, seeking only help. But he couldn't save her from the Captor. One long terrifying night, Rose cried until sweet death mercifully claimed her, ending her suffering, leaving Erik with no hope, only the confinement of his dark cell.

Her cries of "Erik, Erik," soon returned as a nightmare that rang out every night. He could not save his love and could only show his anguish by striking the walls until his bloodied fist could take no more.

"Erik, Erik....," cried Carlotta. Erik opened his eyes. Carlotta was looking at him, fear in her eyes. He still held her long hair in his clenched fist. "Erik, what's wrong?"

Erik studied Carlotta unable to answer straight away. What could he tell her that would make any sense anyway? How could a spoilt diva like Carlotta ever possibly understand the pain he once felt and the love he lost? Then a thought crossed his mind. There was a way he could make her understand.

"I'll tell you what's wrong....but later. I'll tell you everything tonight."

CHAPTER TWENTY

THE OTHER WORLD

Madame Giraud looked on at the rehearsals from high up in her favourite viewing box, Box 39. It offered her an uninterrupted view of the stage and the cast going about their part in the preparation of Macbeth, just two weeks away from opening night.

Like the performers below, Madame Giraud had her own daily routines to complete to ensure the smooth running of opening night. All boxes had been booked just hours after making them available to the public. Modern technology had so changed the audience dynamics, for the better in her view. In past decades, only the privileged were afforded the best seats in the house, but now selection was in the main, based on a first come first served basis. Although, as always, a hundred or so seats were set aside for special dignitaries and members of the Garnier. It made sense that this most famous opera house was frequented by the rich and famous. Politicians, sponsors, business people and well-known artists filled that very special list and Madame Giraud was responsible for its smooth operation.

It was surprising that someone whose three-decade long service was still not well known by the staff. Her knowledge of the Garnier's inner workings was preeminent amongst her colleagues, yet most saw her as a curiosity at best. Even less known, was that Madame Giraud's knowledge extended well beyond that of the physical. She had been gifted with psychic abilities from a tender age, something she valued and disdained in equal measure. Most had heard she had an instinct for the Garnier's spiritual past, but only a few were aware of the extent of her psychic reach — crime investigators, mainly, and soon to include, one Raoul D'Arenberg.

Madame Giraud ate on her favourite Brie cheese and fresh baguette as the sounds of rehearsals filtered up to her box. She always sat in the back row of Box 39 on Level 3. Box 39 was dead centre, facing the stage. No one could see her in its shadows, which was to her liking. She straddled two worlds up in her high box, the world of opera and the 'other world', as she liked to call it.

The opera world had a tension to it that morning. The new diva had been particularly testy, behaving quite abominably toward Monsieur Laloux, a likeable fellow in her mind, whose first and only love was for the opera. Madame Caccini had been true to her reputation, difficult and conniving. It came with the territory of course. World famous singers had to carry large egos just to survive in this cut-throat world and Carlotta had an ego enough for ten divas. She was as flirtatious as Marie Antoinette, too, having quickly won the attention of the usually cautious security manager. It was clear to her that the two were attracted to each other and she didn't need her psychic abilities to see that. But they shared something more than lust and it was the other world that was sending her mixed messages about them.

Voices from the other world had filled her mind all through rehearsals, but she had also sensed other murmurings the night before, again when Carlotta and Erik were together. As was usual, the voices had been many and varied, leading to confusion in her mind. Many years as a psychic had taught her never to interpret too quickly. One thing was clear, Madame Giraud saw darker colours around Carlotta, the colour of unbridled ambition. Erik was similar, but another shade enveloped his aura, one so dark it could only signal great trauma in his life.

It was Erik's dark shade that attracted the voices of

the 'others', too many to understand their true plight. She had to wait and consider all who wanted to supply her answers. Madame Giraud had learnt over time not to accept the thoughts of just one individual 'other', as sometimes the strongest voice wasn't necessarily the right voice. Many strong voices filled her awareness about Erik, both producing a physical manifestation, but more through her clairaudience. Voices, male and female were contacting her and filling her mind with conflicting thoughts, some disturbing and perhaps of interest to the young investigator, Raoul and also to Christine Dubois. Perhaps she should meet with them.

Madame Giraud continued to sit quietly in the silence, as the performers had a break from rehearsals. She loved the silence, for in her world of duality, she had precious little of it. She took small bites of her baguette and smelled the aromas of her coffee flask that she now opened. The precious quiet lingered until a soft voice broke the calm. She thought it a voice from the other world at first, but then she heard it again and thought it emanated from the wall to her right. Other world voices only ever came from her left, so she studied the wall and room behind her, looking for a human occupant.

"Who goes there?" she asked. But only silence followed, leaving her to ponder its ownership. She tried to remember the words that had been spoken, but they were too muffled for her to understand. So she sat in the quiet and considered the many voices that had visited her since the beginning of the new opera — *Macbeth*. Darkness seemed to follow this new production and shadows, particularly those that enveloped the mysterious Head of Security. So many voices sought to offer Madame Giraud impressions about this new evolving atmosphere that inhabited the Garnier. She wanted to say more to the young detective who had returned to investigate yet another disappearance, but she knew she would only confuse him. He wasn't ready yet. As she finished her tasty French treat, she decided it best she remained in the shadows and observe the many plots that were about to unfold. She was certain however, that her hidden scrutiny should remain firmly on the new diva and her equally new lover.

CHAPTER TWENTY-ONE

THE PACT

Carlotta stood in the lower bowels of the Garnier for the first time. It was a world away from the Garnier she knew. She looked to Erik, for reassurance that their underground dalliance would be as exciting as their previous encounter, but Erik provided no such assurances as they wound their way through a series of locked doors and dimly lit corridors.

"Do you have to re-lock every door?" Carlotta asked, eager to reach their destination.

"Why am I Head of Security?" Erik replied, sharply, unsympathetically.

The next corridor was longer than the previous three and at its end was a staircase that wound down several flights.

"I feel like I'm going to the Phantom's lair. Perhaps my new lover is the Phantom reincarnate?"

Erik stopped at the foot of the stairs and turned to Carlotta. His tall powerful frame and dark beard, looked all the more intimidating in the semi-darkness, and his gaze was intense when he answered.

"You'll meet many phantoms where we're going, including a lover. But expect much more if you want to descend these stairs. Phantoms live in the shadows and take exception to prying eyes and loose lips."

Carlotta laughed at first, believing it to be a lover's tease, but Erik's inscrutable face offered her no such surety.

"I have endured the company of men with little talent and even less passion. They were weak and predictable, preferring to count money and conquests ahead of winning the love of a true diva. So I gave them what they deserved, a little fun. But..." She paused deliberately, taking a deep breath, "if I found the right man? Well, that would be quite a union. One that could never be broken. Together, we could achieve anything and take everything."

Erik turned his head sideways and studied Carlotta from the corner of his eyes, analysing her. "I hold more power than you could ever imagine, my beautiful diva. Do you think you are ready to face such power?"

The challenge made Carlotta physically quiver with

excitement as her eyes widened with expectation. She kissed his lips softly, before biting his bottom lip and drawing blood. Erik didn't flinch, reacting with excitement rather than pain. He lifted her from the damp floor and kissed her deeply.

"Then you have sealed your fate."

Erik took Carlotta's hand and guided her down the many flights of stairs. The light faded and the damp overpowered their senses as they descended further to another corridor, the longest, lit by two torch flames — one where they stood and the other many hundred metres at the other end of the corridor. Erik stopped and removed a dark cloth from his coat as they walked the long corridor together.

"This is a mask. You will have to wear it for the final part of our journey."

Carlotta flinched at the thought of being masked. "Do you not trust me?"

Erik smiled. "I could ask you the same question," he said sternly, before presenting the mask to her to put on.

Carlotta brooded momentarily before resigning herself to being masked. Erik tied it firmly around her eyes, ensuring darkness.

"I will take you to a doorway. You will push that door

open and walk through. Then continue to walk forward fifty paces. It is a narrow corridor, so you will be able to feel the walls both sides to help you move in a straight path. When you count fifty paces, then and only then, you can remove your mask. Is that understood?"

Warily, Carlotta nodded her head.

"You can still pull out of this. But once you go through the door, there will be no return. You will be mine. Do you understand?"

"I want to be free from the mistakes of my past. I want to be yours."

"Very well. Put your hands against the door and push it and walk through."

Carlotta did as asked and walked through the final door toward Erik's secret lair. She counted her steps as she purposefully walked through the corridor, her arms spanned out to feel her way forward.

"....twenty, twenty one, twenty two......she counted."

Everything had gone quiet around her. The total silence matched the pitch black. Carlotta was truly blind to her surrounds.

"....thirty, thirty one, thirty two...." Carlotta's confidence shrunk with every step. The corridor seemed to go on for an eternity in her dark confines, but she continued the momentum albeit at a slower pace as she neared her unknown destination. The silence suddenly gave way to the sound of running water. Someone must have opened a door to allow her to continue to move forward, allowing her to hear what lay on the other side.

"Erik, is that you?" No reply.

"Forty, forty one, forty two....." With every step, the sound of the water flow grew until she finally counted fifty. Carlotta removed her mask and found herself standing in front of a large indoor lake. A boat rested on the man-made bank, leaving her wondering whether she was meant to board it.

"Yes, step into the boat, my lady," came a voice from behind her. Carlotta turned to see a stockily built man walk toward her. He was wearing a mask and a gondolier hat and pointed for her to step into the gondola.

"Are you taking me to Erik?" she enquired, but he ignored her, insistently waving her to board, before he went about expertly guiding the boat across to the other side of the lake.

Carlotta gazed to the bank, but it was in darkness, bar a small flame of fire that lit the gondolier's destination. This was exactly as Carlotta imagined the Phantom's lair to be. Had she unknowingly become the lover of the real Phantom of the Opera? The thought filled her with excitement. The gondolier soon moored and the masked man pointed for her to climb the flame-lit stairs into the darkness. She did so, looking back and expecting his further guidance, but he had already started to leave the shore and return to the other side of the lake.

Carlotta stood alone in the cold, darkness, her excitement quickly turning to fear. She remained beside the comforting flames of the single torch, not sure whether to move forward into the pitch blackness or wait for Erik. Time passed slowly in the silent abyss, before several shadowy figures bearing torches moved slowly in her direction from the darkness.

It felt to her that she was on a stage waiting for the curtain call as three torch bearers approached. The surreal atmosphere was further enhanced as she saw a large dog on a leash, leading the three figures. All were in black hooded garments and masked, further adding to the ominous feeling.

"Who are you? Where is Erik?"

No reply came, except the threatening growls of the large Rottweiler dog that led them. Fear overtook Carlotta as she retreated back toward the lakeside flame. The three men stood side by side, not reacting to the dog's aggression. For a minute, Carlotta thought the dog bearer would release the savage beast, but he instead clicked his fingers, silencing it until it sat motionless beside its owner. The eerie atmosphere magnified as four pairs of eyes maintained their unflinching stare toward her. All the men wore masks from the Macbeth opera, accentuating their mystery. Fear had now gripped Carlotta as she stood close to the water's edge, able only to retreat into the water. The first of them finally spoke.

"I wouldn't if I were you," he said, looking to the Rottweiler. "He's strong in the water. It's where he enjoys taking his prey."

"Who are you? I demand to see Erik. If he is your boss, I will make sure that all of you are removed from the Garnier for this outrage!"

The three masked men looked to each other and laughed at Carlotta's threats, before the first again spoke.

"You are in no position to make threats, Carlotta. We can do as we please in this place. You are in our world now and you will do as your ordered," he said, restraining the Rottweiler a second time with the click of his fingers. Then the second man spoke.

"You will come with us now, or die in the water at the hands of our loyal warrior," he said, pointing to the four-legged beast.

Carlotta resigned herself to do as ordered, visibly shaken from the ordeal. She dared not speak as she stared at the snarling dog. The third masked man held his hand out to her, which she accepted. He gripped her wrist vice-like, causing her to cry out. All three laughed at the sound of her pain, before they silently walked into the darkness from where they came. Carlotta walked in terror, believing harm had come to Erik, leaving her at the hands of these devils. At that moment, she truly feared for her life. Had she unwittingly walked into the lair of the real Phantom?

CHAPTER TWENTY-TWO

MADAME GIRAUD'S DREAM

The three witches floated menacingly above Madame Giraud as she guided Raoul around the maze that surrounded the Phantom's lair. She alone knew the way through camouflaged entries and winding corridors down to where the spirit of the Phantom lived on. The Opera Ghost had guided her on numerous occasions, gifting her with sole knowledge of his home. But this was the first occasion she had met resistance to her descent. The witches repeatedly sang their famous lines from Macbeth, *'Fair is foul, and foul is fair'* as they hovered above them in the fog-filled expanse, all the way to the Phantom's torture room.

"The Phantom's princess is in the distance, past the fog," said Madame Giraud, willing Raoul to ignore the witches and find his missing damsel. They both scrambled through the fog to find a masked woman tied to a small crucifix. Raoul rushed to the task of removing the intricate rope work that held her firm to the cross of steel, but it was securely bound. Instead he removed the mask from the hapless victim. Madame Giraud thought she recognised the woman, but her face changed rapidly as if a thousand faces tried to claim the lifeless body that hung from the crucifix.

"I don't understand," she said, making Raoul turn in her direction.

The witches swarmed from the fog and flew around them, then through them, demonstrating their unearthly powers and singing, "*fair is foul and foul is fair*," mocking their unwanted guests and pointing to two other crucifixes in the distance. "For you both," they sung, before swooping and carrying both to their crucifixes and restraining them. "Now, experience real pain," they cried, tormenting their two captives.

Madame Giraud struggled to free herself from her tight binds, feeling only acute pain as she failed to break free. "Help me!" She called repeatedly, but no one came.

Madame Giraud woke with a start from her dream, perspiration falling from her brow. She often had dreams, some terrible like this one. "It's only a dream," she repeated to herself, but she was aware that most of her dreams were dire warnings from another place. She also knew that Raoul's investigations would not fail this time, as it did with his brother's disappearance. That case, along with the disappearance of the ballerina were linked. Even worse, she sensed more disappearances would follow.

CHAPTER TWENTY-THREE

CARLOTTA'S CAPTURE

The march from the lake snaked in various directions, the turns marked by small torch flames, as they silently moved from one to the other. Carlotta's wrist pained her from the constant tugging of her capturer. She struggled across the slippery cobbled surface in heeled shoes suited more for the stage than this underground prison. But her cries of pain and outrage were ignored as they moved forward into the dim underworld.

Finally, their trek stopped at a solid, old wooden door requiring similarly ancient metal keys to enter. Carlotta used the moment's rest to kick her shoes off her red, blistered feet. The water had soaked into the open leather making them extremely uncomfortable. She immediately felt the cold of the damp floor but it was the lesser of two evils, soothing her pain for the moment.

The door opened to a world of light that momentarily

blinded her as they came in from the darkness. Carlotta shielded her eyes with her one free hand, allowing her sight to adjust. She was shocked to see her wrist red and bloodied, intensifying her feelings of fear. What would be her fate, she wondered, wanting to cry out for help, but instead retreating further into her fear.

She looked down to the cobblestones, more in a state of disbelief at her circumstance. Her captor accentuated her grave mood as he tied her free hand to an icy steel pole. She squinted and closed her eyes as a spotlight from somewhere high shone directly toward her. Her captor then untied her bloodied wrist for a moment before securing it against a second secured pole. Carlotta's shock deepened as her mind tried to digest her new and terrifying circumstances. Just an hour earlier, she was excitedly descending into the mysterious world of her new lover, but now she was at the mercy of a band of strangers. She had convinced herself Erik had been murdered. Desperation made her finally speak out.

"Please, my partner is rich. He would pay you anything for my safe return!"

Carlotta's pleas were met only with laughter and disdain.

"Is she secured?"

"She won't be going anywhere quickly, unless the boss wills it," responded the captor who securely tied her.

The masked man with the dog inspected the ropes before nodding his agreement. Carlotta reacted to the closeness of the beast, at first trying to break her wrists free from the tightly bound ropes, but she could not move.

"I wouldn't try that if I were you, unless you want to further cut those pretty wrists of yours."

"Don't leave me here. I can pay you well," Carlotta begged, but did not receive the reaction she hoped for.

The captor tightly held her throat, growling his reply. "You will wait here quietly for our master. Don't make me want to come back. Do you understand?"

Carlotta saw only cruel, steely brown eyes from behind his mask and now knew for certain he wasn't playing with her. Tears streamed down her cheeks as she nodded. He held her throat firm, making her struggle for breath, before finally letting go his grasp. Then, the three men left her alone in the deadly spotlight, occasionally turning toward her as they walked away.

Twenty minutes passed before another man walked from the shadows. He was taller and dressed in a black military uniform. He wore a large brimmed hat and mask. Everything was black except for the shine of his military knife, secured in a holster around his hips. Carlotta wanted to speak but fear and shock had taken its toll on her. She believed she was about to die.

CHAPTER TWENTY-FOUR

THE PHANTOM'S LAIR

Erik saluted his Generals as they silently walked past him in the shadows. They had performed their duties to the letter. None of his Generals joined his subterranean world without initiation. Erik's first female member was no different. He marched toward her, pleased with what he saw. Carlotta's strength and arrogance had been quickly stripped bare, leaving only vulnerability and fear. This was her initiation. To submit to her captor and put survival above any lofty aims. She had shown Erik her world the night before and revealed her inner thoughts to him. He'd even allowed her control over his actions for one brief night, but not control of him. There was a difference. He stopped, two metres short of his captive, allowing her a clear view of the real Erik, dressed in full military uniform.

"Erik, is that you?" Carlotta cried, terror still in her eyes.

He would not reassure her with a reply just yet, instead removing his military knife from its leather holster. He studied it from behind the anonymity of his mask. The captor always maintained control of the captive.

"Please, I can pay you anything. Just release me!" Carlotta cried through uncontrolled tears.

Erik remembered a time when he asked for similar mercy from his Captor, but always failing. Full submission and total obedience was the only acceptable survival strategy. It was a lesson hard earned as he heard the torturous deaths of his loyal soldiers who dared to show resistance.

He moved the knife close to Carlotta's throat, brushing the sharp tip of the blade perilously close to her skin, making Carlotta react.

"Please, don't!"

Erik ignored his captive's pleas, as he continued to wave the knife in front of her exposed skin, before he turned the point of the blade away from her. With one assured action, he cut the rope from her bloodied wrist.

"Welcome to my world," he said, revealing his identity. Carlotta wanted to speak, but too traumatised, she instead wept, releasing a cascade of emotions. Relief, doubt, anger and terror poured from her eyes as Erik held her bloodied wrist and tenderly kissed it. Carlotta pushed him away.

"You knowingly set those bastards onto me! How could you?"

"Just an hour earlier, you said you were ready to face the real me," he said, removing his mask and hat and pointing out to the shadows. "This is my world, Carlotta. I would defend this world with my life, as would my loyal Generals. Would you?"

"You could have fucking asked, instead of releasing those sick bastards onto me. I thought I was going to die at their hands. Do you care?"

"If I didn't care, you wouldn't be seeing me, here and now. You need to understand that from this point on, only loyalty will be tolerated. Anything remotely disloyal and you'll not sing in any opera, ever again."

Carlotta's questioning gaze was wild and unflinching. She went to slap his face, but Erik reacted quickly and grasped her free wrist.

"Now, now, my beloved. That will not help you. Remember you are the one with one hand still tied. I could tie you up again. You wouldn't want that would you?"

Carlotta breathed deeply as she fumed, before she lashed out with her free arm, fist clenched, trying to strike his face, but failing. Erik easily defended every blow, letting Carlotta strike out until she drained all her anger and strength, finally yielding to the hopelessness of her situation. Erik held her close to him allowing the long silence to calm her. Her tears spent, Carlotta looked out into the darkness.

"Weren't you going to show me your world? All I have seen so far are shadows."

"I will show you everything, but never forget the pact you agreed to."

"I seem to remember we made two pacts. My loyalty, if you give me the head of that upstart understudy bitch."

Erik smiled, before cutting the second rope tied around her right wrist, releasing her from his torture chamber. "There's something about you that I like so very much, my darling diva. Are you truly as evil as me, I wonder?"

Erik walked toward the dark, signalling to someone high above them, near the light. Suddenly more lights shone down, showing the large expanse where they now stood. Carlotta saw for the first time, Erik's lair. As he showed Carlotta the cavern in which he lived and described his dual life, both musical and military, he lit the many candles that adorned his subterranean world. Several dozen now lit, he signalled for the spotlights to be turned out.

"Welcome to the Phantom's lair."

Carlotta looked on in wonder, her earlier terror forgotten as she breathed in Erik's secret wonderland.

"The Phantom really exists?" she said, shaking her head in disbelief."

"I'm much more than a mere legend. I've come to shake the Garnier to its core. I want its occupants to know real terror and I won't rest until that's achieved," he said, as he walked around his lair.

"So how do you intend to do that? Frighten people with your band of maniacs?"

Erik ignored Carlotta's sarcasm, choosing instead to pick up one of his musical scores.

"You know, there was a time when music was my life."

"I could tell. When you sang to me last night, your voice lifted my spirits with its purity. Why didn't you pursue a career?"

"What makes you think I haven't?" Erik replied, randomly picking up one of the many musical scores spread across the cobbled floor.

Erik sat at his grand piano and played the score he had selected with the skill of a virtuoso. This was one of his favourite compositions, written when he was barely twenty years old. He remembered first playing it in his family home. He performed most of his new compositions under the discerning eye of his mother, but this piece was only ever to be played for his true love, Rose. Tonight was the first time he had played this, his most intimate of compositions, to another.

He turned his head toward Carlotta, who now stood close to him, turning the pages as he played. Erik knew he didn't love Carlotta. That special place in his heart was reserved only for his beloved — Rose. But something about this selfish, egotistical woman made him desire her. She did have similar features to Rose. His score was meant to be played with a soft intensity, but he felt compelled to play it with greater bravado, as he struck the keys with a power that filled his subterranean world with a Macbeth-like atmosphere. His fingers moved ever faster across the keys, until they became a blur in the unfolding performance. He no longer needed to read the music. Such was the clarity of his recollection, he played it by memory and feeling as if he had truly returned to that special time and place with Rose.

He looked again to his side and believed that Rose stood beside him, not Carlotta, singing the special words he had composed for her. They rode the highs of the dramatic score, declaring their vow of everlasting love. Both completed the challenging duet, riding an emotional wave. Erik finished the score, forcefully sweeping his left hand across the keys and in the same movement he picked Rose up off the floor and held her close, kissing her deeply and longing for more.

Rose sighed, also wanting more. Erik sensed her hunger and accommodated, sliding her strapless dress to the floor, revealing her naked body. Their duet had built an intense hunger in each, stoking fires for immediate sex without foreplay. Erik slid his firmness into Rose's willing folds, all the while holding her writhing body off the ground, so that he could glide her slowly over his desire. He gazed into her eyes, his expression filled with an urgency to fulfil their building climax. Rose reacted, twisting her torso and squeezing his desire in her dew filled sex. Both exploded in an urgent, intense orgasm as if it were the final notes on their special musical score, ending the composition they had created to show their everlasting bond.

"I will always love only you," he softly whispered, repeatedly until the high of their orgasm subsided.

Erik held Rose to him for a time, breathing in the perfectness of the moment, before he moved toward the piano stool and lowered her to it. The magic passed, before he realised he was not with Rose, but Carlotta. He gazed at her with genuine surprise, unable to speak, instead waiting for Carlotta.

"Do you really love me?" She asked.

Erik couldn't reply. His words would reveal his true feelings were for another, so he nodded his head, masking his deceit.

Carlotta reacted, showing her intense pleasure, not only for the urgent sex they had both enjoyed, but for some intangible feeling she had desired for a long time. Was it power? Had Lady Macbeth entered her soul?

"Then our bond is complete. You are my Phantom and I am your Lady Macbeth. Let's rule the Garnier together."

Again, Erik hesitated to put words to his feelings. He knew he could never love Carlotta as he had loved Rose, but there was something in this diva that he found hard to define, something that held great promise, as if destiny had forged their union. Finally, he spoke.

"We shall rule the Garnier or sacrifice our lives in trying to make that happen," he replied, seeking Carlotta's loyal agreement.

She kissed him softly on the lips, then looked directly into his eyes and replied with a purpose in her tone, that Erik had not heard before. "Yes, I would be prepared to give my life to make the Garnier ours. But I want so much more, my love. I also want that we would both willingly take lives to make the Garnier ours."

CHAPTER TWENTY-FIVE

BOX 39

"Time to escape. Have a break. You have earned it, ma chère. Ignore Monsieur Laloux. You sang beautifully." René kissed Christine affectionately on both cheeks then headed off stage. They had just finished rehearsing the first aria in Act Two – *Perché mi sfuggi (Why do I escape)*. Monsieur Laloux, still smarting from his defeat at the hands of the diva a few days ago, had made both of them suffer, constantly finding fault, making them sing the aria through four times.

"Thank you, René. You are being kind, but my voice is tired. I am tired." Christine stood there, feeling decidedly weary. Her throat was dry, her voice a little strained. Carlotta's absence meant that she spent more time with the cast and crew and the increasingly meticulous Monsieur Laloux, rehearsing for two roles. And more time with René, although he made it easier. René was so professional, a joy to work with.

Opening night edged ever closer, but all this effort was to little avail. Carlotta Caccini would be Lady Macbeth, and she, Christine Dubois, an acclaimed rising star, would instead be, but one witch in a chorus. How humiliating to play second fiddle after so many leading roles. Her voice was in its prime. She was in her prime, unlike the diva, but that would be cold comfort on opening night for Macbeth, when all eyes would be turned to Carlotta.

Raoul was waiting in the wings for her when rehearsals finished, as he promised. So reliable and so dependable. So unlike Philippe with his flamboyant, aristocratic ways, yet she was warming to him. Philippe had secrets. Parts of his life had been a closed book, although she knew enough to know his profligate spending meant he was always short of money. He tried to compensate by becoming involved in some shady, possibly nefarious money making schemes. Yet he loved nothing more than historical tales of caches of buried treasure underground in Paris which had financed the city's many revolutions. She wondered if that was what had drawn him to the Palais Garnier. She looked over at Raoul, twelve years younger than Philippe, and wondered whether he knew more about him than she did.

Raoul smiled and signalled to Christine to come

Box 39

join him. She would have preferred to have some time to herself, but he wanted her opinion on something significant. So, instead she nodded and returned the smile, albeit a tired smile, Raoul noticed as she moved towards him.

"Madame Giraud asked to meet with us," he said, kissing her cheeks.

"Madame Giraud? Heavens above, why?"

"She didn't say, but I think it may be about Philippe's disappearance." Christine visibly sagged. Raoul picked up one of her hands, a worried look on his face, "But, perhaps you should rest instead, Christine," he said, patting the hand.

"No, I'll be fine, Raoul. Monsieur Laloux is driving me crazy. Anything to take my mind off opera, please, at least for a while." She looped her arm around his, smiled, squeezed him affectionately, then asked brightly with a pretence she feigned, "Where to?"

"Upstairs to Level 3," said Raoul, returning the squeeze.

Raoul tapped gently on the door to Box 39. Christine was standing beside him, staring off down the corridor. Madame Giraud's muffled voice sounded from inside.

"Enter, please Mademoiselle Dubois and Monsieur D'Arenberg."

"How does she know it's us?" whispered Christine, mystified.

"Magic," said Raoul grinning. "Or, more likely, because we arranged to meet here at this time." He opened the door, allowing Christine to enter before him.

Christine looked at Madame Giraud critically. She was dressed head to toe in black again. Here in this opulent setting, in contrast to the plush red and gold that adorned the walls, ceilings and furniture, her outfit looked incongruous. Sturdy black court shoes were combined with a calf length skirt and a button-through collarless jacket pinched at the waist. No jewellery or adornment of any kind. Severe, closely cropped hair framed a pale face, with not a trace of makeup, not even lipstick. She seemed austere, androgynous even, eschewing the softness and femininity that Christine loved, in favour of a plain, understated style that allowed her to move about almost unnoticed. Whereas Christine loved to be noticed, and took great delight in dressing as a woman. Perhaps Madame Giraud doesn't see herself as a woman?

Madame's Giraud returned the scrutiny, her eyes, rimmed by steel-rimmed spectacles, seemed to bore right through Christine. Christine lowered her gaze. Such an enigmatic character, endowed with psychic powers, and, if rumour be true, the ability to communicate with the

Box 39

dead. Christine shivered. "I wonder if she can read my thoughts," which brought a faint blush to her cheeks. "Oh dear, I do hope not."

"You wanted to see us, Madame?" she asked politely instead.

Madame Giraud smiled knowingly, "Oui, ma chère, I did. I have been given information that could be of assistance to both of you."

"Who gave it to you?" intervened Raoul.

"Someone who is dear to both of you."

"You mean Philippe. He's still alive? Where is he? Where did you meet?" Raoul battered her with questions.

"I'm not sure," replied Madame Giraud, holding up a restraining hand. "Listen to me, please, Monsieur. Sometimes I communicate with spirits, with people's spirit guides." Raoul scoffed at the suggestion, disappointed. Another false lead.

Christine touched him firmly on the arm. "Please, listen to her, Raoul."

"I have someone here coming through. He wishes to connect with both of you, to seek your help," Madame Giraud said in a calming, soothing voice, "but do you understand he is in spirit now?" Words flowed from her lips smoothly, like a hypnotic meditation tape.

Christine nodded, then looked at Raoul, who had

quietened, and was listening intently. "Do you understand what this means, Raoul?" she asked softly, touching his arm again.

Raoul nodded, "But how do we know it is Philippe?"

"It may not be," said Madame Giraud, and lent her head to the left listening as though someone were speaking to her. "Alright, I will," she said to whomever was there, then turned back to Christine and Raoul. "Ask a question that you think only you and Philippe would know the answer to. Do you understand?" Raoul looked at Christine and nodded.

"Philippe gave me a dog for my twelfth birthday. Why? What was its name? Its sex? And what was the breed?" demanded Raoul.

"That's four questions, Raoul," exclaimed Christine.

Madame Giraud put her hand up to indicate it was alright.

"Ask him then," Raoul challenged.

"I don't need to, Monsieur. Whoever is here, can hear you." She leant her head to the left again and listened intently, then sat up straight and faced him. "It was a male French bulldog, a breed you loved. And his name was Lucky."

"But why did my brother give him to me?" Demanded Raoul again.

Box 39

"Because your father was dying and he didn't want you to be lonely. Because there would just be the two of you left. Because he loved you," said Madame Giraud, echoing the words exactly as given to her. Raoul sat there ashen faced as the truth slowly dawned. Philippe was here.

Christine held tightly to Raoul's arm as tears welled in her eyes.

"And your question, please Mademoiselle Dubois?"

"What present did you give me for my thirtieth birthday?"

Madame Giraud leant to the left once more, listening, before speaking.

"A champagne pearl ring set in rose gold," Madame Giraud intoned.

Tears streamed down Christine's face. "It was his mother's ring. His father, Armand, gave it to Philippe, before he died." She sighed, "Armand and Philippe looked so alike. Like brothers, rather than father and son. So handsome and so close."

Raoul nodded, then turned back to Madame Giraud. "What now?"

She leant her head to the side and listened once more. "Philippe is trapped. He's a lost soul," said Madame Giraud. "He wants you to find him, to release him, and to release his troubled soul."

"But where is he? How do we find him?" asked Raoul urgently. "Is he trapped under the Garnier? It's a vast network of underground passages and cellars and, as we found out the other day, guarded by security cameras."

"He told me you already know the answer and to think back. There is a quicker way to go — an underground passage running straight from Rue Scribe to the lake," said Madame Giraud. "It was used by the revolutionaries in the Paris Commune uprising to escape the French army troops."

"But how can we find it?" asked Raoul. "I went all around the Palais Garnier the other day. There are hundreds of stones, perhaps thousands."

"You will find it if you work together. There are two entry points," Madame Giraud continued. "One from the outside which you will find Monsieur, as your brother did."

"I need to know more, please," pleaded Raoul.

"It is the largest of the cut stones. You will know it when you see it. When pressure is exerted it turns and allows you access."

"And a second entry?" chimed in Christine. "Where is that?"

"Through an iron gate, but you will need a key."

"A key?" asked Christine.

Box 39

"He tells me that you know about the key, Mademoiselle Dubois."

"I don't know anything about an iron gate or a key. How could I know?" she asked, a puzzled frown spreading across her brow.

"He says you will remember. He says Philippe gave you something to mind just before he went away. He asked you to put it somewhere safe?"

"I don't remember. It's a year since I saw him last," said Christine anxiously, looking around at Raoul, then back to Madame Giraud, tears starting to well again. "I don't know anything about a key." Christine's voice was rising. She was now visibly upset.

"Don't worry," Madame's voice said soothingly, "He says he is sorry you have been left on your own. He let you down. You deserve better.'" Tears coursed down Christine's cheeks. Raoul stroked her hand.

"Tell me where to find the key, please, Philippe," beseeched Christine desperately.

"He's moving away," said Madame Giraud, holding her head as if she were in pain. "He's having trouble remembering because his head hurts. He's saying, 'Christine will remember.'"

"I don't! I don't!" cried Christine. "Tell me again, please! Please, Philippe!"

"He's gone." Madame Giraud sighed deeply, her face shaken and white. "He had a head injury, a brain tumour."

Christine started sobbing. "No, no! That was Armand, his father."

"Sometimes messages from the spirits can become confused," she added.

"We'll find him," said Raoul standing up. "We'll find out what happened to Philippe. I promise, Christine," vowed Raoul, hugging her close.

CHAPTER TWENTY-SIX

RUE SCRIBE ENTRY

*C*hristine moved restlessly from side to side, impatiently waiting for Raoul to appear in the dimly lit Rue Scribe, at the rear of the Palais Garnier. It was dark and freezing cold. Alternately stamping her feet or running on the spot to keep warm, she was rugged up against the winter chill. Dressed head to toe in black ski gear, mountain boots and gloves with warm thermals underneath. A beanie was pulled down over her head, ears, neck, mouth and throat. All that could be seen of her face were her eyes and nose, through which her breath misted in the cold early morning air. Sunrise was three hours away.

Raoul had offered to pick her up, but she was still too emotionally raw after her meeting with Madame Giraud the day before. Philippe was dead. She had suspected that all along, but had been too afraid to say it out loud, for fear it would make it come true. Philippe had been a romantic fairy tale come true. He had adopted her. She had been on her own for many years, orphaned after her parents died in a car crash. Following in her mother's footsteps, singing became her life and her love. Until Philippe. He had made her feel safe and loved again. And now that was over, too. Or was it? They still had to find him and Christine had no idea where the so called key was. A safe place indeed! So safe she couldn't remember.

A taxi pulled up and Raoul hopped out. Christine smiled at him, a wan smile. He too, had chosen black ski gear and hiking boots. He moved towards her, opening his arms, ready to hug her, but Christine stepped backwards.

"Let's get this nightmare over, please, Raoul."

He stopped, and still looking at her, wordlessly pulled gloves and a beanie from his jacket pocket and put them on. Raoul looked up and down Rue Scribe. Not a soul in sight. Paris was still sleeping.

"This way," he said, "It makes more sense for a getaway to be at the quieter end of the opera house." They walked along Rue Scribe past the rear of the magnificent building, under the balcony adjoining Le Foyer du Chant towards the Grand Salon. Street lighting was dimmed but light enough to see the hundreds of cut stones that formed the base of the building.

"They look immovable," said Christine miserably.

"They do look as if they've been here forever, although the foundations were laid only one hundred and fifty years ago. But there are slight variations in size. See here," said Raoul, pointing to two stones. One above and one below. Raoul passed his trembling hands over the rough surface of the cut stones.

"They are all huge. And there are so many," sighed Christine.

"The larger stones appear to be on the bottom two rows, which makes sense for people trying to escape without being noticed," Raoul went on, ignoring her sigh. "Let's systematically work our way backwards from there. That corner, tucked in under the Grand Salon on the second floor, has the least visibility from the front," he said, looking at Christine. "Please, don't give up now. We must try and find Philippe." He needed to get her moving. "I'll do the bottom row and you following, can do the row above. Look for the largest stones first. Okay?" Christine nodded mutely.

"There will be a counterbalance somewhere. A counterbalance, a spring you press, that lifts the whole of the stone so it can pivot and will swing around. Understand?" Christine nodded. "Alright let's go."

Raoul and Christine worked together in silence, one

behind the other, under the high windows at the end of the Grand Salon, sizing up stones, tapping and feeling around the edges and applying pressure with their gloved hands. What a strange pair of old crones they looked like. All in black, crouched over, knees and heads bent, their breath eerily misting upwards as they felt their way around the base of the building, searching for pressure points on huge blocks of cut stone. Fortunately Paris still slept. Daylight was another two hours way.

"Look at this block," said Raoul excitedly. "It is significantly larger than the rest and still close to the Grand Salon."

"Yes, it is!" Christine exclaimed and stood up, groaning as her back straightened. She watched as Raoul removed his gloves. His fingers tapped firmly, but carefully around every inch of the huge masonry block. Nothing moved.

"Try exerting pressure on each of the corners and see if that helps."

"Okay." Raoul stood up, too, groaning as Christine did, but it gave him more leverage. Using the heel of his hand, he pushed hard, first on the top left and then on the top right hand corners. Then on each of the bottom corners. The cold seeped through the block and chilled him to the marrow, but nothing moved. He looked all around.

Daylight would soon be here. There wasn't much time left.

"This is definitely the largest stone."

"Yes, well around this area, anyway," said Christine stamping her feet trying to keep warm. "What if this is all a joke? She said wearily, "A joke from beyond the grave."

"Philippe isn't like that," defended Raoul. "He would never harm you. Or me, either for that matter."

"Another of your big brother's hair-brained money schemes?" Her voice was rising. "Damn you, damn you, Philippe D'Arenberg," Christine cried out loud, kicking the stone hard. "And damn you, Raoul D'Arenberg," she screamed, kicking the stone again, so hard she hurt herself and was hopping around on one foot. A grinding sound rent the early morning air as the giant stone slowly started to turn on its axis. A stunned Christine and Raoul watched on in amazed silence. The stone stopped moving, revealing an opening just large enough for a person to climb into.

"Come on," said Raoul grabbing Christine's hand, "before anyone sees us. You made enough noise to wake the devil." He pushed Christine ahead of him. "You first." She climbed through followed by Raoul, ducking her head to avoid hitting her head on the foundation stone above. Once inside they turned. A thick dusty cord rope hung just to the left. Raoul tugged on the counterbalance. The stone slowly swung back into place, suddenly plunging them into the deepest darkness.

Silence and cold enveloped them. Christine grabbed hold of Raoul, her whole body trembling as fear gripped her. Raoul pulled out his mobile phone and switched it on. No coverage at all, but at least the light worked. The light played around unsteadily in a large arc from where they stood. Eerie shapes and shadows formed on the rocks and crevices, then disappeared. They were totally on their own, encased in stone, entombed under the Palais Garnier except for a narrow passage that wound its way ahead. It had been carved out of what seemed like solid bedrock. Neither Raoul nor Christine could stand fully upright. They would have to remain in a crouch position if they were to move along it.

Christine trembled once more, wondering. "Did they want to follow the passage? Where would it lead? What would they find?"

"Do you want to stay here?" whispered Raoul.

"No. I'd rather stay with you," she whispered back, wondering if anyone could hear them, and thinking she would prefer to be anywhere else but here.

"Okay, follow me. Place your hand on my back. And keep it there."

As they inched slowly forward, Christine could not help thinking of the past, and how this place had been built. She knew the narrow cutting had been hewn by hand after the foundations were in place, but four years before the Palais Garnier was completed. An escape hatch, supposedly to the safety of the underground cellars that existed long before the architect, Charles Garnier, envisaged a grand opera house atop them.

"How many revolutionaries had passed this way?" wondered Christine, thinking about the French history she had learnt at school. The Paris Commune of 1871 had been one of the nation's greatest and most inspiring revolutionary movements, where the working people of Paris seized political power. The Versailles Government had crushed the short-lived uprising, slaughtering about 50,000 men, women and children. "How many never found their way out and died here?" Christine shivered. "Will we ever find our way out of here?" Her fingers found their way into Raoul's belt. She hooked onto it and held on for dear life. Raoul moved slowly forward. It was hard going crouched down in such cramped confines.

Raoul stopped. Christine looked over his shoulder. Their way head was blocked by a heavy iron gate. They had come to an abrupt end. He rattled the door, but it was locked. The noise echoed loudly bouncing off the rocks around them. Raoul turned and put his finger to his lips cautioning her to be quiet and turned his light off. A diffused light appeared to the right, showing a narrow crawl space over a rocky outcrop. Christine watched as Raoul crawled across the low lying rock, then lay flat on his belly looking downwards. He signalled to her to do the same. Christine crawled into position and looked down onto a large lake below.

The enormous cavern surrounding it was lit with flickering gas lamps set into the walls. They cast a strange glow on the dark surface of the water and the surrounding rocks. A pathway emerged from an opening on the far side of the lake. It circled the lake, leading to what appeared to be a huge, domed, windowless room with a chimney coming through the roof.

"Someone lives down there?" whispered Christine amazed. "It looks like a scene from a horrible fairy tale, a dragon's lair."

"More like a phantom's lair," Raoul whispered back.

"What was Philippe looking for down there? Or was he looking up here, instead?" she asked him. "Aha, I remember some of the message now. Beyond the iron gate is a hidden door that will take us to what we seek.

We need a key to progress. I remember Philippe talking about it, something about money, about two thousand dollars."

"Money? It doesn't make sense. It has to be a cryptic message."

"Well, whatever it means, I'm fairly sure we won't progress much further without it."

"We could... wait." Raoul touched her arm. "Did you hear that? Someone is near." Christine nodded. "We have to go now and return another time."

"Okay, you first," mouthed Christine, and they disappeared into the darkness from whence they came.

CHAPTER TWENTY-SEVEN

DIVA IN DISGUISE

"And, finally, the tinted glasses," said Carlotta to the image in her dressing room mirror, who slipped on the spectacles. "There! No one will recognise you now," she said, smiling with smug satisfaction at her alter ego. "Not even my handsome bodyguard." Carlotta had given Erik the day off just in case, saying she wanted to stay at her hotel and rest all day today. Although she doubted anyone would recognise her.

She looked like any one of the army of ubiquitous cleaning ladies to be found anywhere in the opera house at any one time, dusting, polishing and cleaning. A head scarf roughly tied over her wig, allowed a mass of untidy red curls to escape. Frumpy, baggy, grey pants were topped by an overly generous grey cardigan, unsuccessfully trying to hide a bulging belly. A large cushion taped to her waist made her appear fat. Flat, scuffed plimsolls teamed with hunched shoulders and a stoop, made her appear shorter, and were kinder on her sore feet. Carlotta removed the glasses to reveal, chubby cheeks, a double chin and buck teeth, all courtesy of prosthetics. She laughed at the reflection of the character she had created.

Over the years Carlotta had performed many roles, imbuing each one with a character all its own — *Norma, Aida, Tosca, Lucia, Carmen, Violetta* and now, again, *Lady Macbeth*. She was a master of disguise. Or was it a mistress of disguise? How ironic she thought, looking at the largish woman in front of her. It wasn't that long ago, she didn't need prosthetics to make her look big. She had been big. Fat and frumpy, too. So big, she felt it detracted from her ability to perform the roles to the level she desired. Which is what inspired her transformation from ugly duckling to beautiful swan. But, for the time being, the ugly duckling was back.

Carlotta turned round and around in front of the mirror, checking her outfit, her face, and the clumsy way she moved. Satisfied, she replaced the spectacles and picked up a worn, woven carpet bag full of cleaning products and slung it over her shoulder. She lay a dust cloth over it for special effect. Ready to perform her duties. Carlotta chuckled to herself.

"Yes, this should allow me to move around the Garnier

unnoticed. It's only a week until opening night and I want to know everything that is happening," she said out loud to her alter ego. "About that young upstart Christine, but also about Victor. I can no longer trust him, if I ever could. Something is going on, and I must find out what it is."

Carlotta moved around the first floor, stopping every now and then to inspect, and, if need be, to dust and polish one of the many statues that lined the corridors and balconies. People walked by as if she were invisible. No one gave her a second glance. She was just another one of the army of workers within the Garnier who did their work in plain sight, yet were never seen.

Emboldened, Carlotta moved down to the ground floor into the rear of the auditorium. Starting in the back row, and slowly moving across, she started polishing the dark mahogany moulding on the backs and arms of the chairs. No one noticed her. An unusually large number of the cast and crew had gathered at the front of the theatre, including Victor. Raoul sat inconspicuously to the side, as did Madame Giraud in Box 39 and Erik in Box 5, but all eyes were looking at the simple setting on stage. Ruffled white linen on an unmade bed with a white washbasin on a pedestal nearby. Excited whispers were being exchanged.

Monsieur Laloux, looking particularly dapper in navy

blue pin-striped suit, navy shirt and pink tie, walked on stage. He was looking particularly pleased with himself, too, Carlotta noticed.

"Bastardo!" she muttered, under her breath.

He bowed to the audience. "A very special rehearsal, n'est pas?" He motioned to the actors waiting in the wings. "Lady Macbeth's gentlewoman and the doctor on stage, please." Danielle and Ivan walked out together. "Over here on the left hand side, out of Lady Macbeth's line of vision, please." They moved into position. Ivan wearing a long dark robe cinched at the waist with a girdle and Danielle in a long, drab, button to the neck dress. He motioned to the other side of the stage, "Lady Macbeth, please."

Christine walked slowly onto the stage in bare feet looking almost ethereal. Wearing a flowing, full length, white organdie nightgown that did little to hide her graceful curves, her long brunette locks were plaited and tied at the nape of her neck. The audience visibly sighed at this vision of serene loveliness. Christine flashed them a winsome smile.

Carlotta scowled. "The sleepwalking aria!" She gasped.

"*Una macchia è qui tuttora (A spot is still here),*" said Monsieur Laloux importantly. "Lady Macbeth's famous sleepwalking scene is one of the great soprano showpieces."

"How dare she! How dare she be allowed to sing this?" Carlotta, unable to speak out loud, threatened to implode. "That's an aria I made my own."

Instructing Christine, as well as the audience, Monsieur Laloux continued, "The way Verdi sets this is that Lady Macbeth is so vulnerable at the very beginning. She is consumed with guilt. He looked at Christine who nodded. "At last, this powerful, intelligent and elegant woman, this queen, breaks down with guilt at her misdeeds. And there is nothing that's going to put her back together." Christine nodded her understanding once more. "I think this is a work of genius. And..." he said, looking directly at Christine, challenging her, "it takes a genius to sing it as it should be sung. Someone like you, Christine." She smiled apprehensively, took a deep breath, and then walked to the wings, ready to begin.

Carlotta forced herself to stop and watch. She was so angry she was shaking. "I'll show you who is a genius, Mr. Artistic Director. I'll show all of you how it should be sung on opening night," she vowed silently. A hush fell over the auditorium.

"Ready, Maestro. From the beginning of Scene 4." A nod to Christine, then Monsieur Laloux disappeared off stage. Lady Macbeth entered, walking as if in a trance. The doctor and the gentlewoman stepped forward to sing.

"That lamp in her hand?

It is the lamp which she keeps always beside her bed.

Oh, her eyes are wide open!

Yet she cannot see."

Lady Macbeth put down the lamp and rubbed her hands as if washing something off.

"There's still a spot here.

Away, I tell you, curse you!"

Christine's voice, full of emotion and hauntingly beautiful, instantly transported the audience to another time and place. She was no longer Christine, but Lady Macbeth.

"I'm not listening to this rubbish any longer," said Carlotta, rising to her full height, before realising she was still in disguise. She headed to the exit. The movement caught Erik's eye. There was something familiar about the woman, but too riveted by the performance to care, he turned back to watch Christine.

CHAPTER TWENTY-EIGHT

A NEW DIVA

"Bravissima!" called Victor loudly, from the front row, standing and applauding along with the rest of the cast and crew at the fallen figure of Lady Macbeth on stage. "Bravissima!" he repeated as he walked up the steps onto the stage, followed closely by Monsieur Laloux. Victor offered her his hand to help her to her feet. He held her hand, kissed it and bowed deeply. "C'est magnifique!"

"Bravissima!" Echoed Monsieur Laloux, and "Bellissima!"

"You have the voice of an angel, my dear Christine," said Victor.

"Your bel canto brought tears to my eyes," said Monsieur Laloux.

"A riveting performance," said Victor, sounding like a star-struck fan. A surprised Christine was taken aback that both the Opera Manager and the Artistic Director were so keen to flatter her. It was only a rehearsal.

"Please excuse me," said Christine, exhilarated by the performance, but also feeling a little uncomfortable, "I wish to change out of this nightdress." Not waiting for permission, she headed off stage, wanting to escape the over-exuberant pair. While she knew the effects of her talent for singing and acting, she wondered why the pair had made such a fuss.

A fuming Carlotta, hiding in the wings, was wondering, too. She would stay.

"Time for a private chat, Maurice," said Victor to Monsieur Laloux, his manner serious, but excitement still uppermost in his voice. Rehearsals had finished. The auditorium had emptied, the cast and crew left for the day. Only they were left, standing together on the stage. Or so they thought.

"Christine really does have the voice of an angel," said Victor.

"I know! I've been trying to tell you that for some time."

"She reminds me of Renata Tebaldi, the greatest lyric soprano of all time," continued Victor, "And one of the most beautiful voices of the twentieth century."

"I agree. There is the same exquisite and emotional quality to her singing."

"But," said Victor, still rhapsodising, "also one of the most beloved opera singers of all time."

"She beguiled audiences, in the same way Christine does."

"Carlotta has overriding ambition. She can sing with great dramatic flair, but…"

Maurice finished his sentence, "Hers is not a beautiful voice. And…" he hesitated slightly, but emboldened by the camaraderie, he added, "it is fading."

"Yes, it is!"

Carlotta writhing with anger at the insults, didn't dare breathe a word.

"And, Carlotta is not loved the way Renata was, or the way Christine is even now, at the beginning of her career," added Victor. "Maurice, I do believe we have a new diva on our hands," he said, puffing out his chest with pride and clapping Maurice on the shoulder.

Carlotta, her wrath nearing the point of no return, wrapped her mouth around a curtain and bit hard, to stop herself from screaming. Was there no end to this calumny?

Monsieur Laloux, barely able to contain himself as well, asked, "What exactly does that mean for this opera, Victor?"

"Well it means that if Carlotta is not well enough to

perform, then Christine surely will. We will introduce a new diva to the world. And…"

"Perhaps you can persuade Madame Caccini, it is not in her best interests to sing," said Maurice, praying such good luck could befall him.

"I'll try, but there may be a better way to deal with Carlotta," Victor mused, speaking more to himself than to Maurice, "I must look into the contracts first with my business partner – at Carlotta's and the one for Christine."

"Bastardo! We'll see about that," said Carlotta, *sotto-voce*, brushing the curtains aside and storming off. You will rue the day you met me, Victor Marchand."

CHAPTER TWENTY-NINE

SURVEILLANCE

Erik's monitor remained on pause, showing the entry through which Raoul and Christine were first captured on screen, deep within what he believed was his impenetrable lair. He leaned back onto his chair, sipping a hot coffee, while considering the possible scenarios that led to this breach. Outside of blind luck, there were three ways in which the intruders could find their way into his subterranean world. Outside help from someone with knowledge of the Garnier, such as Madame Giraud, other worldly help from the much heralded phantoms that were oft mentioned; or inside help. Increasingly agitated by the breach, he recalled Jean Claude, for the third time in the last hour.

"Have you finished the perimeter sweep, Jean?"

"Yes. I will be with you shortly to report."

"About time. I need answers," he barked, his agitation growing by the minute.

Erik finished the last of his coffee and threw the paper cup to the floor, before replaying the monitor record of the two intruders. Their access was from a perimeter that had no cameras. It was a large expanse on the outside of the buildings foundations, surrounded by rock. Erik and his team had spent countless hours sweeping that perimeter and viewed it as no more than a low lying cave with no light or flowing air. If there was an entry, it had to be well camouflaged and man-made.

Jean Claude entered Erik's lair, his head slightly lowered, which was always a bad sign. His loyal General had been his closest confidante, since they had both served in military operations in the Middle East. The thought that he could be the traitor in his midst had to be considered, but Erik would review all other possibilities before turning on his closest ally.

"Tell me you have found the access point," Erik demanded.

"The perimeter is unchanged from our last inspection. There are no immediate signs of where they gained access. I'm organising x-ray scanners, so we can do a thorough search of the area."

"And?"

"We will have the scanners shipped by tomorrow. I will personally carry out the inspection. If there are any hidden entries in the perimeter, the scanners will pick them up. We are also installing night cameras throughout, in case they choose to return."

"Very well. I want you to personally oversee all the arrangements and installation."

"I'm confident our team will...."

Erik slammed his fist on the desk and pointed to the monitor that continuously replayed the two intruders."

"Jean Claude, these amateurs came close to finding everything that we have worked so hard to secretly build. Trust no one!"

"Including the diva?" Jean Claude responded, indicating his own suspicions.

"I'll take care of that. You focus on the team. If there is a hint of suspicion around any of our men, let me know immediately. Is that clear?"

"Yes, sir."

"Then do as I say."

Erik saluted, as often he did when seeking Jean Claude's trust. They had been to hell and back together, never forgetting what saved them — discipline and trust in each other's capabilities. As Jean Claude saluted, turned and exited the lair, Erik studied him. He had always listened to his loyal General and trusted his instinct, even ahead of his own, at times. Maybe Jean

Claude's mistrust for Carlotta was well placed? There had been no breach of security until he brought her to his lair. Could she have somehow remembered her way down to the lair, even though she was blindfolded for some of that time? He doubted she would be capable, but even more unlikely, would she dare be disloyal, knowing it would cost her life? Erik shook his head, certain she was not the traitor. The information he needed had to be on the recording, he thought, turning once again to the monitor and watching the replay, particularly the one and only conversation they had while being taped. The sound of their voices were barely audible at maximum volume. He strained to hear.

"I remember some more of the message, now. There is another hidden door that will take us to what we seek. We need the key to progress. I remember Philippe talking about it, something about two thousand dollars," said a voice that sounded like Christine Dubois.

"Money? It doesn't make sense. It has to be a cryptic message."

"Well, whatever it means, I'm fairly sure we won't progress much further without it." That had to be Raoul.

"We could......wait did you hear that.....someone is near. We have to go now and return another time...."

At that, both intruders disappeared back from where

they came. Erik knew now, they had discovered an entry, more than likely the one used by Philippe. They were never able to find out how Philippe gained entry. He took his secret with him. That in itself was concerning, but Philippe had also confided to Christine that a key was hidden, a very important key. He paused the monitor and made himself a second coffee as he considered the new information.

There were a number of people whom he would have to keep a close eye on. Potential outside help could come from Inspector Moreau. He assisted Raoul with Philippe's investigation, so his knowledge of the Garnier was better than most. Madame Giraud was the other potential accomplice. She'd already had many meetings with Raoul and he was sure she was a willing helper. She also had a long history with the Garnier and an extensive knowledge of its inner workings. More fanciful, she'd always quietly claimed a psychic as well as physical connection to its inhabitants, past and present. Erik had considered her psychic claims as more delusional than factual, but given their invidious position, he had to take account of all possibilities, no matter how remote.

Erik turned off the monitor and walked over to his grand piano. He sat and replayed the musical score he had written for Rose and played for Carlotta. Although similar in looks, how different these two women were. Rose had a pure love for art, whereas Carlotta saw it as a means to power. Yet both held great talent as opera sopranos. Ironically, Carlotta excelled in the world of opera, where Rose never had the chance to soar in the artistic world she held dear. Perhaps both were more similar than he cared to believe? It was just a case of time and experiences that changed Carlotta. Could she have been like Rose at a younger age? He played on, lost in his thoughts, remembering a time that he had all too often buried away from his mind. But try as he might to unlock the door, the Captor stepped in his way and locked it shut again.

Erik stopped playing, slamming the keyboard cover over the keys as if they contained the tools of the torturers kit. He walked away from his beloved piano into the shadows of his lair toward the lake and sat by its soothing waters, studying the currents that just a few weeks earlier had taken a ballerina from the Garnier. How many more would be swept away before he could soothe the whirlpool of anger that filled his mind? Perhaps Carlotta really saw the devils that controlled him? Perhaps she could satiate his appetite and allow him to control this savage force and to finally find peace? For her sake, he hoped Carlotta was as strong as she claimed, for if she failed him, she would certainly feel the savage power of his anger, a terror far worse than any of the old folk tales of Phantoms the inhabitants of the Garnier were fond of telling.

CHAPTER THIRTY

THE BODYGUARD

Erik found that his upgraded position required he oversaw the most mundane of jobs. Mercifully, some of the more trivial, such as taking care of Carlotta's hyperactive poodle, were delegated to one of his team. Whereas some duties, such as escorting Carlotta to various functions, demanded it be him. Today was such a day, as he drove Victor and Carlotta to the famous Paris restaurant, Le Meurice. On this day he was asked to join them for drinks to finalise an agreement on his new salary. Victor was as chatty and effusive as always, whereas Carlotta was unusually introspective, although Erik was sure she would return to her outgoing persona on arrival at a public forum. The drive from the Garnier to Le Meurice Hotel in Rue de Rivoli in the First Arrondisement was unusually free of heavy traffic.

"Carlotta tells me you are doing a fine job, Erik."

Erik checked Victor's expression in the rear view mirror, looking for any hint of accusation, but found none.

"I treat my job seriously, Monsieur Marchand. Her ongoing security is tantamount to my interest, now."

"He is a true professional, Victor," Carlotta added, finally breaking her moody silence.

The conversation continued as they neared their destination, most of it suddenly dominated by Carlotta as her excitement and expectation grew about dining in one of Paris's finest restaurants where she was sure to be greeted with adulation. All three stepped out of the limousine, allowing the hotel concierge to organise a driver to park it, before being quickly ushered through the marble floored lobby where high society and not so worthy Nazi invaders, had frequented its famous hotel since 1835. The large dining room had a timeless elegance, inspired by the Salon de la Paix of the Chateau of Versailles. Carlotta strode across the mosaic floored dining room as if she were indeed the Queen of Versailles.

"Merci, Monsieur," she said, as a waiter took her elegant waist length coat and scarf, revealing a dazzling, designer dress, made of titian silk. Both men walked behind her as she drew bows and respectful smiles from the maître d'hôtel.

"Yes, the window seat. The Jardins des Tuileries is so elegant in the evening light."

All were seated and attended to by a number of waiters who efficiently worked under the ever watchful gaze of the maître d'hôtel.

"Madame Caccini, the management are honoured to have your presence tonight. We would be delighted if you'd allow our head photographer to take some photos of this special occasion?"

"Your dining room is so divine. It reminds me of the Garnier, so I would welcome photos of the occasion."

"Merci Madame," replied the maître d'hôtel, smiling obsequiously, before clicking his finger to a waiter who quickly delivered the finest champagne and three crystal glasses to the table. "A small token of our appreciation," he said, before taking Carlotta's hand and leading her to a prominent position in the dining room, which was surrounded by antique mirrors, crystal chandeliers and bronze, marble and frescoes.

The famous hotel was known for its serene elegance, but by the end of the photo shoot everyone knew that the Grand Diva, was dining in Le Meurice. Erik watched on, slightly amused as Victor and Carlotta spoke more to the captivated diners than to each other, a skill finely honed over the years in the spotlight. But once both returned to the dining table, the room quietened and the three blended into the elegant ambience of the hotel. Once the champagne was poured, the tone of the table turned business-like, as Victor negotiated Erik's new salary.

"I wanted to quickly finalise the details of your new position as a sign of our appreciation for your support, Erik. Carlotta hates when I talk numbers, so let's make this a simple deal. Given you are looking after the most precious singer in all of France, I believe you should be suitably rewarded. I want to double your current salary. Does that sound fair?"

"More than fair. I have also hired one extra person to take care of some of the less important duties that I can oversee."

Carlotta was studying her mobile, but interjected. "I'm glad you have finally recognised my importance, Victor. Sometimes I wonder if you really do believe that."

Victor met Carlotta's gaze, before picking up his champagne and sipping it, contemplating his reply. "A toast to the most beautiful and talented woman in all of France!"

Another silence ensued, revealing a tension that had been stewing between them since they got into the car. Erik toasted and sipped on the expensive French champagne, hiding his delight with Victor's salary offer — Perrier-Jouet had never tasted sweeter. All three avoided the tense atmosphere to enjoy the exquisite beauty of their surrounds, before Victor's phone broke the silence.

"Hello..... Yes....... I see, yes. Can I talk with you now?" Victor replied, turning to Carlotta for her confirmation and receiving a sharp glare, before signalling with her hands he could leave them.

"Yes. I understand. In an hour. At your office. Yes."

"So?" Carlotta enquired.

"It was Alexander." He replied. The mention of his name was enough for them to agree he had to leave. "Perhaps Erik could take me....."

"Although I'm disappointed that you are leaving me on this special dinner. Now you wish to leave me alone here?"

"No, no. Of course not. I shall talk with the maître d'hôtel to organise transport," Victor replied, finishing his glass of champagne before rising and excusing himself.

Victor wasn't one to be flustered, but his reaction to the short call was more like a son to his strict father, than his usual air of confidence. Erik wondered who Alexander could be and how much power he exerted over both Victor and Carlotta. He turned his gaze from Victor who was speaking to the maître d'hôtel, back to Carlotta, who surprisingly had a wry smile as she watched Victor's clear discomfort.

"Care to share the joke?"

Carlotta waved farewell to Victor, before taking Erik's hand and giggling. "Can't a woman be happy, now that she is finally alone with her lover?"

"Anyone would think that you planned this?"

"Perhaps," she said coyly. "But let's not spoil this special occasion with business. I have wanted to return to this famous restaurant for many years and now I have my wish."

Carlotta signalled to their waiter to attend them and immediately requested information about her favoured main courses so that she could make a choice. She spent little time charming the young waiter and engaging him in lively conversation as she flirted with an ease, befitting a famous diva, before ultimately making a choice, both for her and Erik.

"I'll have the Brittany lobster with sea potatoes and Monsieur will have chicken from the Culoiseau farm, morel mushrooms and wild garlic."

"Merci, Madame, a perfect choice."

Carlotta watched the waiter disappear to the kitchen with a look of satisfaction on her face, drawing Erik to remark.

"You suddenly look happy with yourself."

"I admit to enjoying control over my surroundings, something we have in common, don't we?"

"We're birds of a feather, but my control can be more deadly. Don't ever make the mistake of forgetting that, will you?"

Carlotta did not react, choosing instead to sip on her champagne and admire the luxurious antique surrounds. "If only you realised that this could all be ours if we stood together," she said, extending her hand across the table. Erik obliged and softly caressed her willing hand.

"So what is Victor discussing with this Alexander gentleman?"

"He would be deep in discussion about his perceived lack of funds to go on sourcing opera in France."

"Believed lack of funds?"

"In all the time I have known my beloved Victor, I have learnt that he believed in just one thing."

"You?"

Carlotta laughed out loud. "Don't be ridiculous, darling. He believes in our finance manager, Alexander, or at least what I get Alexander to tell him."

Erik wanted to ask more, but he knew Carlotta would willingly reveal all, but in her own time. He merely raised his eyebrows in reaction, before signalling to the waiter to refill their champagne glasses. The waiter, along with two others, arrived at their table, with appetisers.

A range of small appetisers made from the finest of ingredients and created by artists more than chefs, complemented the elegant table setting, and their romantic evening. Erik raised his newly filled champagne glass to toast as did Carlotta.

"To us, a long and fruitful union."

Carlotta nodded in the affirmative. "A noi!"

Both savoured the different tastes of food, whilst again appreciating the sensuous surroundings, sharing conversation, longing gazes and fleeting touches of their hands. Slowly, hunger for food gave way to a tidal wave of erotic hunger as the perfect night unfolded.

"We could share something very special if we believe in each other," Carlotta said. The fine food and champagne had long lifted any inhibitions in her. The strong diva, who knew how to perform for a crowd, had given way to a more reflective woman who was prepared to share her vulnerabilities.

"You can believe in me, Carlotta. From what you have told me, the only thing missing in your life is a strong man. I can assure you, there is no man you have ever met that I would fear."

"I think I believe you, my delectable Head of Security. In your arms, it seems I would have no one to fear, except you."

"You would have nothing to fear, as long as you remained true to me. Together, we could conquer all."

"You don't know how right you truly are."

"So, tell me about this Alexander."

Carlotta smiled knowingly at Erik. "Quite the ambitious one, aren't you?"

"No more than you, my darling Carlotta."

Carlotta took another sip of her champagne as if to summon up the courage to reveal her inner secrets, before speaking. "Well, as you know, my beloved Victor is known for his entrepreneurial successes and is considered a very wealthy man."

"It is certainly no secret. You only have to read the newspapers to learn of his business life."

"He is certainly a talented entrepreneur. What is not known, is that his success has always revolved around my fortune, not his."

"Surely you share that wealth as husband and wife?"

"Victor and I married? We are a business partnership. No more."

"You are telling me that Victor is penniless?"

"Certainly not by your standards. But compared to me, I suppose he is penniless."

"Pardon Madame, your Brittany lobster and for Monsieur, the Culouiseau chicken. Bon appetit!

Carlotta looked at her meal with glee. "Come, one never discusses business over a meal," she said, signalling Erik to start the meal.

Erik delighted in the haute cuisine served him. Every taste of the specially produced chicken spelt volumes for the French love affair with fine food. It wasn't too long ago Erik survived on half cooked rice, boiled in water no better than raw sewerage. It reminded him that food was yet another weapon in the Captor's arsenal. Any sign of strength or resistance was met with rationed food, usually no food for a week, before returning to half rations for the following week.

While Erik's taste buds were being tantalised with the finest food Le Meurice could offer, his mind was resisting its indulgence. He had to be ever vigilant, never showing his captors that he was gaining the upper hand. He looked out the window to the dusk filled garden, the royal green foliage slowly turning to shadow. That was his home. In the shadows. He felt an urge to leave the table and hide in the cooling dusk, before a light flashed directly into his eyes. For a brief moment, he thought he was back in his cell about to be interrogated by his captors, before the sound of a man broke his imaginings.

"Could we have one more photo, Madame Caccini?"

Erik reacted immediately to the invasion. He had

to strike back and quickly, to ensure he maintained control. He leapt from his chair and stood close to the press cameraman, holding his throat in a vice-like grip. Unbeknown to the invader, Erik could have ended his life with the smallest of movements.

"Don't ever do that again without asking or I'll snap your little neck like a twig" he whispered, gazing directly into his eyes with an intensity that made the cameraman agree, nodding his head in the affirmative for as much as Erik's grip would allow. "Now go along home and do not cross my path again, tonight. But remember, not a single word of disagreement or you will make me truly mad. Understood?"

The cameraman left as quietly and dignified as his terrified state would allow, trying to avoid attention to the incident. Erik merely smiled to the surrounding tables and shrugged his shoulders, suggesting his frustration with the press, before returning to his meal, as if nothing had happened. Carlotta also continued eating, although with a watchful eye on her moody companion.

"Did I hear you right? You could have killed that man if you chose."

"Standard skills to become a body guard for the rich and famous," Erik quipped.

Carlotta smiled in a restrained fashion, feeling a mixture

of protection and terror in equal part. Quiet remained at the table until the meals were finished and plates removed.

"So define penniless?" Erik said, continuing his probing.

Carlotta shook her head, annoyed and impressed at the same time. "Victor has believed that Alexander is his loyal business advisor and over the years he has increasingly confided in him. Unbeknown to Victor, Alexander and I go a long way back. His undivided loyalty will remain with me for a lifetime. So, I know about Victor's schemes as soon as he confides in Alexander. Unfortunately, his ambition and greed has continued to expand, so much so, that I will need to take action."

"That being?"

"I want to break the existing contract with Victor. His reaction will be extreme, to say the least, so it would be helpful to me to have someone who can convince him that it is in his interest to accept the new contract. I would need someone who knows how to persuade people."

Erik smiled. "Your timing is exquisite, my darling."

"You are a persuasive man, my Head of Security. And I'm convinced together we can make the changes necessary to gain control of opera in France. For the truth is, I own it. I just need the right man to make sure it stays that way, no matter the cost."

"We're birds of a feather, you and I," Erik responded,

barely containing his delight, before reflecting on her generous offer. "Where I come from, there's always a price for that kind of generosity."

Carlotta nodded her head in agreement. "I have the money and ability to control opera in France, but there is one important area that I don't."

"If it's force you require, I can accommodate any contingency. Rest assured."

"I'm certain of that. You convinced me in your lair. But no, my problem is in the art. I want this performance of Macbeth to be my finest, but those who could influence that outcome favour another."

"Christine?"

"The very one. She more than any other, stands in my way. Rid me of her smug, virtuous ways and allow me to garner the awards and accolades that I so richly deserve. Do that for me and we will control French opera together. You have my word."

Erik responded by simply offering his hand and caressing Carlotta's hand. He did not fully know what feelings he felt for the new diva, but he was sure he desired her in a way that could not be easily satiated. He wanted to both protect and control at the same time. They gazed lustfully into each other's eyes, until their moment was interrupted by the waiter.

"Our specialty as per your request, Madame Caccina. Burnt Doyenne du Comice pear, honey and Sarawak pepper. And the same for you, Monsieur."

Both delighted at the perfect desserts placed before them and enjoyed their delicate textures and flavours. Little was said between them as their taste buds were caressed. Carlotta also caressed Erik's inner thigh with her foot, further building Erik's desires. He returned her sexual hunger with his gaze and then later, after leaving Le Meurice, fulfilled their physical union late into the night. Erik never responded in words to Carlotta's offer of a business union, nor did he have to. By the night's end, they both wanted more of the erotic union they had quickly built, much more.

CHAPTER THIRTY-ONE

WHERE IS CHRISTINE?

Carlotta rehearsed under the guidance of Monsieur Laloux with a vigour and enthusiasm that brought a happy smile to the Artistic Director's face.

"Madame Caccini, if you sing like that on opening night, I'm sure it will be a resounding success," he said, his praise more generous with every repeat of the song.

"Perhaps one more time, before I hand you to the rest of the cast, Monsieur Laloux?"

He responded, merely shrugging his shoulders, showing both surprise and delight for Carlotta's new work ethic. Before signalling to the pianist to commence, he called a stagehand to alert the other cast that full rehearsals would commence in fifteen minutes. At that same moment, Victor walked from behind the curtains toward them.

He kissed Carlotta on both cheeks with an affection

that belied their recent tensions. "I'm so sorry to have missed dining with you, my love, but I'm sure you still managed to enjoy yourself?"

"I made the best out of my disappointment, my darling."

Victor managed a forced smile before turning to Monsieur Laloux. "Bonjour, Monsieur Laloux. I trust you are not over-working my angel?"

"Carlotta insisted on an early start, Monsieur Marchand."

"Oh really?" He replied, turning to Carlota.

"I'm surprised you would have the energy, my love?"

"A true artist always performs best when opening night approaches. But I'm sure you are both aware of that. It's why I know I have your complete support."

Monsieur Laloux laughed nervously, before bowing slightly in deference to his star diva. Victor on the other hand, ignored Carlotta, preferring to finish his conversation with Monsieur Laloux.

"I expect a faultless opening night, Monsieur. Our very survival may depend on it," he said tersely, before striding past Carlotta, "and we need to talk," he snapped, before departing the stage. If Carlotta was angered, she did not show it.

"*La luce langue (The light is fading)*. One more time, Monsieur, if you please." An appropriate theme she mused.

Macbeth is now king but cannot enjoy his power, despite his wife's encouragement. He is obsessed with the witches' prophecy that Banquo's descendants will be kings, and together with Lady Macbeth, he plots another murder.

As the music re-commenced, many of the cast started to arrive, their gathering crowd spurring Carlotta to sing to even greater heights, dazzling cast and stagehands alike.

"El suprema!" Monsieur Laloux cried, inspiring Carlotta to sing as if she were at her peak again. As she reached the crescendo of the song, her new lover, Erik walked out from the shadows of the theatre and stood among the cast and crew. He, like them, was spellbound by the power and intensity of her voice. It felt like opening night, such was the atmosphere. All stood and applauded her performance, drawing the Artistic Director to take Carlotta's hand and bow in appreciation of their ovation. Even Monsieur Laloux was swept up in the moment.

"Flowers immediately for Madame Caccini," he ordered, snapping his fingers at a stagehand, who quickly delivered a bouquet of flowers to him.

"You are our diva supreme, Madame," he said admiringly, before handing her the bouquet. "All of you must strive for this level of artistry. Then our performance on opening night will never be forgotten."

Carlotta held her arm out to Erik, who quickly joined

her on stage. "Take me to the front row. I wish to watch rehearsals for a short time." Erik sat with Carlotta in the centre seats of the front row, where they both waited for Monsieur Laloux to organise the cast.

"Well you heard our diva! Could I have the Witches' chorus to the stage please," he cried, clapping his hands to the scurrying cast and crew.

Musicians, extras and eleven of the twelve witches assembled, leaving Monsieur Laloux dismayed.

"Christine? Where is Christine?"

"She is ill, Monsieur," replied Danielle.

"She is ill? Are you serious? Bring her to me, now,"

Danielle reluctantly replied, knowing it would not satisfy her Artistic Director. "I did not see her, Monsieur. She left a note on her dressing table," nervously handing him the hand written note.

Monsieur Laloux's mood quickly changed from rapture for Carlotta's brilliance to rage, given Christine's failure to attend rehearsals just three days from opening night.

"Christine's extra please come to the stage," he barked at the surrounding cast. Almost instantly, Christine's young extra joined the witches, clearly excited for her chance.

"Why is there a delay, Monsieur?" Came the voice of Carlotta from the seats below.

Monsieur Laloux could only shrug his shoulders as he passed Christine's note down to her. "Christine is ill, apparently."

"Amateur!" She cried out loud, ensuring all heard her spiteful remark. As all eyes of the cast turned her way she passed the note to Erik and walked closer to the stage. "Let me see her understudy perform. If she is ready for the part, I will have her replace Christine immediately.

Erik watched on as Carlotta imposed her influence on the rehearsals. Monsieur Laloux appeared less than impressed that Carlotta, who had attended very few rehearsals, was now demanding Christine's head for missing just one. Christine's friend, Danielle appeared even less impressed as she was forced to help the less talented extra to perhaps replace her best friend.

Erik watched on with satisfaction. A new, deadly partnership was imposing its will on their unsuspecting cast. Erik had demonstrated his support for Carlotta and had abducted Christine, who he knew now faced an uncertain future. He sat back, contented with the proceedings of the last few days, knowing his dream of controlling the Garnier was coming to fruition.

But then he felt a sudden chill brush the back of his neck, making him feel as if someone was observing him. He looked to the back of the theatre and saw a small figure leaning against the balcony rail of one of the private viewing boxes high above. It was Madame Giraud. She too had a contented smile on her face. He gazed directly at her and opened his hands in a questioning gesture. Madame Giraud's smile broadened as she tilted her head slightly to his left.

Erik immediately looked in that direction, then to the note he held, the one he had made Christine write just before he took her to his lair. He looked at the familiar message bearing Christine's handwriting and signature, but noticed that a second signature appeared directly below. Two simple initials in red lay on the paper that were not there before — the initials O.G. Erik turned his gaze back to the opera box, to show his dismay and anger, but Madame Giraud had disappeared.

CHAPTER THIRTY-TWO

SPIRITS OF THE PAST

Madame Giraud felt a familiarity in the opera-like events washing over her life. The Garnier, the home of high drama, emotion and music, was again occupied by deadly spirits intent on reigning terror. The Opera Ghost sensed this too, beguiling those who sought to play in its famous corridors. She felt his ominous presence all around her and desperately reached out to him for help.

Erik's reaction to the note convinced her that he was at the centre of the Phantom's gaze. She retreated from the balcony of Box 39 to avoid Erik's accusing glared, seeking the safety of her private space, a small hidden room unknown to all but her and one other, the true owner of the Garnier.

She unlocked a concealed panel at the back of Box 39, revealing her own private portal between the opera house of today and the past, quietly re-locking the secret door behind her, before lighting a single candle and shining a light on a canvas — the Phantom's only portrait ever painted. As was her custom, Madame Giraud sat on a small chair placed in front of it, preparing herself to contact her spirit guides.

She breathed rhythmically and relaxed back into her chair, all the while looking at the Opera Ghost's portrait, a nineteenth century depiction of her most famous guide. Sufficiently settled, she lit a second candle cradled in a rose coloured flask, illuminating the small square space with a softer hue. She took ever deeper breaths as she summoned those spirits that wished to speak to her.

Surprisingly, three of her most valued guides appeared together, standing side by side, in front of the Opera Ghost's canvas. Their union was an unusual event, occurring only on significant occasions. The three were dressed in medieval clothing, that was not dissimilar to the wardrobe used by the current opera cast. One of the spirit guides, the only male, pointed to the portrait behind him as he spoke.

"The Garnier is home to an opera within an opera, more bloodied and stained with sorrow than Macbeth could ever imagine."

Madame Giraud studied the portrait before responding. "Has the Garnier a new Phantom?"

"You will find many phantoms. Journey cautiously through the blood of many," said the second apparition, a young female.

"Has love lost?"

The third apparition moved forward, the eldest of the three, stern in face and with long, straggly hair that flowed to her waist.

"Love has many voices, but only one true heart."

She then whispered a spell in Latin that Madame Giraud knew well. All three guides spread their arms, releasing a flow of spirits into the room. They continued to speak in unison, but their voices were drowned out by a sea of sorrowful cries. Male, female, young and old sang a mournful chorus, as if the world of the tortured spoke as one, overpowering Madame Giraud's senses.

"Leave me!" She implored and the guides recalled the spirits of the damned, bringing silence to the room. The two candles flickered until the old woman spirit exhaled her other-world breath into the room. Madame Giraud heard the spirit's breath firstly as a distant whistle, before she felt the force of the old woman's breath blow across her face, extinguishing both candles, leaving her in darkness bar the face of her spirit guide.

"You face dark forces. Be bloody, bold and resolute, for true love can never be vanquished by those who only seek power."

The old guide vanished, leaving Madame Giraud alone in her secret room to contemplate her guides' warnings. The two candle's magically re-ignited, shining a light on the Phantom's portrait. She knew now that all faced great danger from the secretive forces that sought to control the Garnier. She studied the Phantom's portrait for some time, her body slouched and her face despondent, before finally whispering a heartfelt plea. "Help me. Help us all!"

CHAPTER THIRTY-THREE

CHRISTINE'S ORDEAL BEGINS

Christine woke to darkness, unsure of her where-abouts, she habitually reached out for her bedside timer, only to feel the chill of a stone floor. The pitch black slowly gave way to the dimmest of light, emanating from a small barred window high above her. The comfort of sleep soon turned to horror as she realised she was in a small cell. Her body ached all over, as she drew herself off the wooded frame of the bed she lay on.

Christine's recollection of what had happened slowly resurfaced. Someone had grasped her face; and there was a pungent odour. Her head had spun as she stood up straight, which made her realise she had been drugged. Stretching both arms to relieve her pain and fully wake from her drowsiness, Christine's mind began to fill with questions. How long had she been here? She had no idea of knowing, as her watch and possessions had been taken.

She reached for the window sill and lifted her head up to peer outside her cell.

"Help!" she cried, terrified for her safety. Then she remembered that preparations for the opera were nearing completion. She had to attend rehearsals.

"Help me, please!" Her cries growing desperately louder.

For all Christine knew, opening night may be upon them. She had commitments to fulfil, to the performance and her friends and cast. She cried out for several minutes, before her arms tired and she fell to the stone floor. She repeated the process, but her cries echoed across a seemingly empty twilight surround as foreboding as the cell she inhabited. Finally, she dropped to the floor, too exhausted to continue. Christine hunched against the cold wall, head in hands, sobbing uncontrollably. Why would someone do this to her?

Silence ensued for what seemed an eternity, before she heard the sounds of approaching footsteps.

"Help!" She cried, hoping her rescue was at hand. Hope grew in her as the sound of a key and the cell door opening lit the cell, affording Christine a better view of her confinement. Dampness was all around the small stone-filled cell, except the wooden framed bed. A silhouette of a man stood in the doorway, the shape of a stockily built man in a period costume. A mask hid his identity, as did a voice-altering device that distorted natural sounds.

"I'll only tell you once. No crying out through the window. I don't want to hurt you, little lady, but believe me, I will if I have to return," he threatened, before leaving her a bowl of water. "Behave yourself and you keep the water."

"Please help me. Opening night is close. I have to perform at the Garnier."

The masked man gripped Christine's throat, hissing his threats through clenched teeth. "Not another word or you will displease the master and I assure you that you would regret it!"

He pushed her to the ground, signalling one last time for her silence, before leaving Christine in the dank enclosure, sobbing for her uncertain future.

Erik looked up from the monitor long enough to wave Jean Claude to join him. Jean Claude went to speak but Erik signalled for silence and pointed to the monitor.

"We are located at the banks of the Seine, just one kilometre from the Notre Dame, where a morning jogger made the grisly discovery. The police are yet to identify the body, but they did report that it was a female in her mid-twenties, of average height, slim build and blonde hair. At this stage, they are treating the death as suspicious and investigations are ongoing."

Erik paused the monitor and reflected for a time, before turning to Jean Claude. "It won't take them long to identify the body. Have you secured all entries to the lair?"

"All the known entries are secured. Not even a hundred police could penetrate it."

"And the unknown entry?"

"We are still waiting on the delivery of the detection equipment."

"Then we are not secure, Jean Claude!" Erik cried loudly, showing his disappointment.

"We will act as soon as they're delivered."

"Tell me when they are delivered. I want the whole team to secure that hidden entry, including me."

"Yes, sir."

"And the girl?"

"She is suitably terrified," replied Jean Claude, with more certainty.

"Good. Keep all the troops on full alert. We will soon have the police on our doorstep, so we can't afford a single mistake. Take over all my duties for now, so I can deal with our other problems — Madame Giraud and Philippe's little brother."

Erik stood up and put his jacket on, ready to carry

out his investigations, but not before casting a concerned look toward Jean Claude.

"I'm counting on you," he said, saluting Jean Claude.

Jean Claude stood straight and saluted his leader, his expression resolute and determined. Jean owed his life to Erik and he would carry out any order given for him.

Erik put his hand on Jean Claude's rigid shoulder as he walked past him. "We may need to act with deadly purpose in the next few days and clean up any trails that could lead to us. You know that don't you, my friend?"

"We have faced this before. Have I ever let you down?"

Erik smiled with a confidence born from their decade's long friendship. "Then let's secure our impenetrable fort. Identify any foes and eliminate the threat," Erik ordered, before leaving the lair.

Jean Claude stood at attention until he could no longer hear the sound of Erik's footsteps, as was expected from his leader. He still wore a costume from the Macbeth wardrobe, making him look almost comical as he stood tall and erect, saluting. But a salute was more than just an official response. It was a statement of the belief in their lifelong struggle, a cause written in blood, forging a bond never to be broken. Jean Claude would stand still for a lifetime, if Erik willed it. There was nothing he would not do for him — nothing he hadn't already done.

CHAPTER THIRTY-FOUR

STANDOFF

Raoul arrived late at the rehearsals after an early reconnaissance of the Garnier lower levels. He spent most of his time searching the west wing of the building in a hope of finding a link to the hidden entry outside the building. His search found nothing as he suspected, as every visible entry was secured. However, his real interest was to look for any hidden entries, but an hour of searching proved fruitless, so he decided to meet with Christine again in the hope she'd recall details about the vital key.

Rehearsals were in full gear on the Garnier stage and Monsieur Laloux was at the front, orchestrating the scene. The full cast were in attendance, listening to their Artistic Director, the orchestra and conductor with a focus motivated by an opening night just two days away. It was a dress rehearsal, too, making for a colourful ensemble. Raoul was not surprised by the number of cast and backstage crew, who completely filled the stage back to the first curtain. Raoul looked for Christine, but failed to see her after making several scans. He figured she was hidden in the crowd, so he sat toward the back of the theatre, waiting for Monsieur Laloux to finish his presentation to the cast and crew.

"You will be waiting for quite some time," whispered the distinctive voice of Madame Giraud from the seat directly behind Raoul, making him flinch.

"Madame Giraud, you surprised me!"

"Hush!" She replied, looking around her as if they were being watched. "You have come to meet Christine, yes?"

"That's right."

"Then come with me, quickly," she insisted, standing and heading for the theatre exit, not waiting for a reply and forcing Raoul to hurriedly catch up with her.

"What is wrong?"

"Hush! Not here." She whispered, walking quickly through the back corridors of the theatre to Christine's dressing room. "Close the door behind you, please."

Raoul dutifully secured the door behind him, before joining Madame Giraud at Christine's dressing room table, sitting on a chair beside her. The lighted dressing room mirror highlighted Madame Giraud's ageing face, just as her serious demeanour accentuated the wrinkled lines across her frowning face.

"You look like you've seen a ghost!" Raoul joked.

"Many ghosts, actually. But three important ones."

Raoul quickly reacted to her words, his attempt at humour quickly replaced by concern. "What has happened?"

"Christine has disappeared."

"What! When?"

"I don't know. But she failed to attend rehearsals."

"Perhaps she's ill?"

"That's the excuse, but I fear it is far more sinister than that."

"I knew I should have searched the lower grounds alone. They must have seen us. There were cameras everywhere, no doubt recording our movements."

"It's possible, but you weren't to know the extent of their plans."

"Their plans? Who are you referring to? Do you know who is behind all these disappearances?"

"No, I'm not sure exactly who yet, but there are many. We will have to act with great caution."

"I will contact Moreau and the police. This is getting out of hand."

"You could, but I fear that could lead to inevitable retaliations."

"Christine. You believe they are holding Christine hostage?"

"I'm not sure, but we must fear the worst. You believe you were caught on surveillance cameras?"

"Yes. The last room we entered probably had a number of surveillance cameras in it. We almost certainly tripped an alarm by entering it. That's when we heard someone approaching. So I decided to leave immediately and cover our tracks."

"You don't believe they have found the hidden entry?"

"It's possible they did, but it is a well camouflaged area. We found it, so it would only be a matter of time before they discover it, too. Time is running out Madame Giraud. I need to return there, if Christine is in trouble."

"It would be no help whilst you are unable to progress further."

"The key. We must find the key."

"Yes. It would appear it is our only chance of gaining access."

"Christine remembered more of Philippe's words when we were down below. She said that he referred to money – two thousand? I don't know what she meant, but she was sure that was the only clue he gave."

Madame Giraud sat back in her chair, preparing to

seek help from another world. "Please, lock the door. I sense danger is approaching."

Raoul quickly locked the door to Christine's dressing room and returned to sit beside Madame Giraud, who was already in a trance-like state as she sought to make contact with her spiritual guides. She sat perfectly still, breathing rhythmically and occasionally whispering to her left side as if in conversation with someone beside her. This continued for some minutes before she opened her eyes and looked directly at Raoul.

"The key to the inner lair can be found within the two G's. That's what the two thousand reference meant."

The silence outside the dressing room was broken by the sounds of footsteps approaching, making Madame Giraud speak more quickly, as she sensed danger.

"The two G's refer to the Garnier and the hidden grid entry. You will find the key positioned to the Grid as the Garnier is positioned to Paris central's most famous landmark."

The sound of footsteps drew closer, making Madame Giraud stand up.

"One of our threats is approaching. He must not find me here. His nemesis has warned me. It is important he does not speak to me," she said, as if channelling another's words.

"Tell me what to do," Raoul asked.

"I know another way out of this room. You must stay behind and confront him. Do not fear his words for he can do nothing, for now. But delay him, so that I may escape. Will you do that for me?"

The footsteps grew ever closer, before Raoul saw the handle of the door turn. Time was running out. He nodded to Madame Giraud to make her escape, as he prepared to open the door. She quickly disappeared behind a curtain covered area of Christine's dressing room, as someone knocked loudly on her door.

Raoul thought for a moment to follow Madame Giraud, to evade the pursuer, but he heeded her words, stalling for time instead.

"Coming!" He cried, annoyance in his tone. The pursuer knocked louder, demanding entry.

"Are you deaf? I'm coming. Hold your horses!" Raoul said, waiting until he could no longer hear Madame Giraud. Then he unlocked it, trying to appear calm. But the truth was that if Madame Giraud's instincts were to be heeded, he could be facing the killer of his beloved brother, Philippe. He took a deep breath and opened the door to events he could no longer control.

Erik stormed past him and inspected the room, before speaking. "What are you doing in Christine's room?"

"I heard Christine had disappeared, so I went to look for her."

"Disappeared? She reported in ill, as I understand."

"I tried to call her. She's so ill she's not taking calls?"

Erik ignored Raoul's taunt. "I heard voices. Who were you talking to?"

"It's none of your business, but I was leaving a message for Christine."

"Behind locked doors?"

"I mistakenly turned the lock on the handle. But again, this is none of your business. Christine is my friend. I can come and see her anytime I please."

"Security of the Garnier is my business, as is taking a keen interest in people who roam around corridors that are clearly marked as non-access areas. Is that clear, Monsieur D'Arenberg?"

Although a few centimetres shorter than Raoul, Erik stood close to him in a threatening manner, but Raoul stood firm, showing he would not be intimidated.

"I think you overstep your mark, Monsieur Destler. I have been asked by the police to investigate a disappearance. As Head of Security you'd have to agree with me that there seems to be a pattern of disappearances occurring on your watch?"

Erik tilted his head slightly as if studying Raoul,

before smiling wryly. "Are you trying to intimidate me, Monsieur Detective?"

"I've met your kind before. Nothing you have to say will stop me from finding out the truth about this place."

"You think you know me? How bold of you. You can presume to know me, but that would be the biggest mistake you ever made," said Erik, before he pushed Raoul's chest with an open hand, inviting conflict.

Raoul welcomed the challenge, forcefully pushing Erik's shoulders with both hands and tripping his legs so that he fell heavily to the ground. "Threatening a detective hired by the police to investigate disappearances in the Garnier. That will read well in court, Monsieur Destler."

Erik stood up, his expression impassive, hiding his intent. "Maybe, but will you ever make it to court?" he sneered, before unleashing a furious blow to Raoul's face.

Raoul fell heavily to the ground, dazed and bloodied. The room momentarily blurred. He felt a trickle of blood flow from his nose, so he wiped the blood away, all the while warily watching his combatant, a few metres away. Erik had an absent look on his face, as if he were in another place, before finally turning his gaze back on Raoul. Suddenly he glared, showing a deadly intent as he advanced toward Raoul. Erik picked him up with his one arm, showing the strength of a bear and the hostile gaze of a killer.

"What will you do now, Monsieur Detective?" He mocked, throwing Raoul across the room with ease.

As Erik approached, Raoul reached inside his jacket and drew a pistol, cocking it and aiming it toward his adversary. "I'm placing you under arrest for assaulting a detective. Stand where you are!"

Erik stood still, seemingly unaffected by having a loaded gun aimed at him. Raoul stood and cautiously approached him. "Hands behind your back and together, so I can cuff them."

Erik obliged as he beamed a wry smile. "Quite the man with your gun, aren't you?" He taunted.

Raoul didn't respond, concentrating solely on walking behind Erik and cuffing him. That done, he read Erik his rights.

"Why are you wasting everyone's time, Monsieur Detective?"

"I'll find out the truth about you and then you won't see the Garnier for a very long time."

"Maybe. But then you won't see your special friend for a very long time, too. Is that what you want?"

Raoul clenched Erik's cuffed arm and turned him around. "Where is Christine?"

"Keep threatening me and you'll never see her again."

"Are you admitting you abducted her?"

"I'm admitting nothing. But I know that certain people would not take my arrest too well. These certain people are prone to displays of anger that may not be in your girlfriend's best interest. Arrest me and you'll never see her. Release me and we'll forget our little disagreement. What do you say?" Erik said, turning his cuffed hands toward Raoul.

Raoul considered Erik's words before grudgingly unlocking his hands from the steel handcuffs. Not another word was spoken between them as Erik left Christine's dressing room, but Raoul kept his gun held high as he left. Alone in the room, he opened the chamber of his pistol and studied its empty contents. He knew the next time they met, his gun had to be loaded.

CHAPTER THIRTY-FIVE

COVERING TRACKS

Erik felt the cold noose of captivity circling him once again, a place he vowed never to return to. Three years of torment and captivity had changed him to such an extent, he made a vow never to be the person he once was. In the quietest of times, he dared to question that vow, searching the deepest recesses of his mind, where a storm circled a precious memory he could never fully recall. Was it his vow or one instilled by his Captor? An inner storm was raging, testing his resolve to resist the circling demons.

He stormed into the lair, where Jean Claude was waiting, kneeling at the lake's edge, studying its flow. Erik's mind turned back to their captivity and the daily visits to the river bank where they were ordered to dispose of the Captor's tortured bodies. The survivor's task was to carry the corpses, many of them from Erik's loyal troop, to the river. Erik saw every corpse, except one. Jean Claude mercifully released the body of his beloved, Rose into the river of death. He stood beside Jean Claude for a time, holding a supporting hand on his shoulder as they both re-lived past pains.

"You found the psychic?" Jean Claude asked.

"Not yet, but soon enough. I talked to the detective."

"And?"

"He wasn't too accommodating. We are going to have to cover all tracks."

"You want me to take care of the detective?"

"No. Let him try and rescue his princess. That way we'll find out where Philippe's old entry into the lair is, if he finds the key. Put a tail on him, but let him find our lair. Then we'll deal with him."

"It's risky. He might go to the cops."

"He won't risk losing his princess. I've met his kind before," said Erik, his expression pained, as he fought off bitter memories.

Jean Claude stood up, putting his hand on Erik's shoulder, reading Erik's thoughts. Both had changed so much that their former lives were no more than a vague memory of strangers they once knew.

"And the girl?"

"Leave her to me, Jean Claude. You take care of the

detective. Don't lose sight of him and make sure the new cameras are in place."

Jean Claude nodded before saluting and leaving. As he walked away, Erik spoke.

"Also, make sure our exit strategies are in place. We may have to disappear if there is too much heat."

"Already in place, sir."

Erik stood by the lake for a time, his mind calculating all the possible scenarios that could unfold. They faced three people who could break their cover — Raoul, Christine and Madame Giraud. The police would also inevitably follow, so he had to work quickly and efficiently to cover their tracks. His first problem, Christine, was securely held captive in her cell. She had to be silenced.

CHAPTER THIRTY-SIX

PHANTOMS

Erik shivered when he approached the cell. It was not too different from the dungeon he inhabited for three years. Both were confined and austere spaces, but his Garnier prison was cold and dank, rather than humid and oppressive. His prisoner would be terrified, having endured lonely hours in isolation. Masked and dressed in sombre tones to ensure his captive remained in a state of disorientation, he whispered "fitting" to himself, as he admired his executioner's attire. The Captor, too would have admired the air of foreboding he had created.

Create psychological fear in his captive's mind, he remembered a far more powerful instrument than physical pain, particularly in drawing out valuable information. He needed the knowledge Philippe had shared about the secret entry and key to the lair, in case Raoul did not lead them to it. Satisfied with his outfit, he picked up his carefully wrapped present for Christine, the fallen diva, a small box wrapped in a blood red ribbon, a gift certain to convince her to cooperate.

He crossed the darkest area of his lair toward a dividing corridor that led to the cell. Two large stone pillars dominated the space of this little used area. None of the men liked to walk along these columns, including Erik. Rumours had abounded that this was where the original phantom lived. He could easily see why, as he slowed, thinking he heard a voice. The chilliest of breezes flowed around the massive columns, making uninviting ghost-like noises, heightening the feeling of tension. Erik stared into the shadows between the columns and felt certain he heard a voice come from the pitch black.

"Who's there?"

There was no response, bar a sudden chilly gust that stung his cheeks. He looked all around, believing someone was watching him from a distance, before a single person peered out from the right hand pillar, someone he knew.

"I have returned to claim what's mine, Erik," came the whisper of his Captor.

Erik shook his head in disbelief. Both columns took on a light hue as if they both bordered a large subterranean theatre and the master of ceremonies was his torturer.

"The Captor is dead. Who are you?"

"Forgotten me already? Did you really believe I would ever leave you?" The Captor taunted, smiling, before pointing to the shadows between the columns.

"But you won't forget this, will you Erik?"

On cue, ghost-like figures began to walk across the dark expanse from the left column to the right, heads bowed, seemingly remembering the ordeal their Captor had put them through. Erik recognised them all — his fellow soldiers and locals, young and old — trudged across the makeshift theatre as if they had marched for an eternity.

"This can't be true," Erik said, turning in all directions, looking for the perpetrator, projecting the ghost-like figures, but no one was there.

"This is no trick, Erik. You will always be mine, you know that, don't you?" The Captor cried, walking to the middle of the columns and signalling for Erik to join him.

"I don't believe this is real," he said, looking away, but then a single cry for help made him look back toward the apparitions.

"Help me," Rose cried.

"This is not real," Erik said to himself, but still looking earnestly for Rose.

"This is very real, but don't look to him. Look to me."

Another apparition walked out from behind the left side column. He was tall and wore a plain white mask, covering half his face. His attire was from another era, common to the late nineteenth century. A long black cloak lined with white flowed around his dark brown cravat and single breasted waistcoat of floral maroon silk. His appearance on the surface was one of civility, yet his veiled gaze, mask and dark clothes hid a torment Erik understood. Could it be that he was looking at the real Opera Ghost?

Erik's mind was a whirlpool of thoughts, making him doubt what he now saw. He stood before a collage of terrifying memories presented on a subterranean stage, an ancient nightmare that threatened to claim him. And the more he studied the scene, the more it challenged his world, as new figures advanced across the stage. He closed his eyes, willing the apparitions to disappear, but on opening them a new corner of his past life emerged from behind the column. Rose obediently joined the Opera Ghost. There was fear in her eyes, resurrecting the intense pain Erik had buried in a secret chamber in his mind.

"Help me," she repeatedly cried, tearing Erik's carefully crafted world into an earthquake-like rubble.

"This can't be real," he cried, advancing toward the unearthly stage, striking out with all his strength to rid himself of this terrible haunting. His fists thrashed at the darkness as the apparitions vanished, but their voices grew louder as all the lost souls cried out for his help. All the while the Opera Ghost's voice grew louder, thundering through his mind.

"I am real. You must believe," he cried ever louder, until Erik responded.

"Yes. Yes, you're real. Make it stop!"

Only then did the Opera Ghost's baritone-like cries cease. Peaceful quiet ensued for a time, leaving Erik in the shadowy silence, before Rose's voice cried for help yet again. He followed the sound of her voice in the darkness until he found the location. He stumbled at the end as his desperation took over, jarring his hand hard against the wooden door he fell on. Only then did he realise that the voice was not Rose's. He was standing outside the cell that contained Christine.

"Help me please," came her desperate cries, as she hit the door repeatedly.

Erik looked around him to see if he was alone, before wiping the sweat from his brow and steadying himself before entering the cell. Had his mind played tricks, or was his world haunted by deadly apparitions?

"Come to me now, if you're real!" He cried into the darkness, challenging that which he didn't understand.

There was no response, except that of his captive.

"I am real. Please, help me!" Christine cried.

Erik regained some composure before responding. "I hear you. Now stand back from the door or I shall have you rot in that cell until you die."

"Please! I have done nothing..." she replied, her voice trailing off as she moved to the back of the cell.

Only then did Erik open the cell. The image of Rose filled his vision. He reached out to her, "Rose."

"No, I'm Christine." Disoriented, his first feeling was one of disappointment. They were so alike, except when they spoke. But then his anger returned as he peered down at the slight frame of Christine. How dare she try and fool him.

"You cry out to me about your innocence and yet just some hours earlier, you were showing your precious inspector friend through corridors off limits to the public. What were you doing there?"

"Please. I'm sorry. I didn't know it was off limits."

Erik smirked as he shook his head. "Quite the brave one back then. Now you claim ignorance. Your type are all the same. Living in privilege, seeking thrills you have no knowledge about. Tell me why I shouldn't let you rot in this cell for the rest of your life?

Christine could not reply immediately, so shaken by

her dire circumstances, that any attempts were restricted by her sobbing. Erik patiently waited for her reply, all the while gazing at the small gift he held in his right hand.

"I don't know who you are, but I can't believe that you would kill an innocent person for no reason. Please, tell me what you want and I'll help you," she pleaded.

"Not the answer I was looking for. But I won't let you rot here. I will come for you when the time is ready. For now, I have a gift for you. It may help you understand your situation a little better," he said, tossing the small gift wrapped box into her lap, before leaving the cell.

Erik breathed heavily as he left the cell, finally submitting to the unearthly experiences he had witnessed. Had it all been in his imagination or was he facing a threat far more deadly than the phantoms that had haunted his mind?

He walked away gloomily, but his mood lifted as he heard Christine's scream. She had clearly opened his gift — a ring Philippe had given to her and which she had returned, requesting he propose to her on his return from abroad. Philippe's last known journey.

CHAPTER THIRTY-SEVEN

THE PLOT THICKENS

Raoul searched for Madame Giraud to warn her of Erik's threats against him, but unsurprisingly, she had gone into hiding. He sat inconspicuously in the theatre for a time in the hope that she would come to him, but instead it was the inspector. Moreau walked in unobtrusively, his gaze hawk-like as he studied all corners of the old theatre, before he slumped back into the seat next to Raoul, maintaining a watchful eye on his mobile phone as he greeted him.

"You've been quiet?"

"As have you, Inspector."

Both observed the cast rehearsals for a time as Inspector Moreau answered an incoming text. Even sitting in the comfortable surrounds of the theatre, he constantly fidgeted and moved his body, no doubt a habit born from the never-ending demands of his profession. He squinted at his phone with tired red eyes as he responded to text messages.

"Busy night?"

Inspector Moreau shrugged his shoulders helplessly. "Always. Unfortunately, crime does not sleep."

"You will always have clients. Do you ever take holidays?"

Moreau laughed. "Never ask my wife this question! Both smiled, as another text sounded on his phone, making Moreau shake his head in frustration, before turning his phone off. "Peace at last! For a while. Perhaps you'd join me in a coffee?"

"I would, but I'm waiting for someone."

"Another time perhaps. I wanted to update you about a new case on my list. A body found in the Seine. You heard the news?"

"Yes. A woman in her twenties."

"It seems this woman is the missing dancer," he said casually, waiting for Raoul's reaction.

Raoul was not totally surprised, given the occurrences of the last day. He had briefly read of the discovery in the papers and wondered if it were the ballerina. Having it confirmed by the inspector built even more dread in him. Raoul was almost certain he had traced the killer, yet he dared not brief Moreau of his suspicions.

"The plot thickens. Was she murdered?"

"It looked suspicious, but I am waiting on the forensics.

With luck, I'll have the report in my hand by day's end. Anything happening at your end?"

Raoul could only think of Erik's implied threats against Christine, as he pondered an answer.

"Nothing tangible at this stage. As you told me, they are a tight-knit group, so I have precious few leads. I've decided to use Madame Giraud."

Inspector Moreau raised his eyebrows in response. "We have another ghost?"

"I hope not. One is enough! I just wanted to exhaust all my leads before giving a final report."

"I could have the forensic report go public, if you think it may flush out any guilty parties?"

Raoul knew Moreau was testing him, but he didn't react. If he pushed Moreau too far from the case, he would make him suspicious.

"Do what you think is best. It can't hurt," Raoul replied, turning his gaze toward the stage.

Moreau studied him for a time, before he turned his phone back on. Several moments ensued until he finally responded.

"Let's wait for the forensics before we shake up any wolves in the hen house. Don't you agree?"

Raoul casually nodded his head in the affirmative. "There's enough rumour swirling around about the television coverage of the murder as it is, so if anyone has heard anything, they will talk about it."

Inspector Moreau studied messages that streamed on his phone, before standing up. "I will pass by later in the day. Keep me informed, won't you," he said, slowly buttoning his overcoat as he studied Raoul.

Raoul knew the inspector would be suspicious. Thirty years in the force had developed a natural instinct for detecting deception. At best, Raoul had the day to rescue Christine. He knew it was a risk, but his instincts were also finely honed, and he knew the look of a cold blooded killer when he faced one. He sat for another half hour, hoping Madame Giraud would come to him, but she had disappeared. He sat in the dark of the theatre wondering whether she had met a similar fate to Christine, before he pulled out his pistol and filled it with six bullets before returning it to the holster inside his jacket.

His time for waiting was over as he stood and headed outside to return to the secret entry. He hoped that Madame Giraud's last instructions were accurate enough for him to locate the all-important key to where he believed was the suspected murderer's world. "This is for Philippe," he whispered to himself as he walked out of the theatre, determined to finally solve the case that had consumed his life this past year.

CHAPTER THIRTY-EIGHT

BUSINESS MATTERS

Carlotta was dressed in a striking silver and dark grey patchwork, Chanel coat dress, teamed with knee high black leather boots by Lesage, a chic feathered hat by Massaro, gloves by Causse and exquisite Goosens drop earrings – amethyst, diamonds and silver. Haute couture was another passion. An expensive one. Ever since the house of Chanel brought back a number of artistic crafts that had been headed towards extinction back into the mainstream, its couture runways had been spectacular. Within their ateliers, these couturiers, in the utmost secrecy, poured all their talent into the original Coco Chanel's creativity. A creativity Carlotta gloried indulging in.

Today's meeting would be life-changing, as she sought full control of the business she had partly shared with her partner for many decades. She entered the office of their trusted accountant, Alexander, and haughtily glided past his personal secretary, into his office, despite her strong remonstrations. Carlotta walked into his office as if she were a model on a catwalk, immediately gaining the attention of those in the office.

Alexander and Victor both stood as Carlotta swept in, flaunting an outfit befitting a princess. She slowly and deliberately removed her gloves.

"Sit down, both of you, please!" She commanded, imperiously, choosing not to sit, as she approached Alexander's grand teak desk. She leaned her right hand on the desktop, flashing a huge diamond ring, to further demonstrate her opulence.

"Have I interrupted something?"

Alexander looked to Victor to respond.

"I am discussing the future of our business, my darling. I don't think you are fully aware of the gravity of our situation," he replied, casting a sardonic eye toward her glittering ring.

"Oh, I think I know a lot more than you give me credit for, my precious," she replied, before sitting on a chair beside Alexander.

"I don't think you do. Your strength is spending money we do not have, the sole purpose to inflate your over-indulgent ego. Tell her our true financial situation, Alexander." Victor commanded.

Alexander cast a nervous eye toward Carlotta, seemingly seeking her approval to do so.

"Yes, I want to know the financial position of Marchand Enterprise," agreed Carlotta.

"Well, as I was explaining to Monsieur Marchand, the financial situation is dire. We may be able to extend its operation until the end of the season, but only if we secure funding that would attract very high interest re-payments."

"Or perhaps sell half of my darling's couture clothing and jewellery," interrupted Victor.

"Charming as always, my dearest."

"Carlotta, you don't seem to want to accept the gravity of our situation. Perhaps when the debt collector comes to take all our belongings, you will actually listen to my sound advice."

Carlotta stood up in anger, a wrathful expression etched in her glare.

"I understand very well what you have done with this business and I also know where you intend to take it. Don't I, Alexander?" she said, turning to him, demanding a reply.

"I have signed a contract of silence, Madame." He nervously replied.

"Of whom only one person can ask you to break. I am requesting you inform Monsieur Marchand now, please."

"Very well," replied Alexander, as he opened a drawer beside him, took out a folder and opened it to read its contents.

"This is to certify that I, Alexander Dumont, shall be entrusted with the management of two business accounts. Firstly, Marchand Enterprise, owned by Monsieur Marchand and Madame Caccini; and secondly, Caccini Enterprise, owned exclusively by Madame Caccini. The details of this enterprise, I have sworn shall remain in confidence between Madame Caccini and me, unless she requests otherwise."

Alexander closed the folder, nervously avoiding Victor's look of betrayal, before nodding to Carlotta.

"While you have planned and schemed all these years, supposedly behind my back, I have continued to build my company through astute investments, thanks to sound, professional advice," she said, acknowledging Alexander. "These investments have afforded me the freedom to indulge at times, but given my standing in the opera community, it is an indulgence that benefits our businesses and is tax deductible. Unfortunately, your wasteful self-promotion under the guise of entrepreneurship built nothing but poor headlines and strategies that I will no longer support."

Victor stood up and walked around the room in an

indignant manner, responding incoherently and showing his surprise at what had been said.

"I have devoted so many years of my life, supporting you. And you now tell me that you have systematically betrayed me and kept secrets! How could you allow me to struggle these last few years, when all along you were financially sound?"

"Betrayal? How dare you talk of betrayal to me, given your plan was to replace me as the diva of our forthcoming opera, without a word!"

"It was to save the business."

"Well, like you, I intend to save my business. Alexander has drawn up a generous financial offer to buy you out, if you accept all of the contract conditions. It will be a one and only offer. I advise you to accept it."

Alexander withdrew a contract from the folder and handed it to him. Victor quickly skimmed through its many pages, stopping only to read its key elements. His cheeks reddened as he clenched his jaw, trying to contain his anger, occasionally looking at Carlotta and Alexander with accusing eyes. Several minutes passed before he threw the contract hard onto the desk, breaking the tense silence that had ensued.

"I have sacrificed so many years of my life and you offer me this? I'll see you in court and rightfully claim half of everything," he snarled.

Carlotta maintained her composure, not reacting to Victor's threats, instead sending a text from her mobile, before responding.

"I have organised the limousine to pick you up, as I have nothing more to say, except consider this offer. It is the first and last time I will be this generous. Consider it seriously."

"I will ruin you," he threatened before charging out of the office and slamming the door behind him.

CHAPTER THIRTY-NINE

TOOLS OF THE TRADE

Erik sat in the limousine waiting to pick Victor up. Carlotta's instructions had been very clear, 'convince Victor to accept her financial offer'. He wasn't clear what the financial offer was, but he was sure he could convince her partner to accept it. This was a craft he'd learnt over a lifetime in the military and he would quickly show it, firstly to Victor, then more importantly to Carlotta, sealing their bond in blood.

The offer was clearly not to Victor's liking as he slammed the limousine's back door closed and gruffly ordered Erik to drive him home. Expletives aside, Victor's only other words were, "I don't wish to be disturbed," which suited Erik perfectly, as he quietly secured all doors and the security window between the back seating and himself as driver. He occasionally checked his rear vision mirror to check his agitated passenger, who seemed to be seeking refuge in drinking from the well-stocked mini-bar.

Erik smiled to himself as Victor failed to see he had not taken the usual turn to his apartment, such was his agitation. It was a good half hour before he raised some concern, buzzing the intercom.

"Sorry, there was roadwork on Avenue du Général de Gaulle. I have had to take a detour," he lied, satisfying Victor for sufficient time to reach his intended destination, the home of his loyal General, Jean Claude.

Erik's passenger had drunk his fifth whisky as he drove through the electronic doors of Jean Claude's garage. Victor's suspicions turned to fear, when Erik quickly closed the doors behind them. His first reaction was to call for help on his mobile, causing Erik to quickly open the back door of the limousine.

"I wouldn't do that if I were you."

Victor fumbled with his phone, trying to think of who he should call. "Are you threatening me?"

Erik extended his hand, "Give me your phone, Victor."

Victor retreated to the other side of the car, trying to make a call, before Erik reached in and snatched the phone from his hands, throwing it hard against the brick wall of the large garage, instantly smashing it. He stared at Victor for a time, saying nothing, letting the threatening silence build Victor's growing fear.

"What the fuck's got into you?"

"Get out of the car, Victor."

"No. Drive me home, now! In case you forgot, I'm your boss!"

Erik shook his head in annoyance, before reaching out and dragging him from the car and throwing him hard against the brick wall, dazing him. He laughed tauntingly as he stood over Victor, delighting in his discomfort as he tried to stand up.

"Wrong, Victor. Carlotta is my boss, not you."

"Are you insane? You'll all go to jail for this outrage," he said, wiping the blood that was trickling down his face from a head wound.

Erik smiled wryly, as he shook his head in annoyance.

"Are you threatening me, Victor? I don't like being threatened. It brings out the worst in me."

"You're fucking mad!"

"Oh, you don't know the half of it, little man," he said, picking Victor up again and forcing him from the garage into an adjoining room — Jean Claude's torture room.

"I'll say this once and I recommend you listen very carefully to me. You will agree to all the conditions of

Carlotta's contract or I will make you suffer terribly, before you die."

Erik then held Victor firmly around his neck and forcefully showed him the 'tools of the trade' that he would unleash on him.

"You don't seem to understand the gravity of your situation. You're only getting one chance, because of Carlotta. I wouldn't think twice about snapping your podgy little neck, so I wouldn't play any games if I were you. Agree to sign, or suffer before I kill you."

Victor initially held a defiant gaze, but Erik's cold glare convinced him he was truly facing death. Fear took over disbelief as he began to shake. Erik played on his fear, as he drew a knife from his coat pocket and held it to his throat.

"You know, the truth is I don't like to inflict pain," he said, as he slowly pushed the cold steel blade across his throat, drawing blood.

"No. Please don't. I'll pay you well if you let me go."

"With what, little man? You're bankrupt." Erik slowly moved the blade across his throat, widening the small gash he had made. Victor started to sob, uncontrollably.

"What I truly enjoy is convincing people when they are so horribly wrong, to do what's right. But when they won't yield to my control, it makes me mad. Mad enough to do the craziest things."

Erik held the knife still as he ran his free hand over Victor's neck, before showing him his own blood. "Last chance, Victor."

"I'll sign it. I'll do anything. Just let me go," he pleaded.

"That's a good boy," he said victoriously, before dropping him to the ground. He wiped the blade clean before throwing Victor the bloodied towel. "I suggest you wipe your neck. We don't want to upset Carlotta so close to opening night, do we?"

Victor did everything asked of him, too shaken to speak.

"I will drive you back to Alexander's office, where you will sign the contract and behave exactly as Carlotta dictates. If you ever have a stupid thought, like reporting anything to the police, I, or one of my many colleagues, will find you and we will unleash a fury you can't begin to comprehend. Is that clear?"

"Yes. Yes. Anything... please..."

Erik lifted him up, gripping his throat tightly and issued his final warning.

"I will get the car now and take you to Carlotta. You will do exactly as she says. From that point on, I never want to hear that you didn't honour our agreement. Do that and you will have the chance to live a normal life, but if you share our agreement with the authorities, we will exact a terrible revenge on you and your family and friends."

"Never. I promise you," he gasped, before Erik released his grip.

"Then we will now do exactly that. Do not speak to me again until you tell me that Carlotta's contract is signed. Is that clear?"

"Yes."

Erik smiled for the first time, before slapping Victor's face lightly. He could have made him do anything at that moment. Both men knew that. He was the captor who had turned his prey into the captive, just through the hint of torture. This was Erik's skill, finally crafted by the horrors of war and captivity. As he gazed deeply into the eyes of his prey, he knew he had delivered on Carlotta's wish. Like Victor, she would do anything for him, now.

CHAPTER FORTY

THE KEY

Raoul carefully paced out the distance that he had calculated on his mobile phone, scaling down the equivalent of the Garnier to central Paris. He paced thirty metres south from the hidden entry into the Garnier's under-world. The stone formation of the Garnier building was exactly the same as the entry, larger stones laid on its bottom two rows. Unlike the entry, he was looking for a smaller stone that was hiding a single key, so he inspected every stone within a ten metre radius by passing his hands over the rough surface of the cut stones. He spent the best part of an hour searching for any tell-tale signs of a false compartment, to no avail.

Once convinced it wasn't there, he looked away from the building across Rue Scribe, focusing his search to a ten metre radius from the wall. It was a normal narrow Parisian street, enclosed by limestone three-storey apartments built close to narrow walkways and curbs lined tight with cars. Raoul considered looking under the parked cars when a small plaque caught his eye, no more than thirty centimetres square, containing commemorative words for those who had fallen in the revolution.

He skimmed the words, thinking nothing was unusual, until he came to a small diagram on its base, containing various codes, including a symbol of a key. Raoul ran his hands around the surrounding limestone blocks, searching for a hidden compartment, without luck. In frustration, he punched the plaque. "I must help, Christine," he thought, before noting the sound from hitting the plaque had a hollow vibration. "Could the key be here?" Raoul pulled out a small Swiss knife and immediately started to pry at the plaque, quickly breaking it free from the building wall. To his delight, a key was attached to the small plaque, which he hoped was the entry to the hidden lair.

Raoul quickly descended to the lower bowels of the Garnier to the gated entry that had earlier blocked his and Christine's way. To his surprise, the key opened the ancient wooden door. Raoul expected new barricades would be in place to block his way, but instead he had easily gained access. He moved forward into the darkness, now with his pistol in hand. All was still, bar the sound of running water in the distance. As his eyes adjusted, he learnt that he was walking towards an underground lake. Torches burned at the lake's edge where a single small boat was moored. He thought to board the boat and row out onto the lake, but heard a sound in the distance, making him retreat into the shadows of one of the many large stone pillars that formed an imposing column in this gothic world.

Raoul moved cautiously from pillar to pillar, toward the only other light he could see, another torch that lit a second large wooden door. He stood in the darkness of the nearest pillar, the door his only way forward, except for the lake. Both directions were likely traps set by Erik, who would be anticipating his attempt at rescue, so Raoul re-checked his loaded gun as he decided the next move. He had no other recourse, but to accept Erik's deadly invitation, so Raoul held his pistol ready as he tested his key on the second wooden door.

For a second time, his key unlocked an entry into another hidden passage. He silently crept into the pitch black, holding one hand out to feel his way forward and the other holding a loaded gun, cocked and ready to fire. He blindly moved forward in different directions for several minutes, before touching something metallic and cylindrical. A light suddenly switched on revealing the room where he stood was empty but for one large structure that he stood beside. It was a steel framed platform that contained a single rope at its centre — a hangman's noose.

He stood in an open area, vulnerable to attack, so he swept around in a 360 degree arch, his pistol aimed and ready to fire. At first he thought he was alone in the room, before he heard a sound behind him, making him turn.

"Who's there? Show yourself," he demanded, but another sound blasted from the opposite direction. He reacted, turning and pointing his gun in that direction, before he felt a stabbing pain in his back. The room started to spin as his vision faltered. Raoul let fire a shot into the empty room, before he staggered to his left and fell to the cold stone floor, unconscious.

CHAPTER FORTY-ONE

MURDER CASE

Inspector Claude Moreau sat in introspective silence at his desk, which was unusual for him. His dingy office was usually a hive of activity, crowded with open 'case folders', weary investigators and the constant reverberation of his mobile. Claude used the rare moment to enjoy another hot coffee, his fifth for the day. Between sips, he pondered the open folder in front of him, the case of the dead ballerina, as he waited for Inspector Andre Martin to arrive and brief him on forensics' findings.

Claude's well-honed instinct for criminal activity was telling him that recent events around the Garnier were likely foul play. He was surprised that Raoul had not uncovered anything in his investigations and would likely ramp up investigations if forensics confirmed his fears. So, either they faced criminals, expert in covering their tracks, or Raoul was not sharing information with him. As was

Claude's habit, he shuffled the many press clippings and reports in the Garnier folder in an orderly fashion on his desktop, in preparation for the update from Andre.

Andre arrived with a report in hand, quickly sitting down and waiting for Claude to ask him to report. Andre was an enormous man, with an equally large ego. He always reminded Claude how small his office was when they met. He sat on two of his chairs to be comfortable and noisily chewed on gum, seemingly as a way to slow his incessant chatter. Claude quickly acknowledged him, knowing the extended silence would aggravate his talkative colleague. Besides, he was tired and busy.

"How's Michelle?"

Andre raised his eyebrows, "Don't ask!"

Sometimes, Claude would engage him, encouraging conversation about Andre's family, about whom he could endlessly speak, but not today.

"Agreed. What did forensics uncover?"

Andre opened the report, slight disappointment in his expression at the rebuff, before reading the findings.

"The body was confirmed to be that of the ballerina reported missing from the Garnier three weeks ago. Her death was from drowning, but they believe she died of asphyxiation from a form of torture known as 'waterboarding'."

"How could they know the difference?"

"Not from the waterboarding, but from the stress placed on her neck and shoulders as a result of using that technique. She had an unusually high number of tears to her neck muscles. They believe she had been under duress for some time, perhaps a week. There were also abrasions to the shoulders and back, signalling a struggle of some sort. They concluded that she had been restrained by a person or persons with a high level of military knowledge and training."

Claude took the report from Andre and skimmed its contents. "Get the team to do back checks on all personnel in the Garnier. Do any have a military background? Start with their Head of Security. I want it by the end of the working day," he said, with an urgent tone.

Andre nodded and left quickly, not needing to ask any more. Claude's demanding deadline meant a long day of tedious follow-up and little time for small talk. The Garnier case had shifted from a simple disappearance to a murder case, requiring more resources and a second visit to the opera house, where Claude would demand more answers from his undercover, Raoul.

CHAPTER FORTY-TWO

CARLOTTA IN COMMAND

Raoul woke where his search had started, at the location in Rue Scribe where he had found the key. Someone stood in front of him looking down to where he lay. Raoul slowly sat up and rested his back against the wall, adjusting his sight to the midday light and rubbing his eyes to clear his blurred vision.

"Take it slowly," said the familiar voice of Madame Giraud.

"How long have I been here?"

"I don't know. I just arrived. It's just after twelve midday, if that helps," she replied, checking her watch, before helping Raoul to his feet.

"I've been here for a few hours. How did you find me?"

Madame Giraud smiled and looked up to her left side. "I think you know the answer to that question."

"I found the key!" Raoul said, suddenly remembering and checking his empty pockets.

"You went to the underground lair?"

"Yes. I found the door and entered a large dark area. I remember now. I heard a sound. There was a noose, before I felt a stabbing pain in my back," said Raoul, rubbing his back, still feeling the pain.

"It had to be a drug-tipped dart. I heard a whistling sound, then the next thing I remember is waking here."

"You're lucky to be alive. Where was the key?"

"It was right here," Raoul replied, turning to the building and finding that all traces of the plaque had been removed. "It was behind a small plaque that was attached to this building, but they have removed all traces of it."

"They're beginning to cover their tracks. I'm sure the hidden entry you found has been secured, too."

"But Christine is still in there. We have to try."

"They would have only released you because they are focused on covering their tracks. Another abduction would have created too many complications. The best way to help Christine now would be to work with the police."

Both returned to the Garnier, where rehearsals continued, but with opening night was just a day away, there was an extra sensation of urgency and frayed tempers.

Many of the cast were gathered around Monsieur Laloux whose face was becoming redder as he talked. Three of cast designated to be witches stood to the side, in conversation with Carlotta. A full dress rehearsal was scheduled for this evening.

"I know you feel unprepared, Nadine, but this is opera. You must learn to take your chances and show you can perform under any conditions," Carlotta snapped.

"When will Christine be returning?" Nadine enquired, trying to hide her thrill at having the chance at a bigger role.

"As I understand, Christine offered her resignation. She was unhappy with the part offered her and has left Paris." Carlotta exclaimed, ensuring all around her heard, before turning back to the three witches.

"I have met her type before. Full of bravado and confidence, but unprepared to accept that only hard work and sacrifice will deliver success. You girls must remember this, or you too will fall short. Now, I want to hear a sublime performance. Follow Monsieur Laloux's guidance. I will be in the front row listening, so I want you to imagine that I am one of the dozen critics who will be in the audience at tomorrow's opening. Make your performance unforgettable for all the right reasons," she demanded, before clapping her hands and directing Monsieur Laloux to begin the rehearsal.

Carlotta then sat in the front row, acting more like a manager then the leading lady. Everyone scurried to her commands, including Monsieur Laloux.

"Perhaps she has assumed command," Raoul thought, as he and Madame Giraud sat a few rows behind Carlotta. Raoul cast a vigilant gaze around the theatre, looking for Erik and his team of cronies, but none appeared to be in the building. He then looked toward Madame Giraud who held a trance-like gaze on Carlotta. Some minutes past before she uttered words that seemed to come from another world.

"Remember in the darkest of times, men can find their way out of the shadows. You are in a play that has long ago cast its deadly plot. Play your part with courage and conviction, knowing that by the plays end, your part may be over, but eternal love will play on."

Raoul felt as if he were no more than a pawn in another, grander opera of which he had no control. His feeble attempts to rescue Christine had fallen far short, perhaps putting Christine's life at risk. He had been far too confident that he could deal with the likes of Erik and his cronies and he wouldn't make that mistake again. He would tell Inspector Moreau all he knew, now, hoping together they could stop the evil force that had again been unleashed on this most beautiful and undeserving home of music.

CHAPTER FORTY-THREE

IN THE TORTURE CHAMBER

Standing behind his hooded captive, listening to her erratic breathing, Erik looked around, admiring his torture chamber. Another expression of his art. Six gothic pillars merged into a vaulted ceiling to form a small, stone, subterranean cellar. Candles burned in niches carved into the stone.

The only way in or out of this dark, dank space was an antique, gothic, wooden door. Studded with iron nails, it was secured with a heavy, cast-iron lock and giant key. The walls were adorned with instruments of torture. Instruments of obedience, Erik preferred to call them, sourced from his various nefarious contacts around the globe. In this domain, he was god. He held the power of life and death.

Erik smiled as he tapped a small leather drawstring bag hanging from the ceiling, *the bag of life and death*. It swung backwards and forwards like a pendulum. His captive's life in the balance. Ropes bound the captive's hands, chest and feet to the chair. Time to let her know I am here. He pressed his hands down hard onto his captive's shoulders. She jumped, startled. Erik held them there, immobilising her further. She whimpered and trembled all over, unable to escape his forceful touch. Unable to turn. Unable to see her attacker.

"Where am I?" Christine asked, her voice cracking.

"Welcome to my lair, Ms. Dubois, the phantom's lair," Erik said, in a threatening manner. "Or, more accurately, a special annex to my lair."

Christine swallowed. Her mouth was so dry. This man sounded different from the others, like pure evil. "What do you want from me?"

"Information, of course."

"I don't have any information of interest to you!" Christine said, with a bravado she didn't feel.

"Come, come now, Ms. Dubois. That's a lie," he said, digging his thumbs hard into pressure points either side of her neck, Christine winced with pain and struggled to move away, but was bound too tightly.

"Please. I'm not lying."

"Well then, tell me how you found your way into my lair from Rue Scribe."

"It was by accident." Erik's fingers ground into her.

"It was!" Christine screamed as his thumb screws bored into her. "It's true. I was angry and kicked a stone. And it started to turn."

"Where was the stone?"

"I don't remember exactly. There are hundreds of them." Erik pressed again. There was no need for words. Pain seared through her. Christine nearly fainted. "Between the Grand Salon and the Foyer du Chant," she replied, her voice weak, unable to help herself, knowing that the only way she would get out alive was if she were rescued.

"Ah, that's a good girl," he said, patting her on the shoulder, rewarding the prisoner for her compliance. "So much easier to do as you're told, Ms. Dubois. It lessens the suffering. Doesn't it?" Erik was a master of torture, knowing all too well the psychological bond that needed to be forged between captor and captive. "Which row was the stone on?"

"The bottom row," said Christine, chancing a lie.

"Liar!" roared Erik, as the thumb screws were tightened once more. Christine twisted, struggling to escape, but to no avail. Erik knew it hurt, but unlike him, she had not yet learnt the trick of not minding that it hurt.

"I can tell when you are lying, Ms. Dubois," Erik's voice was a low throaty growl. "You must obey my command," he warned. "It's no good hoping that lily-livered Raoul D'Arenberg will come and rescue you. I'll soon get rid of him the same way I got rid of your lover, that arrogant snob."

"You're a monster. An evil monster!" Christine spat the words out.

"Yes, I am," chuckled Erik. "Perhaps you would like to see this monster?" He whipped the hood from Christine's head, leaving her hair in disarray, like her clothes. She blinked rapidly. Her eyes were assaulted, first by the light, then by what hung right in front of her — a hangman's noose, close enough to slip her head straight into.

Christine screamed again, her throat now raw. A soldier stood behind the rope. Wearing light grey combat fatigues and black boots, his face was covered by a black balaclava. To intimidate her further, he set the noose swaying.

"No need to cover your face. I know who you are, you coward." Christine's eyes were wild. Erik liked that. The beast in her was starting to emerge. Everyone becomes an animal when stripped of their humanity. Even someone as beautiful as his precious Rose. It was the law of the jungle. A jungle Erik had learned to survive in, and to thrive in, but he knew it would never be this woman's milieu.

"Beware of unmasking the phantom," his voice menacingly deep. "I decide whether or not you will leave here."

"You have no intention of letting me go," said Christine, tremulously.

"That is not true, my dear little princess," said Erik, oozing charm, disconcerting and disorienting her with another of his guises. "Your fate lies in this leather bag here — *the bag of life and death.*" He set the bag swaying, then tapped the hangman's noose again. Two deadly metronomes swayed back and forth in front of Christine.

"Your destiny is up to you, my angel," Erik smiled, an evil smile. "And I am the master of your destiny," he said, whipping off his balaclava and bowing. "Erik Destler at your service, Mademoiselle Dubois," he said, sarcastically. An icy blast of air came from nowhere and passed over them. Christine shivered, whilst Erik looked behind him uncertainly.

CHAPTER FORTY-FOUR

THE TORTURE BEGINS

Such evil belied by the handsome man who stood before her. Christine looked at Erik, watching him, watching her. What was going through his tortured mind? A phantom who looked strangely out of place in this forbidding subterranean underworld. Tall, tanned, muscular, sculpted body, upright, almost regal mien. Strangely, he reminded her of the aristocratic Philippe and Raoul.

His light brown hair was expertly groomed, his beard neatly trimmed and his watchful, dark brown eyes rarely left hers. She hardly knew the man, and yet she knew enough to know that his ugliness was masked by a cultured veneer. But why such enmity towards her? What had she done to deserve such ire? Surely not just breaking into his lair? There must be more to it. What was he hiding? Or, more to the point, what was he planning to do? What was in *the bag of life and death*? Was he truly the monster he claimed to be?

"Let me introduce you to the instruments of your obedience." Erik's voice cut savagely into her thoughts.

"I don't understand why I'm here. What do you want from me?"

"Not much. Only the truth and your unquestioning obedience. Not a lot to ask." His voice oozed an equal mix of charm and menace. Christine shivered uncontrollably.

"I'm sure you are wondering what's in the bag," he asked, setting the bag swaying to its deadly beat once more. "I have assembled some instruments of obedience, just for you." Erik pointed around the room, one by one, to his medieval torture tools, as if delivering a lecture. "Some designed specifically for women. Recalcitrant women, like you," he added, bringing his face close to hers and baring his teeth. Christine tried to draw back, but was constrained by the ropes that bound her.

"*The bag of life and death* holds four cards, each with the name of an instrument," he said, setting the bag in motion again. "Do you understand?" Christine nodded mutely, mesmerised by the bag moving to and fro.

"We'll start off with this," Erik said, gleefully, taking what looked like an oversized pair of scissors off the wall. A screw was fixed between the ends of the handles. "An iron

Tongue Tearer, particularly useful for liars." Erik menacingly opened and closed the scissors near Christine's face. "Once a firm hold is maintained on the tongue, the screw can be tightened and your tongue roughly torn from your delicate little throat." As he brought the *Tongue Tearer* closer to her mouth, her eyes widened in horror. He stopped and studied the *Tearer* carefully, momentarily lost in his thoughts. His mouth quivered and an evil look appeared in his eyes. Erik grabbed Christine by the neck and yelled,

"Open your mouth," he demanded. Christine wrenched her head away and clamped her jaw shut. Her gut was churning. She wanted to strike this monster with all her strength but she was shackled by the burning ropes. She looked down to her chafed arms. Blood was trickling down towards her white knuckles. Her hands shook uncontrollably. Was this the end?

"Please, tell me what you want," she pleaded.

Suddenly Erik loosened his grip, and flung the instrument of obedience to the cold stone floor.

"I think you're getting the picture, princess." Erik said, enjoying his captive's terror. He stroked her hair almost lovingly before pulling his next of tool of torture from the wall. He smiled longingly as he twisted the handle of the pear-shaped tool, which opened up into four leaves or quarters.

"Say hello to the *Pear of Anguish*, or the *Choke Pear*," said Erik, opening and closing it, admiringly. "This is particularly good for punishing liars. And other deviants." Erik gazed menacingly into her eyes. He clamped the *Pear of Anguish* shut, then gently stroked her cheek with it, before positioning it right in front of her mouth, close to her horrified gaze.

"Do you know where this can go?"

Christine closed her eyes, hoping to rid herself of the unfolding nightmare. She could only shake her head.

"Oh you don't. Open your pretty little mouth and let me show you." Tears flowed, but she dared not speak a word. "Once inside your mouth I open it up and twist it to cause maximum damage," he said opening up the leaves of the *Pear of Anguish* once more. Christine sobbed loudly and uncontrollably, resigned to her grisly fate. Only then she noticed a change in his demeanour. Erik drew back and walked away from her, only turning to lean against the wall. He loosened the top button of his uniform, studying her all the while. Something in his gaze made her feel it was her last chance. She stifled her sobs and found the courage to speak.

"I don't want to die, Erik. Please, tell me what you want."

"It's simple, my little princess. I just want to know exactly how you found your way into my home."

"I'm not sure," she replied, truthfully. "We were working our way along the wall between the Grand Salon and the Foyer du Chant." Christine took an uneasy breath. "I got angry and kicked a stone and it turned. But I can't remember exactly where it was," she gulped.

"Oh, dear, Ms. Dubois, that is not what I wanted to hear," shaking his head, disappointed. "We'll have to continue with our instruments of obedience." He selected another device, a metal cage the shape of a head. "A *Scold's Bridle*," Erik announced, triumphantly. He positioned the instrument over the top of her head.

"Please don't. I've told you all I know."

Erik ignored her pleas. "Well, then there's nothing more to say." He lowered the *Scold's Bridle* over her head before putting the bit in her mouth, pressing down on her tongue, and securing the apparatus firmly around her throat so she could not speak. "They will indeed be your last words, Ms. Dubois," said Erik, walking out of the room and closing the door loudly behind him, leaving her on her own.

Christine could barely breathe, or swallow. She felt she was slowly choking to death. She had never felt so helpless or so alone. "He's left me here to die." She tried to scream, but no matter how hard she tried no noise came from her mouth. It was firmly clamped shut. Pain was radiating through her body. Her bladder was threatening to burst. Panic took over. She stamped her feet on the flagstones, desperately trying to attract Erik's attention.

After what seemed hours, the door finally opened. Christine was beside herself with fear, her eyes flashing wildly.

"You called, my dear Ms. Dubois?" Erik's charming, aristocratic demeanour returned. "And ready to confess all, no doubt?" Christine nodded in desperation. "Well, let me show you a final inducement, one I feel will particularly appeal to you, my dear – to the opera singer, the artist within." "Let me try it on for size." He walked back towards her, picked up the noose, and placed it around her head. Christine, shocked to the core, started shaking. "The art is to not tighten the noose so tightly that you hang." Erik suddenly jerked the rope up, and held it there, restricting her airways and sending Christine into a panic. "Just enough to crush the larynx and the vocal chords, so you can never sing again." He dropped the rope dramatically. Christine's whole body was wracked by violent shaking. She started to retch.

"Oh dear! I've upset you. Please forgive me." Erik, now penitent, removed the rope gently from around her neck and offered her a clean handkerchief. Christine retched into it, then looked up at her torturer. Her heartbeat was so loud she could hear it, her emotions on a rollercoaster ride. She shook her head in disbelief. Surely she was trapped in some kind of nightmare. Feeling utterly powerless, the tears started to fall, silently. She closed her eyes, so her captor couldn't see them, and started to drift off into unconsciousness. A kindly voice broke the spell.

"Here, let me free your hands, Christine. You'll need them." Erik untied the ropes.

"Thank you," she mumbled, gratefully rubbing her sore wrists and numbed fingers.

Erik pulled the leather pouch down from the ceiling towards him – *the bag of life and death*. Christine's eyes were irresistibly drawn to the bag as he opened up the drawstring. "I'll mix the cards up a little." He spoke calmly and gently, as he moved two fingers slowly around inside the bag, beguiling his captive, all menace gone.

"How did you find your way in?" he demanded, very loudly and aggressively in her ear, catching her unawares and making her jump with fright.

"By accident. I kicked a stone by accident. Please, please believe me," she replied shakily.

Erik suddenly thrust the bag at her. "Choose a card, Christine." His demeanour was now deadly calm and menacing once more. "Choose the instrument of your obedience." The blood instantly drained from Christine's face and she fainted.

CHAPTER FORTY-FIVE

INSIDE THE MIND OF A TORTURER

E rik looked down on the unconscious form of Rose as he carried her from the torture chamber to his inner lair. He pulled aside a curtained area and laid her on his bed. Her hair and clothes were dishevelled. Dried tears and dirt stained her cheeks. Even in this state, she was stunningly beautiful, and so helpless. Those bastards! What had they done to her? She was scared to death. I'll take care of her, now.

To avoid disturbing her, he removed her outer garments slowly and carefully, then brought a bowl of warm water, soap and a sponge. He gave her face and body a sponge bath, wiping slowly and gently, admiring her in the peace and quiet of his lair. Rose looked so peaceful, a Sleeping Beauty, a princess in his castle. He had rescued her, saved her.

Suddenly his vision blurred, as the present intruded.

Erik angrily thrust the thought away as he saw who it really was who lay before him. There would be no fairy tale ending. This was Christine Dubois, and she was a threat to all he'd created, to the man he was now. He had to kill her. As Erik continued to stare down at the lifeless woman before him, his vision blurred once more and the past returned.

Erik finished Rose's toilette, towelled her dry, and then brushed her hair, her glorious brunette mane. Satisfied, he lifted her head gently off the pillow and cradled it into his chest, while he pulled a beautiful white gossamer nightgown over her head. He threaded her arms through one by one, before laying her back on the bed. He drew the nightgown down over the rest of her body. She was so limp, like a rag doll.

He pulled a blanket over her and leaned in to listen to her breathing. Satisfied Rose was just sleeping now, Erik tenderly brushed a stray strand of hair from her face. She looked like an angel lying there so peacefully. As he stood over her and watched her, he was reminded of a time when life was kinder, gentler and infinitely more loving. A time when the finer sensibilities of life were uppermost in his mind. Unable to resist, he leant down and kissed her forehead. Once upon a time a love like this was possible. My life was so different then. When did I become so hardened, such a monster? Am I a phantom, he asked as he looked around his subterranean world? "Is there no going back? Am I past the point of no return?" Erik ran his fingers through his hair, tearing at his scalp. I must stop thinking. I am exhausted. He extinguished the candles in the bedroom and lay down beside his beloved. Sleep, sleep. I must sleep.

When he awoke, his arms were still cradled around Rose who was nestled in beside him. As she stirred, he pulled back, aghast. Christine Dubois was in his bed. How was this possible? He extricated himself carefully, without waking her. The phantom was playing with his mind?

Erik stood over her and watched her sleeping. She seemed at peace, although he knew there was little safety in sleep either, unless it were the sleep of the dead. Even asleep his Captor had tormented him, ruthlessly. Nightmares and sleep deprivation plagued him. Music was played so loudly, day and night, he couldn't sleep. The theme song from *Apocalypse Now*. It was a waking nightmare. Erik thrust the thought aside. He needed to calm his thoughts. What was he going to do next with his captive?

Upstairs was a fever of activity. Opening night was but twelve hours away. Inspector Moreau and the police were crawling all over the place yesterday. And he knew

Raoul would never give up. There was so little time left. He didn't want to leave his captive, but he had business to attend to. Erik left some food and drink for Christine, but securely locked the door to his lair. There was no way out. No escape. And no one would hear her.

CHAPTER FORTY-SIX

EXIT PLANS

Erik spent the morning reviewing security footage, finding out what was happening upstairs. Carlotta, now in charge, was puffed up with her own self-importance. But Erik was more concerned about his team. They were getting antsy. Having the police around disturbed them. He wondered how much longer he could count on their loyalty. Loyalty indeed! A wry laugh escaped him. Their loyalty to him was bought. And for a high price. None of them were who their papers said they were. Not even Jean Claude. He offered them safety and anonymity. They were like the sewer rats that thrived under the Garnier. But, if their cozy nest was threatened, they would just scatter in all directions and disappear down another sewer.

Erik summoned Jean Claude to Box 5, a rare event brought about by the unfolding emergency. Both men had an instinct for self-preservation, born from the hideous events they had shared as soldiers. Erik came straight to the point, revealing his restlessness about their situation.

"What is Raoul doing?"

"He went straight to Moreau, as expected. He's still there."

"They're working out their strategy as we speak. Time is short, Jean. Is the weapons cache secured?"

"Yes, just completed."

"Explosives positioned and set?"

"All done, bar one."

Erik removed a note from his pocket and gave it to Jean Claude. "This is the approximate location of the secret entry. The nearest I could find out. Position targeted explosives around that area and secure the entry, permanently. I expect Moreau's team will swoop on the Garnier on or around opening night." Erik looked at his watch. "That's just six hours away. Finish the job in no more than two hours."

"As good as done. Then?"

"The team disappears and leaves no traces for the likes of Moreau and D'Arenberg to find. We will be as invisible as ghosts as of 1800 hours."

Jean Claude stood up immediately, and saluted, ready to finish the job. Both gazed at each other, aware this may be the last time they ever met. Both revealed a small but knowing smile, before again showing a demeanour of stony-faced determination. Their life's work was slowly being caught in a net of investigations that had to be escaped. Erik saluted Jean Claude and then he was gone.

CHAPTER FORTY-SEVEN

POLICE PREPARATIONS

Raoul watched on from the back of the room as Inspector Claude Moreau addressed his team of investigators for the final time. His mouth was in a grim line. Dark circles surrounded his eyes. Worry etched his handsome features. He had hardly slept since Christine disappeared. That his abortive efforts to find her ended so ignominiously, still rankled. Tonight, finally, there would be a coordinated effort — to break the stalemate with Erik and rescue Christine.

The police team was assembled in a very large briefing room at the Paris Police Prefecture. Well out of sight of the Palais Garnier, the cast and crew, and Erik and his henchmen, in particular. At the prefecture, one hundred men and women, in innocuous-looking casual dress, had gathered. Despite appearances not one of them was innocuous. They were a highly trained special operations group, often at the forefront in the response to terrorism.

Over the past three days, all the senior officers had participated in a guided tour of the opera house, purportedly part of a specialised media campaign, orchestrated by Carlotta to cover the premiere performance on opening night, Carlotta's triumphant return to the stage as Lady Macbeth, and her grand plans for the future of the Palais Garnier. Pleased with the idea, she had given over management of the tours to Enzo, the Stage Manager. Enzo, ever the opportunist, responded to Raoul's subtle suggestion, by opening it up to a wide range of journalists and influential donors and supporters, including, unknowingly to him and Carlotta, the police.

At the rostrum at the front of the room, wearing his familiar sand-coloured knee length coat, Moreau moved restlessly about, like a prize fighter before a fight. So did his large grey eyes, hidden behind the dark glasses. Inspector Claude Moreau missed nothing. He continued in his rapid colloquial French.

"Although many of you have already met him, I wish to formally introduce Monsieur Raoul D'Arenberg." Moreau motioned to Raoul to step forward. "He has been conducting some undercover inquiries these past few weeks which has given us some valuable intelligence for tonight's raid."

Raoul moved to the front of the room. "His inside knowledge of the Palais Garnier, opera, and the cast and crew has been invaluable." Moreau held out his hand to Raoul. "He will be joining us on our raid, this evening. Please treat him as a member of our team." The team clapped.

Raoul shook hands with Moreau. "Thank you, Inspector. I am glad to help in any way I can." Raoul looked around the room, nodding and making eye contact with the members of the team. He had a good memory for faces, but there were far too many to remember. He just hoped there would be enough to get rid of Erik and his henchmen, once and for all.

Moreau went on, "Tonight is opening night. It is now exactly 1400 hours, six hours until the curtain goes up. Please synchronise your watches. Timing is crucial to our raid this evening, although it will need to be synchronised with the running of the opera as well."

Each officer checked and nodded to Moreau. "No detail must be overlooked. No stone unturned. We are looking for a murderer, and, I believe, a kidnapper. They may be one and the same person. But..." His gaze roved over his team, ensuring he had their full attention. "He will be protected by a ruthless team. Our background checks have elicited several men and one woman who are extremely dangerous and will not hesitate to kill."

He paused to allow the thought to sink in. His hand went into his coat pocket and withdrew a pistol – a Sig Sauer SP2022 — standard issue for his elite squad. "That is why each one of you will be armed." He handed the gun to Raoul. "You may need this, Monsieur. It is fully loaded, but check for yourself."

"Thank you, Inspector," said Raoul, checking immediately that it was loaded. Unlike the last time when he tried to arrest Erik.

"We will be in position one hour before the opera begins at 1900 hours, to be precise. Each of you have been assigned a position. Yes?"

"Yes, Inspector," they chorused.

"And the clothes you need to wear, to blend in. Yes?"

"Yes, Inspector," they chorused again.

"You will be hidden in plain sight, covering every door, every entry, every exit and every box." He paused to draw breath, "in the theatre, backstage, underneath the stage with the scene shifters. Even in the orchestra pit. We will be observing entries and exits at every level – above ground and underground. Understood?" His alert eyes took in them all.

"Yes, Inspector."

"Just nod assent, from now on. You're beginning to sound like performing monkeys." Muffled laughs reverberated around the room.

"You all have detailed maps of the opera house. Study them carefully, so you are aware of where you are at any time." He paused to allow each point time to sink in. "There are significantly more of you dedicated to the underground areas, but to our knowledge, there only four ways in and out. One from Rue Scribe, thanks to Monsieur D'Arenberg's intelligence." He nodded gratefully at Raoul.

"The only way you will have of recognising if someone is in the team, will be this oak spray." He held up a small spray of oak leaves tied together. This also conceals your microphone. Wear it somewhere it can be instantly seen, on whatever costume you are wearing." He looked to Raoul and smiled. "This was your suggestion, mon ami. Tell them the significance."

Raoul stepped forward. "Tonight's opera is Macbeth. Macbeth has usurped the throne. The witches have prophesised that he won't be defeated until Birnam Wood comes to meet him." A few doubtful faces were seen and sly murmurs were heard amongst the group, but he went on. "The rightful king, Malcolm, orders his troops to cut down branches of the oak trees in Birnam Wood to hide behind. In this way they march right up to Macbeth's castle for the final battle." He gazed around, a stern mask over his handsome face. "Which they win, you'll be happy to know, and take back the opera house. Oops, the throne," he said, trying to inject a levity he did not feel. A few laughs could be heard.

"In more serious vein," Raoul went on, "the oak tree is a symbol of strength and this spray symbolises our battle to wrest control of the Garnier back, this evening. And, the rescue of Christine Dubois, who will one day be a queen of the opera — someone I love dearly. I wish you, God's strength, everyone." Heads nodded in sympathy and understanding of the unusual context to this police raid.

Inspector Moreau took over again, still restlessly moving back and forth as he spoke. Two hundred eyes following his every movement and every word.

"I say again, tonight is opening night. We do not wish to disrupt the performance in any way, but to use it to our advantage, whilst everyone is engaged in the opera." Only Claude Moreau would dare such an audacious raid at such an audacious time. "Yes?" Nods again. "And…"he added interjecting a sombre note, "if we get it wrong, everyone will know. But…" he said waving a hand over all of them, "we will not get it wrong. Over to you, Monsieur D'Arenberg.

"Timing is critical, but it can only be approximate as our timing is synchronised with the opera, which will vary depending on how long the audience applause goes on," Raoul spoke slowly, yet confidently. "Act 3 begins straight after interval — a Witches' chorus with thunder and lightning. Singing with loud orchestration. This signals the beginning of the raid, when every door and every exit inside and outside the theatre and the opera house is to be locked. You will hear the female voices in the Witches' chorus, accompanied by drums and cymbals clearly in your ear pieces. Loudly. Very loudly. Is this understood?" Heads nodded all round. "Thank you." He stepped aside.

Inspector Moreau stopped walking and faced them. His face was earnest. "You then have exactly forty-five minutes to check your area thoroughly, apprehend any suspicious person, and report to me. We will then unlock the doors to the auditorium and the opera house, just before the opera ends. The underground exits will remain guarded at all times. Any questions?"

A woman standing to the side put up her hand. "Detective Inspector Sophie Giroux, sir." Moreau nodded to her. "Approximately what time will the raid start?" He turned to Raoul, who answered.

"The opera begins at 2000 hours. Running time, including interval, is two hours forty-five minutes. Interval is approximately 2120 hours for twenty minutes. Act 3 will start at 2140. This is when the doors will close and the raid will begin," he looked at Sophie, to ensure she was following his rather obtuse logic. Her alert manner told him she was. "Forty-five minutes later, at the end of the sleepwalking aria, when the stage is darkened, and the audience is applauding loudly, the raid will conclude." He smiled, "we are choreographing our own opera. No?"

"It seems that way," replied Sophie. "Thank you, sir."

"Any other questions, please?" asked Moreau.

A giant of a man standing next to Raoul put his hand up. "Inspector Andre Martin, sir. Where will you be, Inspector?"

"At the beginning, I will be atop the Grand Staircase, in black tie and tails, and with my opera glasses, surveying the scene. Once the opera begins, I, and these six boffins here," he indicated to his technological team, all standing together, and "will be in Box 39 on Level 1 which has an overview of the whole auditorium, including the infamous Box 5." He paused to take a breath.

"We will be listening to you via the devices you are wearing, monitoring where everyone is, and..." he paused, a pregnant pause, "recording everything. So please, mind your language." A laugh went around the room, relieving the tension. "No one is out of contact at any time." He turned to Raoul, "And Monsieur D'Arenberg and Inspector Martin, here, will be leading the team backstage." He turned back to the group. "Any further questions? No? Alright, then you have a few hours to rest before being in position. Bon courage."

CHAPTER FORTY-EIGHT

CRI DE COUER

When Erik returned to the lair, Christine had opened the curtain briefly, seen him, and then retreated, terrified. I used to be such a noble character, Erik mused. Like Macbeth, temptation came to me in the form of lust for power. After I'd first killed as a soldier, there was never any hope of regress. I was cursed. Temptation begat sin, and sin yet further sin.

From then on, the tragedy unfolded. One sin led to another with a remorseless fatality, until now, the bitter end – the utter ruin of moral sense and even, I think, of reason itself. Erik sighed. Punishment was sure and inexorable. He was bone weary. Death would come as a relief. But for now, a brief respite in the form of music.

"Stop thinking for a moment and start feeling," he told himself. "Listen to the music and let your mind unwind." Erik moved to his piano and sat as his fingers hovered over the keyboard. He closed his eyes and slowed his breathing, before giving his fingers and mind free reign.

The pulsing strains of the overture to the *Phantom of the Opera* filled the lair, bringing his underground castle and him alive. Erik throbbed in time with the power of the music as he pounded the keys.

The world of music was his spiritual home, one he loved and thrived in. It was the deepest expression of him, before his world and his heart were ripped apart. He looked around him in desperation. Now, he was forced to live his life as a phantom, in this underground prison.

In another lifetime, he could have played the phantom. *Phantom of the Opera* was the most successful musical of all time. Erik's high baritone voice had a unique timbre and quality, but now he was condemned to play and sing here in this hell hole. Unable to let go, he aggressively played the theme song next, *a cri de couer* for a life lost, for a lost love — Rose, his angel of music. From behind the curtain in his bedroom, an angelic voice answered his passionate outpouring.

"*In sleep he sang to me,*
In dreams he came..."

Erik looked over as Christine emerged sheepishly from behind the curtain, an angel in a flowing white nightgown. A vision of loveliness, of a world untainted. He kept on playing. Christine went on singing. Her voice resonated around the walls of his lair, full of warmth and lyrical poignancy. Christine moved towards him, as if in a dream. Who was this man? This phantom? Such talent.

Erik bowed his head, as Christine stood beside him, another angel of music. Her light shone from within. Lost in time and space, the power of music enveloped them. They slipped into character, and sang, captivated by an old love story. A love that never died.

"*Sing!*" The Phantom commanded. Christine sang.

"*Sing!*" He commanded again. Christine's voice rose higher.

"*Sing!*" And higher. Her vocalising becoming more and more extravagant.

"*Sing to me!*" Erik roared. Christine's voice soared to another level. She held the high note. Their eyes locked together. All she could see was the sadness and solitude that radiated there. She smiled, softly, sadly. Solicitously, her hand reached out and touched him gently on the cheek, but all Erik could see was her pity. Enraged, he lashed out, grabbed her by the throat, threatening to strangle her.

"How dare you pity me!" He snarled. His handsome face, once more hideously transformed into a menacing mask. Evil incarnate, just inches away from her face, raged at her, again. "You piteous creature, I can abide anything but pity."

Struggling to breathe, Christine cried, plaintively. "No!"

"No!" An echoing voice roared. Suddenly the ghostly apparition of the masked phantom appeared, bolts of flames shooting from his right hand. "Let her go!"

"No! No one tells me what to do!" Yelled Erik, wild and beyond control.

Whoosh! Flames shot everywhere — high in the air, across the table, and then directly at Erik, licks of flame swirling around his arm and dangerously close to his hand and the fingers which held Christine's throat in an iron grip.

"You will curse the day you did not do, all the Phantom asked of you," the Opera Ghost thundered at him, sending two lightning bolts of flame streaking over Erik's head, and setting his hair alight. Erik let go of Christine's throat, and beat wildly at his head to put the fire out.

In the face of all the pain and madness, Christine passed out, again.

CHAPTER FORTY-NINE

THE LAST SUPPER

C hristine woke once more in the Phantom's bed. How many hours had she been asleep? She looked at the clock beside her. Seven o'clock. Was it night or day? You couldn't tell down here in this underground prison. In spite of the warmth of the room, she lay there, shivering. Winter had descended with a vengeance, the cold penetrating into the deepest crevices of her mind and body.

Looking down, she saw another white nightdress, a beautiful, gossamer lace one, laid out across the foot of the bed. This one a costume, the one she wore when playing Lady Macbeth. It floated like a cloud when she wore it. Nearby lay some stage makeup. A note lay on top of the nightgown. Christine picked it up and read it.

It is opening night. Please get ready for your final performance.

Christine shivered. Am I expected to perform down

here, too? Would this nightmare never end? First Christine Daaé from Phantom of the Opera, and now, Lady Macbeth. All the while confusing me with his lost love, Rose. Will this madness never end? She listened. Not a sound. Perhaps Erik had gone off and left her here alone. Maybe she could escape. She stood and tiptoed to the curtain, parted it with a finger at eye height and peered through into the lair. It was in total darkness. Despair seeped into her soul. Her final performance. Would she never sing again?

"Well, Christine," she answered herself, "best make it the performance of your life." She closed the curtain. "Time to dress for it, to transform into Lady Macbeth." She sat in front of the mirror, applied the thick stage makeup and the deep red lipstick, then started plaiting her long brown hair.

When Christine peered into the room again, it was lit, but only with candles. Erik sat at a large banquet table, but he had transformed again, too. No longer the Phantom. It was a clean-shaven Macbeth who sat there, face made up, in a long robe and wearing a crown, staring straight back at her. His eyes dark and brooding. His mood unreadable. Macbeth stood and walked over to her. There looked to be a real dagger hanging from the cord around his waist. Christine's heart started palpitating wildly.

"Come, my Lady." Erik extended his hand. She drew back in fear, wishing he would just go away, leave her be. This was no opera. Singing was her love, her passion, but there would be no performance from her. Her chest heaved. The thought of never singing again a punishment too great to bear. And then she wavered, resigned to her inevitable fate. The show must go on. Destiny awaited. Lady Macbeth took hold of Macbeth's proffered hand and walked as regally as she could to the banqueting table.

"Never fear, my Lady, this opera is nearly over. Soon the king and queen will be dead." Christine gave a sharp intake of breath and stopped mid-stride to steady herself. Her legs threatened to fold beneath her. Taking a deep breath, she forced herself to continue. "But, we are overriding Verdi, and creating a new, final scene. A more modern interpretation." Erik sounded fatalistic, ominously resigned, which scared Christine even more.

The banquet table was draped in red velvet and laden with platters of delicious food. Christine counted silently. It was set for eight. Why eight she wondered? Who was joining them? And why? Her curiosity about the guests was forestalled when Christine saw the extravagance of the setting. Such wealth and decadence on display, a setting fit for Versailles.

Four candles burned in each of the exquisite pair of carved ormolu candelabra. Antique gold cutlery, embossed wine glasses, and gilded fine French porcelain china, with matching platters, and the finest embroidered napery, were arranged with military precision.

Seeing her wide-eyed gaze, Erik commented, "The candelabra date back to Louis XV, but the cutlery and tableware are a century later, after the monarchy was overthrown. He picked up a knife, and ran his finger over it. "Exquisite isn't it, the rarest antique Vermier gold on sterling silver?"

"Yes," said Christine, overawed, despite herself, "fit for a king and queen."

Erik laughed mirthlessly. "Indeed. Here, my Queen." He pulled out a chair at the far end for her, "this scene is to be the last supper. Our last supper," he said, solemnly, his voice the tone of a cathedral bell. Christine trembled and started to sway as her legs folded beneath her. Macbeth caught her, steadied her, and then placed Lady Macbeth on the chair. "We are dining with the ghosts of the past."

CHAPTER FIFTY

GHOSTS OF THE PAST

As Christine and Erik sat down, a deep chime sounded. They listened in silence. Eight deep chimes resonated throughout the underground lair. Opening night performances, upstairs and downstairs, had begun.

"Eat and drink, my Queen," Erik commanded, "I'll introduce you to our guests, soon." He filled her goblet, then sat down at the opposite end of the table, and filled his own. "A toast." He raised his gold goblet and nodded to Christine, to pick up hers. "To Lord and Lady Macbeth, the king and queen."

Slipping into character once more in the macabre setting, Christine replied, "To my liege, Lord. They sipped their wine in silence, and ate sparingly, whilst studying one another intently. Circumstances had brought them together. Two characters of totally different mould and fibre – one a man, the other a woman; one realising himself in action, the other in thought and music. The grandfather clock announced each minute as it ticked by, the air around them suspended, as Erik mentally summed up the consequences of killing Christine.

Might be the be-all and the end-all here,
But here upon this bank and shoal of time,
We'd jump the life to come.

Breaking the impasse, Erik suddenly stood up and went to his piano. "Time to meet our guests, the ghosts of the past." His hands moved across the keyboard, "my father, the mailed fist of fate. Prokofiev's *Dance of the Knights* depicted a diabolical sword fight." The dark, brooding passages, played so powerfully by Erik, sent chills up Christine's spine and set her heart racing.

The music suddenly changed, to an exciting piece. Richard Wagner, *The Ride of the Valkyries,* which depicted the female messengers of the god Odin, as they rode into battle on their flying horses to take the souls of dead soldiers to Valhalla. Or the deafening flying horses of modern combat taking endless body bags to boxes covered in starry flags and the dubious love of a grateful nation. Erik bowed his head, "My Captor and tormentor. Bastard!"

Erik's mood changed to darkest grief, an open wound

announced by the unutterably tragic *Funeral March* of Chopin, borne on its stately way through a sea of tears and the bewildered laments of incomprehensible agony. A foretelling of doom, slashing and stabbing like a demonic razor at the composer's will to live. He looked directly at Christine.

"Philippe." She sat there, stunned, turning the ring, round and around on her finger, tears flowing, finally grieving. There was no escape

the raw blackness of the music destroyed all hope.

And then there was hope, and love, and devotion. *Ave Maria.* "My mother." Erik's fingers caressed the keyboard, giving life to the transcendental beauty of Schubert's hymn to the Holy Virgin. And, to his mother.

"Blessed art thou among women, and blessed is the fruit of thy womb." Christine sat and wept, amazed at the duality of this gifted and tortured individual.

Erik paused, sat there in quiet contemplation for a moment. Tears welled in his eyes, then another melody, in his tribute to the past, rang out – *A Time for Us.* Heartbreakingly beautiful, and hauntingly sad — *The Love Theme from Romeo and Juliet.* Of hurting and hope, of sorrow and peace, of a love lost, but never forgotten. "My Rose." Christine nodded. His pain was palpable.

"And finally, my nemesis," he said, looking at her, "the

Opera Ghost. A figment of mine and everyone else's imagination." The strident notes of an organ filled the room. The Opera Ghost appeared before him. Erik leapt to his feet, shouting and gesticulating wildly. "No, you are not real." Christine jumped up, startled. What was happening? The Phantom's voice drowned out Erik's ranting.

"The bridge is crossed, so stand and watch it burn
We've passed the point of no return."

"Go away, go away," Erik raved. "You are not real." He closed his eyes. "I can't see you." When he opened his eyes his nemesis was gone, but Christine was looking at his chest with horror. He looked down. A shadow of the Phantom of the Opera was emblazoned on his chest – a stigmata. "No, no!" He screamed, scratching at his chest, trying to erase it.

Christine was shocked. Erik was unravelling before her. She grabbed his hands. "Erik! Look at me," she commanded.

Erik looked at her, bewildered. "Rose. Rose. You've come back for me." He wrapped his arms around her and kissed her, passionately. "I love you, Rose." Time stilled for a moment, a blessed moment.

Then an alarm sounded and their world was rent apart. A klaxon blasting non-stop, reverberating off the stone walls. It was hideous. Christine covered her ears to block out the sound. Erik looked at the red lights flashing all over his security screen. The entrances leading to his hideaway had been breached. In several places. They were coming for him, again. No warning. His men had already gone. A deadly calm came over him. It was past the point of no return.

Thrusting his hand into the grand piano, he grabbed a gun. He hefted the trusty, Glock 18 automatic pistol. It was fully loaded, able to fire thirty-three rounds in a few seconds, if needed. And he was going to need it. He tucked it into the pocket in his robe. Followed by his mobile phone which controlled all the explosive charges. Erik then grabbed Christine's hand, trying to tug her out of the chair. Too frightened to move, she sat there. He could see she was panic stricken,

"If you stay here, you will surely die." He held up the mobile phone. "You will be trapped here forever because this lair is about to be blown up." Erik slowed his breathing and spoke in the gentlest voice, "I could not save Rose, but I can save you. Please, Christine?" He pleaded with her, willing her to trust him, to move. Erik was back in charge again, the present overriding the darkness of the past. Tears filled her eyes. This monster was capable of love. She had seen that, felt that. Christine stood up. "There is no time to lose." They fled the lair hand in hand.

CHAPTER FIFTY-ONE

OPENING NIGHT

Carlotta studied her reflection in the dressing room mirror, surrounded by flowers from well-wishers. The art of performing was transforming into different characters, and differing moods, using costume as well as music. She loved the simplicity of the costume she was wearing. Her costume for the final aria of the night – *The Sleepwalking Aria*. A beautiful embroidered white nightdress and an intricately plaited brunette wig. The long plait lay over her left shoulder. As she spun around, the nightgown floated up like butterfly wings, heartbreakingly vulnerable, like Lady Macbeth in her last scene.

Carlotta's mood was buoyant. What a triumphant return to the Paris opera scene it had been. Not a spare seat in the house and the audience had loved her, applauding and shouting brava after each aria. The ruthlessly ambitious Lady Macbeth was a great dramatic role, and was an extraordinary opportunity for her to show-case her talent in Paris once more. Carlotta knew she was at her powerful best, capturing Lady Macbeth as Verdi envisaged. Her voice had created, along with her huge, penetrating eyes, her gestures, a sense of drama and glorious music, that captured her audience. Carlotta preened in the mirror as she congratulated herself on her performance so far.

This final aria really had no parallel in the drama. It was an invention of Verdi's to give Lady Macbeth a connection to her other worldly side.

She said, *"'la luce langue' (the light is languishing)*, time is running out... we have to get rid of the next person in this little chess game!" This was her last big moment before she began to crumble with guilt. Carlotta smiled at the irony of her ordering Erik to kill Christine. Unlike Lady Macbeth, she felt no remorse, no guilt about getting rid of anyone who stood in her way — Christine or Victor. And she certainly wouldn't die. But where was Erik? Her Head of Security, lover and, soon to be, her partner in managing the Palais Garnier? She hadn't seen him all day. A knock at the door.

"Ahh, on cue. Here he is at last," she thought.

"Curtain call, Madame Caccini. Act 4, Scene 4, three minutes."

"Damn Erik! Where is he?" she cried out loud, picking up the vase of red roses he had sent her. "Damn him to hell!" She hurled the vase at the large mirror on the wall shattering the vase. Glass shards, water and roses flew everywhere, leaving the mirror with a maze of fine cracks radiating outwards like a spider's web and water dripping down.

Christine instinctively ducked. Unbeknownst to Carlotta, she and Erik were hidden behind the large one way mirror on the wall, still trying to catch their breath from their flight. Erik had told her it was the fastest way to gain access backstage. No one knew of it, but him, and perhaps, a phantom of long ago, but he didn't tell her that. His raving and ranting had disturbed her enough. As had the series of small explosions behind them as they fled.

Erik and Christine had been waiting for Carlotta to leave, so they could slip into the opera house, without being captured. They would hide in plain sight, as the police had done. It was usual for understudies of the lead characters to be in costume, ready to step in if anything untoward happened during the performance. The cast and backstage crew would not think it strange if there were two Macbeths or two Lady Macbeths. All they had to do was keep far enough away so as not to be recognised.

Christine had been bemused by watching Carlotta

prancing and preening, getting ready for Lady Macbeth's final aria, almost the climax of the opera. They were both wearing the same costume, their makeup dramatic and their hair identically plaited. At a cursory glance, to an audience, they would look very similar, but there the similarities ended.

"How strange it seemed to be watching her without her knowing," thought Christine. Certainly it confirmed her thoughts about Carlotta's vanity, which seemed as boundless as her ambition.

The antithesis between Macbeth and Lady Macbeth had echoes in Erik and Carlotta, Christine reflected. Macbeth was bold and resolute in the moment of action; he could kill a king, but he became prey to countless terrible imaginings and he was wildly superstitious, as Christine had seen in Erik's lair. Lady Macbeth was the exact converse; she had banished all superstition from her soul; she could scheme and plot, but she could not act; she left the doing of the deadly deed to Macbeth.

Christine looked from Carlotta to Erik. Despite both of them being in costume, they were not characters in an opera, and Carlotta was not faint-hearted. She was a conqueror and had won her triumphs, not in war, but in the training of her voice and mind and the subjugation of her will to opera. Had she been the instigator behind her kidnap? Erik was prey to his ambitions and the ghosts of the past. What had Carlotta promised him? Had Christine now become a threat to them both? Was she right to trust him? Would he kill her, too? "Or would she, too, one day succumb and become prey to such vanity and ambition? Doubts swirled in Christine's mind.

CHAPTER FIFTY-TWO

THE BLUFF

"Finally," Erik breathed a sigh of relief, as Carlotta blew herself a kiss in the cracked mirror and opened the door. Watching this vainglorious woman so closely had shown him what a fool he had been. He wanted to be shot of her. Timing now was of the essence, to blend in and gain valuable cover amidst the cavernous backstage props and curtains during the final act. Once there, they would be safe. He would no longer need Christine for cover and he could disappear, perhaps forever.

Christine watched as Erik checked his watch. He put one finger up and mouthed, "One minute." He tapped the gun reassuringly under his robe, then adjusted his crown, so it sat firmly across his forehead. The king had recovered his brave spirit. Erik was poised ready for action, for the final battle. Would he come to the same ignominious end as Macbeth?

And would she, Christine, come to the same wretched death as Lady Macbeth?

Erik pulled a lever to the side of the panel. The wall slid back and they stepped into the dressing room. Erik put his finger to his lips, opened the door and looked both ways. "All clear. Let's go." She took the hand he proffered and together they walked quickly towards backstage. As they rounded the corner, a well-dressed woman in front of the entrance, stepped forward, looking puzzled. Detective Inspector Sophie Giroux wore an oak tree spray on her lapel. Christine didn't recognise the danger, but Erik did. Both saw the query in her eyes, and Christine went to stop. Erik tightened the grip on her hand, put his other hand in his robe, wrapped it around his pistol, and then quickened his pace.

"Smile, Christine." He whispered. Christine beamed at Sophie.

"It's alright, Madame. You haven't got double vision," said Erik, blithely, unleashing a charming smile to bluff his way past, "we're the understudies and we're running late." As they hurried past her, Sophie said,

"Dieu merci. You had me worried, there for a moment."

CHAPTER FIFTY-THREE

THE FINAL ACT

Raoul was nearing despair. Christine was nowhere to be found. Neither was Erik. He was sure they were together, but where? Were they trapped together underground? Only ten minutes until the end of the raid, but not one of Erik's crew had been sighted, let alone found. Access to the lair was blocked by rock falls, disguised by the rousing chorus scenes at the beginning of the third act. But, it seemed, the rats had already deserted the sinking ship.

The sleepwalking aria was up next. Raoul and Inspector Andre Martin were doing one final sweep of the backstage areas.

"All clear out here, Detective Inspector Giroux?" Asked Andre Martin.

"Yes, sir. Just the diva and then the understudies a couple of minutes ago."

"Understudies? What understudies?" Raoul barked at her.

"Macbeth and Lady Macbeth, sir." She stood to attention, adding, "In costume, sir."

Raoul turned to Andre, excitement mounting, "There are no understudies tonight, Andre. It has to be Christine and Erik."

"Which way did they go?" demanded Andre.

"Through there, sir. To the wings, backstage."

"Come on, let's go," said Raoul, moving off.

"Wait! Sophie, call Moreau. Tell him to surround the backstage area. Give descriptions of the two people and what they are wearing."

"Yes, sir."

"Was he armed?"

"He had one hand in his robe and was holding the woman very close with the other. I would assume now he was, sir," Sophie was looking decidedly downcast.

"Sophie, he's a killer. If you had challenged him, I doubt you would be alive. Let Moreau know. Erik Destler is trapped now. We will get him." Then to Raoul waiting impatiently, "Come on, Raoul. Very carefully, though." Guns drawn, they inched open the door.

On stage, a chorus of refugees from Macbeth's reign of terror were collected on the border with England, among them Macduff. Malcolm arrived with a troop of English soldiers to lead his men against Macbeth, all carrying branches from Birnam wood as camouflage. Their voices now combined in a rousing aria, to rescue the oppressed — *Ah, la paterna mano (Ah, the paternal hand)* — and destroy the villain.

A crack of light appeared, as the door where Erik and Christine had entered, opened once again. From his hiding place, Erik watched as two shadows eased their way into the backstage area. One, a giant of a man, the other unmistakably, Raoul D'Arenberg. He heard Christine catch her breath, then the light disappeared. Erik could no longer see them, but he knew they were there. And so did Christine. They both knew, that others knew, he and Christine were hidden somewhere close by in the wings, too. Erik and his beloved were being hunted, again. But this time, he would never allow them to be captured, alive.

The music and the singing stopped. The stage was plunged into darkness as the soldiers and refugees exited the stage. Knowing he only had a minute, Erik propelled a reluctant Christine further into the stage area, in amongst the voluminous folds of the curtains and ropes and pulleys at the side of the stage. It was a risky manoeuvre. They might be seen and their cover wouldn't last long, but no one would risk getting near to them whilst the opera was on. And, Christine, ever the professional, would never dare to interrupt a performance. For now, it would give him some breathing space, time to think what to do next. The noose was closing ever tighter.

CHAPTER FIFTY-FOUR

THE SLEEPWALKING ARIA

A hush came over the audience, until all was silent. It was night-time on stage, the setting a darkened bedroom in Macbeth's castle. To one side, huddled in the dark together, peering into the bedroom, were the doctor and Lady Macbeth's gentlewoman, Danielle. They conversed softly, the doctor first.

"We have waited in vain for two nights."

"She will appear tonight."

"What was she talking about in her sleep?"

"I must not repeat it to any living man. Here she is!"

Lady Macbeth entered with a lamp, walking slowly. Ever so slowly, as if in a trance. The doctor and gentlewoman, watched on, continuing to converse.

"That lamp in her hand?"

"It is the lamp which she keeps always beside her bed."

"Oh, her eyes are wide open!"

"*Yet she cannot see.*"

Lady Macbeth put down the lamp and rubbed her hands as if washing something off.

"*Why is she rubbing her hands?*"

"*She thinks that she is washing them.*"

Carlotta now sang. "*There's still a spot here. Away, I tell you, curse you!*" Her sonorous voice penetrated the darkness, reaching into every recess of the opera house, and touching every soul.

"*One, two, it is time!*

Are you shaking? Don't you dare go in?

A soldier and so cowardly?

Shame! Come on, hurry!"

Lady Macbeth incarnate, inciting her husband to murder. Two accompanying instruments from the orchestra repeated again and again. One from the string section, as she tried to rub the blood from her hands, whilst sleepwalking, lost to the world. The other a horn, like the lament of an owl. Her sin was ever present awake or dreaming she could think of nothing but that awful night, and the stain upon her hand and soul.

"*Who would have thought that there would be so much blood in that old man?*" Carlotta's ethereal beauty and rich, mournful tones told that deep within Lady Macbeth's unconscious there lurked the memory of the moment Duncan met his death, when an owl cried out at night.

"*Shall I never be able to clean these hands?*"

After reliving the night of Duncan's murder, Lady Macbeth's overtasked brain broke down. The audience was awed, witnessing the spectacle of Lady Macbeth's mental agony, as she moved, ever more desperately, to and fro. Carlotta looked at her hands, bemoaning.

"*Here's the smell of blood still. All the perfumes of Arabia could not clean this little hand. Alas!*"

The police and Erik and Christine, peeping from behind the folds of the curtains, were as spellbound as the audience, by the exquisite and deeply moving performance. In Lady Macbeth, the witches' curse had worked itself out, not in fear, but in remorse, with remorseless fatality. She was entirely isolated, headed for the most wretched death. Opera at its dramatic best.

"*To bed, to bed. What's done cannot be undone.*
Someone is knocking! Come on Macbeth,
do not let your pallor accuse you."

Now, thought Erik. He has to be now. The aria was nearing the end.

"*Come Macbeth.*
Come, come.
Come Macbeth.

Come.

Come."

As her voice faded into silence, Lady Macbeth sank on her knees, the stage lights dimming, as the scene slowly ended. Needing to reconnoiter, Erik tentatively began moving back the folds of the curtain, slowly exposing Christine and himself. Out of the corner of his eye, Erik saw a movement in the wings and looked over. Feeling him tense, Christine followed his glance. Raoul was pointing Erik out to the giant. They pulled their guns out and had them trained on him. He would not escape this time. Erik's heart started racing. He was being hunted again, trapped like a rabbit in the spotlight. Fear threatened to overwhelm him once more. He became deathly still.

Christine could smell the fear and indecision emanating from Erik. This wounded soul, this phantom, had struggled in and out of the darkness for too long. He was haunted by the past, but there was so much goodness in him, too. He had brought her to safety. Now it was her turn to give him a chance. Christine suddenly stepped in front of Erik and wrapped her arms around his neck, trapping him, against the curtains.

"What are you doing?" Erik struggled to break free.

"Kiss me. They won't shoot if you kiss me."

Erik, sensing a trap, looked deep into her eyes. This

time he saw only love and hope and redemption. His spirit soared and he kissed her. They became trapped in a time warp, of lost loves overcome by the power of hope and redemption. Raoul and Andre Martin watched on, their guns wavering, bewildered by the turn of events.

Meanwhile, Carlotta was centre stage, down on her knees, in the last throes of the aria, already revelling in the thought of the accolades such a divine performance would bring. *La Divina* indeed! The movement near the curtain at the side of the stage attracted her attention. Looking across, she saw her lover and her rival with arms wrapped around each other, kissing passionately. Bile filled her mouth. Traitors. Both of them.

"Perfidy!" mouthed an enraged Carlotta. "I will take great pleasure in seeing you both die, a horrible death," she promised. A stabbing pain struck at her chest. Erik gaped as Carlotta looked down with horror, at the jet black stigmata of the phantom emblazoned on her nightdress. She gasped and clutched at her heart, as her body slowly collapsed onto the floor. The music faded into nothingness. As the spotlight on Lady Macbeth's body dimmed, darkness returned, and the audience started to applaud.

Christine's voice broke the spell. "Go! Go now, Erik. Save yourself." She unlocked her arms from behind Erik's neck and moved back a little. Their eyes locked once more, searching each other's soul for meaning. Christine touched his face gently, pleading with him to go. "Please, go. Leave me." More than anything else, she wanted this man to live. Thunderous applause broke out all around the Garnier. Erik went to leap onto the ropes at the side of the stage, then hesitated and turned back towards her.

"You will find Philippe in Rome, in Suburra." He took her beautiful face in his hands and kissed her again, before leaping onto the ropes. A gunshot rang out. Christine screamed.

CHAPTER FIFTY-FIVE

CURTAIN CALL

The magnificent, heavy red canvas curtain, painted to represent a draped curtain, replete with golden braid and tassels, slowly closed over leaving a triumphant Malcolm, Macduff and the chorus standing there. After their rousing finale, *Vittoria! Vittoria! (Victory! Victory! Macbeth is dead!)*, rapturous applause erupted once again, echoing all around the auditorium. Opening night of Macbeth in the Palais Garnier, had been a resounding success, electrifying the audience. They stood and clapped and stamped their feet. Just as they had done earlier, at the end of Lady Macbeth's sleepwalking aria, for fifteen minutes, before the opera was allowed to continue.

The curtains opened again on the final scene. The clapping continued as the curtains closed. Then opened once more. Malcolm, Macduff and the chorus stood silently, still in character, acknowledging the applause. The curtains closed over again, but the applause continued.

Behind the scenes, Raoul stood on his own, the gun in his pocket still warm after firing. He watched on with mixed feelings. The organised chaos and jubilation after a successful opening night performance, was something to behold. The Artistic Director, the Opera Manager and Madame Giraud, were running back and forwards, struggling to summon up order for the curtain call. Pandemonium again as there had been when they discovered Carlotta had collapsed. What to do about curtain calls. No leading lady.

Adding to the confusion, was Christine's return. She was surrounded by a dozen people, cast and crew, overjoyed at seeing her again. Eager to know what had happened. Eager to let her know she was loved. A beaming Monsieur Laloux, forgetting his anger about her disappearing, clapped as he approached the group around Christine.

"Come, come. Not now, my angels. In place for the curtain call, please. Your reward for a performance. C'est magnifique!"

"We'll be back," said Danielle, kissing Christine on the cheek. "Soon." She kissed her again and grabbed her hand. "It is so good to have you back where you belong, ma chère amie." Danielle planted another affectionate kiss, this time on Christine's hand, not willing to let her go.

"Shoo! Shoo! Christine will still be here, when you return," said Monsieur Laloux, pulling Danielle off with his hands. He picked up the hand Danielle had dropped. Holding on to it, gallantly, he said, "Welcome home, Mademoiselle. All is forgiven. The Garnier needs you." He kissed her hand and bowed slightly, before moving on, leaving Christine bewildered.

As the group scattered, Raoul's eyes scanned the lit, cavernous interior once more, searching for any sign of Erik. Instead he was greeted with the sight of Inspector Moreau, Andre, Sophie, and other police, watching the celebrations from the sidelines, defined less by their oak sprays, than by the disconsolate looks on their faces. There was absolutely nothing to show for their raid. Except for a few drops of blood, Erik had vanished like a phantom, as if he were never there.

With the chorus finally settled in position across the stage, the main actors and the orchestra conductor, waiting either side, in the wings, Monsieur Laloux gave the signal to open the curtains. The clapping turned to thunderous applause once more, the warmth radiating around the auditorium. Lead by Angelique, the Witches' chorus ran on stage, hand in hand. They bowed then moved to the side. They were followed by the Doctor and the Lady in Waiting. Danielle's face was alive with joy. Then one, by one came Malcolm, Macduff and Banquo. The applause grew louder and louder, in anticipation of Lady Macbeth.

René Bourdin looked around, but Carlotta was nowhere to be seen. René looked at Monsieur Laloux, who looked at Victor. Victor just shook his head, unhelp-fully. Monsieur Laloux threw up his hands in despair. René turned to Christine and offered her his hand.

"Please, Christine. The audience must see a Lady Macbeth before Macbeth." Although wearied to the bone, Christine stood and, holding his hand, they walked onto the stage together. The audience erupted.

"Bravo! Bravo!" René and Christine bowed, then moved back whilst the conductor came out and bowed. Then the cast and the conductor joined hands and moved forward and bowed, then backwards, before bowing again, and again. During an agonising fifteen minutes of curtain calls, Christine was recalled again and again, by an audience so blinded with delight, they saw *La Divina*, not Christine Dubois. Leaving her, and everyone else, in no doubt whose night this was.

From high in his eyrie, Erik lay there watching Christine on stage, unable to take his eyes from her. He winced.

He mopped at his left cheek with a make-shift bandage. His face was a bloody mess. The bullet had shattered his cheek bone and was still lodged there. But it was nothing to the pain he felt for the loss of Christine. She had saved his life, given him a chance of redemption. Even after the treatment he had handed out to her at Carlotta's behest, she had kissed him, then set him free. But what kind of freedom was it?

He looked around his secret dungeon. His crown lay on the floor, along with his gun and the torn and tattered robe. The robe had slowed him down. So had the blood pouring from his wound. After Christine said go, he'd leapt up the ropes behind the stage curtains, but was momentarily stunned when he was shot. Through sheer willpower, he'd hung on and kept climbing. The darkness had both protected him, and made it doubly dangerous. First he had to access the network of ropes and wires that held the scenes in place. Once there, he removed his robe and tied it around his neck to free him for the next part of his ascent. The extended applause after the sleepwalking aria continued to provide cover. Erik was amused by the irony in thinking Carlotta would be beside herself with rage if she knew her performance was helping him escape.

Working from memory, and his highly attuned sense of balance, Erik had then climbed up the combination of steps, ladders and knotted ropes to the narrow viewing platform. From there to the bridge, then across the make-shift rope ladder, to the ceiling entry. And, finally, the long crawl through the narrow duct to the safety of his Box 5 *oubliette*. Without pausing to draw breath, he opened the front viewing space and peered down at centre stage.

It was the curtain call, the final choreography of the evening's performance. But why was it Christine on stage doing recall after recall, and not Carlotta? Something serious must have happened for her not to wallow in the adulation of her adoring fans. And, for Christine, after what she had already endured, being on stage, standing in for Carlotta, would be another waking nightmare.

Christine faltered. She trembled and started to sway, a spent spirit. Her soul was slipping away. Erik's hands automatically reached out to save her. As he did, the chandelier trembled and swayed, and the curtains closed for the final time. He looked at his hands. As empty as his life. Christine had made him realise he wanted to live again, to love again, to be in the light, for music to be his life. To be rid of the phantoms of his mind.

Erik reached forward and closed the door to his view-ing space. Darkness overwhelmed him. Shivering from exhaustion, he sank into his velvet pillows, and closed his eyes, seeking peace, and praying for the happiness and the love that eluded him. Then a warm breeze gently flowed over and around him. It enveloped him like a soft blanket, and the dark gave way to the quietest of whispers.

"Love never dies." The whispers continued, over and over, comforting him, warming him. When Erik finally fell into a deep sleep, for the first time, in a very long time, he dreamt of a future and not phantoms.

Christine could barely stand, but she didn't have the strength to move. The closed curtains in front of her had finally brought an end to the humiliating farce. She looked around at the happy throngs of people, but a sadness came over her. There was nothing to celebrate. Philippe wasn't dead. He had left her. She saw Madame Giraud and Raoul watching her from the wings. Concern etched in their faces. Tears welled. Her chest heaved. Sensing her distress, they walked over.

Madame Giraud took both of her hands, and held them, reassuringly.

"I see guardian angels hovering over you, my dear, protecting you. The danger is over."

When Christine saw Raoul's probing look and the many questions she knew he wanted to ask behind it, she trembled and started to sway again. Her emotions still on a rollercoaster, forces within her, beyond her control. Raoul put a steadying arm around her shoulders. Tears streamed down her face.

"Where is Carlotta? I feel like such an imposter."

"You are not an imposter," said Raoul, giving her a hug.

"One day," she vowed, "I will be lauded as a diva in my own right."

"Soon. Very soon, my dear," said Victor, coming over to where she and Raoul and Madame Giraud were standing, and interrupting their chat. "Sooner than you might imagine," he said, smiling smugly.

Christine was about to ask what he meant when Inspector Moreau walked over to join the group. His face serious, he turned to Christine and said, sternly.

"I am pleased you are safe, Mademoiselle, but we will need to interview you, tout suite."

Christine nodded. "Of course, Inspector."

Then Moreau turned to Victor. "Pardon, Monsieur Marchand. I am very sorry to hear about Madame Caccini. Our thoughts are with you. We pray she will pull through."

"What's happened?" asked Christine, concerned.

Victor shrugged and turned to Madame Giraud said, "You tell her."

"Carlotta has had a suspected heart attack. She is in

the Critical Care Unit at La Pitié-Salpêtrière Hospital. And, she is not expected to live."

"Oh, Victor, I am so sorry," said Christine, aghast at the news.

With surprising equanimity, Victor quoted Shakespeare.

"Life... What does it matter?

It is the tale of a poor fool:

Wind and sound signifying nothing."

As indifferent to his partner's demise, as Macbeth.

EPILOGUE

Three days later...

The crowds spilled out of the famous Paris opera house onto the streets. Their excited chatter floating up like will-o-the-wisps into the chill night air. All they could talk about was the brilliant new soprano who had stepped in to play Lady Macbeth after the collapse of *La Divina.*

"*A radiant presence.*"

"*A beautiful face and a beautiful voice.*"

"*The beginning of a new love affair.*"

Hovering nearby, soaking it all in, was a wraith-like figure dressed in a dark cloak and hat. A white mask covered the gruesome horror that was his face. He rarely ventured out. Not that anyone could see him, unless he chose to reveal himself. And precious few had the gift to even sense his presence.

He looked up at the principal façade of the Palais Garnier. The home of art and music, and his beloved home for the past century, preserved once more. The building was lit up like a Christmas tree. *Harmony and Poetry*, Gumery's gilded sculptures atop the façade, cast a golden glow against the dark background of the sky. The chatter continued.

"Love across the footlights."

"A heartstoppingly high pianissimo."

"The voice of an angel."

Christine Dubois did indeed have the voice of an angel, as did the Phantom's protégé, Christine Daaé, a century earlier. He had intervened and saved her, given her this opportunity to shine in her own right. Earlier in the evening he had briefly looked in on her arch rival, Carlotta Caccini. She still clung to life in the Critical Care Unit. Whether she survived, or whether she would emerge changed after her experience, was moot. Her destiny was not within his power. It was up to Carlotta.

Head down, he swept past the retreating audience into the building. He paused before the *Bassin de la Pythia*. Pythia was a high priestess at the Temple of Apollo.

"A new diva!"

He smiled and echoed the sentiment. "A new diva, indeed!" Adoring fans were already worshipping at the operatic altar of Christine Dubois. He turned and marvelled at the theatrical entrance, flanked on each side by *le Grand Escalier*, with its magnificent vaulted ceiling and paintings of the muses of classical mythology — Apollo, Minerva and Orpheus.

Patrons and excited, rapturous comments continued to flow down the marble staircase from the well-lit foyers and various floors above, like a moving sea, but this time, with the tide going out. Past him, past *Les Torchères*, the two female allegories holding torches, bouquets of light, to greet spectators, at the bottom of the stairs, a true theatre within the theatre. Their job well and truly done tonight.

He moved through auditorium. How he loved the Baroque sumptuousness, rich with red velvet, gold leaf, cherubims and nymphs. Following the gaiety and laughter, he slipped through the closed curtains, backstage. He, too, was in a buoyant mood. Madame Giraud was momentarily taken back, when she looked in his direction, before flashing an enigmatic smile.

Champagne was flowing and the celebrations well underway. Groups gathered everywhere. Cast and crew. It had been a magical performance. René, Marias and Julien were waxing lyrical with Danielle and Angelique. Monsieur Laloux, Enzo and Madame Giraud were toasting each other. Raoul stood with his arm lovingly around Christine's waist, listening to Victor rhapsodise about her performance and managing her future as a diva. In spite of her triumph, he could see Christine's mind was elsewhere. On Philippe. Would she try and find him? On Erik Destler who had disappeared. On the phantoms who invaded her thoughts day and night.

Time to return to my subterranean world. Moments later, he was sitting in the prow of a boat moving across the lake. A figure in a dark cloak, wearing a white blood-soaked bandage on his face was rowing, totally oblivious of him. Two phantoms in one lair. Life so often resembles opera, he thought, and this tale is not yet told.

MICHAEL LEON

Michael Leon is a Melbourne based speculative fiction writer with two published novels, *Cubeball* and *Emissary*. Besides those, Michael has written *Extinction*, *Adaption* and *Sentient*. Michael Leon's work has been labelled by reviewers as science fiction thrillers.

www.michaelleon.com.au

CHRISSIE ANTHONY

Chrissie Anthony is the romantic alter ego of Melbourne writer and editor, Christine Lister. After a successful career in education, Christine started writing. Her books are *The Hidden Journey – Melanoma Up Close And Personal, Tahlia You Can Do It!* and *In the Garden of my Delights.* Chrissie's books are *Quiver – Awakening the Goddess Within* and *How Do I Love Thee?*

www.chrissieanthony.com

www.australianinspiration.com.au

Phantoms
The Sequels

Phantoms Act 2

Phantoms Act 2 continues the story of Erik Destler, a latter day Phantom of the Opera. Three years on, he returns to the Palais Garnier in new guise as Enrico Rossi, a wealthy operatic producer harbouring the secret ambition to compose and stage his own opera. To succeed he must again face his demons — the Opera Ghost and Carlotta Caccini, the diva whose life he almost destroyed during his reign of terror, and the new opera manager — Philippe D'Arenberg, a phantom from the past. **Phantoms Act 2** is set in Italy, and then that famous Paris opera house amidst the staging of Verdi's *La Traviata*.